"I completely release y⋯⋯⋯⋯
the wager. I feel I was misled as well."

"Misled?" Gabriel asked, eyes narrowing.

With her eyes down, Marie's smile was directed at herself. "I thought your cousin was to be the prize. He and I are acquainted enough that we have been introduced, and I thought he would understand, and would laugh it off. I could not dissuade my aunt easily and your grandmother would have wagered almost anything because she planned to win. It was over almost before I knew what was happening. I hoped Pierce would understand and assist me, and get the wager canceled."

"Might I hear what the wager consisted of?" He moved to the floral settee, beside where the woman now stood. "Please..." He waved a hand, indicating she make herself comfortable—or at least less frosty.

He settled himself into the seat beside the young woman.

"What did the wager consist of?" he repeated, studying the way she appeared to retreat inside herself.

"A proposal."

Author Note

Years after my great-aunt penned her memoirs, I carefully read and reread every page, wishing she'd written more and thankful for the insight she gave into family history. This helped inspire me to write about the viscount's grandmother, a woman wanting to share her memories with future generations. I hope that if you have been thinking the slightest bit about writing your personal family story—and haven't yet started—that you begin. Family anecdotes can mean so much to your children, grandchildren, nephews and nieces.

The Viscount's Wallflower Wager

LIZ TYNER

HARLEQUIN
HISTORICAL

Recycling programs
for this product may
not exist in your area.

ISBN-13: 978-1-335-59608-6

The Viscount's Wallflower Wager

Copyright © 2024 by Elizabeth Tyner

For questions and comments about the quality of this book,
please contact us at CustomerService@Harlequin.com.

TM and ® are trademarks of Harlequin Enterprises ULC.

Harlequin Enterprises ULC
22 Adelaide St. West, 41st Floor
Toronto, Ontario M5H 4E3, Canada
www.Harlequin.com

Printed in U.S.A.

Liz Tyner lives with her husband on an Oklahoma acreage she imagines is similar to the ones in the children's book *Where the Wild Things Are*. Her lifestyle is a blend of old and new and is sometimes comparable to the way people lived long ago. Liz is a member of various writing groups and has been writing since childhood. For more about her, visit liztyner.com.

Books by Liz Tyner

Harlequin Historical

The Wallflower Duchess
Redeeming the Roguish Rake
Saying I Do to the Scoundrel
To Win a Wallflower
It's Marriage or Ruin
Compromised into Marriage
A Cinderella for the Viscount
Tempting a Reformed Rake
A Marquess Too Rakish to Wed
Marriage Deal with the Earl
Betrothed in Haste to the Earl

English Rogues and Grecian Goddesses

Safe in the Earl's Arms
A Captain and a Rogue
Forbidden to the Duke

Visit the Author Profile page
at Harlequin.com.

Dedicated to Maggie Bennett

Chapter One

The bedchamber door slammed into the wall, causing a lamp to rattle. Only one person in all of London would dare wake him so abruptly. His grandmother.

Gabriel's jaw locked. He opened his eyes, staring up into an amazingly innocent perusal.

His grandmother stood at his bedside. A woman who had to go on tiptoe to give him a kiss on the cheek—and who could make an executioner cry—smiled while her perfume hit him with the force of a sword blade.

A normal person in his presence would have trembled beneath Gabriel's glare, but his grandmother didn't notice.

'Good morning,' she chirped, marching back to the door. 'Or should I say good afternoon, slugabed?'

'How did you get past my valet?' he asked, knowing the man was assigned to stand sentry in his sitting room on the mornings his grandmother was in residence.

She ignored the question. 'We need to talk.'

'I have a perfectly good valet you could have asked to wake me. Where is he, by the way? Still alive?' he persisted.

'He's a bit stodgy. That turnip-head wouldn't let me into your bedchamber.' She waved a hand, dismissing his words. 'I had to take a circuitous route and someone left a mop and bucket in front of the entrance,' she said, annoyance evident in her tone.

She must really be determined if she'd used the servants' stairs.

She turned to his mirror, patting her silver bun and trying to make it taller, the rings on her fingers knocking together.

After adjusting her dress, which would have suited a virginal debutante better, she muttered to her reflection, 'Still got all your teeth, old girl.' She gave a grimace, inspecting them. 'Or at least the ones that count.'

She whirled to him. 'You need to get that valet of yours doing his duties. Making you presentable to your guests...' She barely paused. 'I meant to tell you eventually, but you know how Agatha is. She wants to see you. And you've slept much too long.'

Agatha—Lady Andrews—and his grandmother were friends...of a sort. Hissing and snarling friends, but close nonetheless. His grandmother had invited Lady Andrews to stay and he had thought it would keep her entertained.

Apparently not.

'Wear that black waistcoat with the embroidery on the buttons that I ordered from your tailor,' his grandmother continued. 'And try to look pleasant. Not like now.'

She pinched her forefinger and thumb together, then put them against her lips, scowling as she stared at him. Then she opened the draperies halfway and blinked at the light before turning back to him.

'And you could certainly use a bit of a hair-trim—that unruly mess is covering your face. Such a shame for that healthy head of hair to be wasted on a male. And don't let your valet give you any distressingly scented woodland soap. Use that ambergris I gave you. I don't care if it's from a whale's gut—it smells clean and tart.'

'Grandmother, why would Lady Andrews wish to see me?'

'That cauldron-stirrer should be horsewhipped for the way she cheats at cards. Don't let the lace handkerchiefs fool you—she uses them to hide the cards.' She gave an angry shake of her head. 'I had that king in my reticule—and she played it.' Her eyebrows flew up and she looked at him, chin down. 'And everyone knows how I manoeuvre, so it really *doesn't count.*' She stressed her last words. 'That's what I get for having such a disreputable woman as a friend. But I lost fairly. She out-cheated me.'

She moved, dashing towards the sitting room door, and then jumped back just after she'd opened it. His valet appeared, eyes wide, gasping at the sight of her. She peered at him and shut the door while still inside the bedroom. Her next words were almost hidden in a mumble.

'I lost you in a card game to Lady Andrews.'

Then she hurled herself out through the door at full speed.

'Watson!' he shouted. 'Stop her!'

He would never have told his mother he'd keep watch over his grandmother if he'd had any vision of the way his grandmother truly thought.

In his youth, he'd hardly seen her. The tales he'd heard had seemed humorous then, but now he understood the facts, and he realised his mother had sheltered him from many family upheavals.

The door opened again and Watson herded Gabriel's grandmother back inside, his arms outstretched, corralling her as if she were a sheep darting about.

'My pardon, sir,' the valet said. 'She... Your grand-mother—'

She slapped the servant's outflung arm, stopped moving, and peered at Gabriel. 'I do not want your valet learning about my misfortune at cards. It is not for his ears. If he will leave, I will explain. Agatha knew where I'd hidden the king but she didn't accuse me of cheating. Just let me carry on. Deceitful.'

'Do you know anything about this card game?' he asked Watson, seeking the truthful answer he knew his grandmother would not provide.

The valet stepped towards him. 'It was last night. In her sitting room. A ruckus erupted late in the evening, and no one dared disturb them except a maid. She said the table was upended and cards were strewn around the room. Some had been ripped into pieces.'

His grandmother sneered. 'I have to give Agatha credit for her card skills. I would never have believed someone half my age could be so treacherous. The old bat...'

He stared at his grandmother. 'When she came to stay, you told me she was your dearest friend.'

She shrugged. 'Oh, let's be truthful. She's my only friend.'

She waved the valet away with a flick of her fingers.

'Get my grandson his clothing. I've already summoned someone to bring his shaving water. I need to introduce him to Agatha's niece, and he likely will want to wear breeches.'

'Likely,' Gabriel said.

'Don't sound so irritable.' His grandmother pointed a finger at him after Watson had left the room. 'No one would ever expect you to marry her, so no one will blame you when you don't go through with it. The poor thing is too thin, too tall, has no taste in fashion and reads books about plants…' She put a finger to her lips. 'I wouldn't call her a wallflower exactly. More of a wall weed.' She smiled. 'Yes. The child is a spindly weed, and it's easy to see how she's remained unwed.'

'Did you tell this mystery woman that I would wed her?' he asked.

His grandmother blew out a puff of air. 'Of course not.' She wrinkled her nose. 'I merely wagered a proposal on your behalf. How you get out of it will be between the two of you. It's not as if you aren't experienced in that.'

'Grandmother…' He spoke softly, but clenched his teeth.

She studied him. 'You inherited your grandfather's shoulders and height, and his ability to escape marriage until he met me.' She clucked her tongue in pride. 'And where would you be without me? Now, don't make a fuss. Causing a woman to end a betrothal should not give you any trouble.'

He clamped his jaw, worried about what he might say if he did not.

'The jest is on Agatha,' she said, laughing. 'You're too much like your father and me.' She slapped at her skirts, then paused, standing on tiptoe. She looked into the mirror and pulled the skin tight at one side of her face. 'Oh, I must stop laughing. It causes wrinkles.'

'Grandmother—'

'I think Agatha should explain to you. After all, I had every intention of winning that game, because I so badly wanted those pearls. But Agatha must have seen something, and she spilled her punch on my reticule—which concealed the winning card. Still, I thought I could brazen it out, and Agatha accepted the wager. But it was I who fell into the trap.' Her voice softened and she hid a smile. 'Or *you* who fell into her trap.'

He stared at her, completely flummoxed.

He'd seen two kinds of marriage in his life. His parents' bond, which had been one of incessant determined warfare, and his grandparents' union, in which his grandfather had waved away his wife's misadventures, oblivious to the detriment she caused. His maternal grandparents hadn't fared much better. They spoke only through intermediaries, such as Gabriel's mother. She lived with them—in part to keep the peace, but also in order to keep herself away from the upheaval his paternal grandmother caused. He'd tried to talk his widowed mother into visiting Town more, worried about her isolation, but she had refused, pointing out that it was best for her and her former mother-in-law to be separated.

'Really, all you have to do is propose to Marie. It's not even as if you have to kiss her or pretend she's lovely. And she's not going to accept your proposal, because she knows she is too unattractive and tedious to keep a man's attention. She's mentioned to me that she doesn't believe a woman should ever wed. I tried to tell her about my happiness. She didn't believe me.'

She put her fingertips together and rested them below her bottom lip.

'I know that I am generally not celebrated for my honesty, but I had a wonderful marriage with your grandfather and it would be lovely to see you find that same happiness—be it with Marie or someone else. After all, it is well past time you provided heirs.'

He knew that. That was why he'd considered the best

way to propose to the stunningly beautiful Rosalind. And considered it…and considered it. He was intending to act… eventually.

Flouncing to the door, his grandmother added, 'Agatha and her…um…passable niece are waiting in the main sitting room. Make sure you make a few jests when you meet Marie. I love it when Agatha laughs.'

'I refuse to have anything to do with this.'

He spoke softly, but firmly, and she took a step towards him, face crumpling in defeat.

'Gabriel, you have to,' she insisted. 'If you don't make good on this wager…'

'No.'

'You don't understand… I possibly had been drinking too much punch, and I might have written out a note stating the details—a sort of contract…' She looked heavenward and puffed a breath in the same direction. 'Which Agatha might have kept. She's so distrusting… Anyway, you really only have yourself to blame. Take this as a lesson to you on what will happen if you don't wed a suitable woman with due haste.'

'Grandmother.' He glared at her. 'You must get this sorted out—and without my being involved. I do not want any tales of it in society. It would devastate Mother. She cares very deeply about her courtship with the widowed Duke of Bellton, and he is a stickler for propriety—particularly because he has a daughter about to enter society.'

His grandmother put the back of her hand to her forehead, shut her eyes, visibly wilted, and then said, 'Very well. I will see what I can do.'

She left, humming some funeral dirge, and he rolled out of bed with a frown on his face. Perhaps *he* needed to

worry about getting wrinkles while his grandmother was
nearby…

He had known Lady Andrews had brought a niece with
her on her visit, and frankly he didn't trust either of them
any more than he trusted his grandmother. They were
likely fortune-hunters.

Footsteps sounded and Watson stepped back inside.

'Find out from the maids which room belongs to my
grandmother's young guest,' Gabriel instructed, taking his
breeches from the valet and dressing. 'But don't let anyone
know I'm curious about her—particularly my grandmother.
Then get the maid to invite the woman to the music room
and summon me. I don't want to hurt her reputation, but
I think it's time I see what kind of woman Grandmother
has brought into my home.'

'Of course. But perhaps you might wish to wait? Your
cousin Pierce's mother has just arrived, and she and your
grandmother are going to have tea. There is the possibility
that your aunt might seek you out.'

'Fine. I will wait,' Gabriel said. 'After she leaves, however, we will need to move quickly.'

'I agree, sir,' the valet said as he moved into the dressing room.

Gabriel followed and took a comb from Watson's hand.
'I knew my grandmother had her friends visiting, but how
long have they been staying?'

'I thought you knew, sir? Their stay has stretched for
longer than a fortnight now. The younger lady has very
little by way of baggage. At first the maids assumed she
would only reside here a few days, because she brought almost nothing. Now the staff is all aflutter with speculation.'

Gabriel would have to get to the truth of the matter and

find out more about these women living under his roof. He knew of Lord Andrews, and was fairly certain his wife had wed him for financial reasons and brought her niece into her husband's home. Andrews had probably displaced them because they were draining his funds, buying fripperies and whatever else would waste money. Or they'd wagered everything away and were now worming their way into his grandmother's good heart—well, her not so good heart—so that she would pick up their bills.

He should have been watching his grandmother's activities more closely.

While he waited in the music room, with the scent of beeswax polish wafting in the air, Gabriel plucked at a few strings on his grandmother's harp. He winced at the sound he created, thankful that any so-called music from the instrument rarely carried to his rooms.

He looked up when Watson opened the door, and put out his hand to still the strings.

The valet gestured into the room with a wave of his arm and then left, the door remaining ajar.

A woman walked slowly through the door, her head bowed.

Her hair was about as severe as a woman could manage to make it, pulled into a knot and pinned onto her head in a fashion so tight he wondered if she had trouble closing her eyes. She wore a dress with flounces reminding him of strewn autumn leaves—which a few carriages had rolled over. She did appear thin, and her dress certainly covered her with plenty to spare. The neckline was puckered, and the round spectacles she wore sat primly on her nose.

The woman in front of him was perhaps fifteen or

so years older than he was and, given that until now his grandmother had always pointed out the virtues of women younger than he, he wondered if she was trying to send him a stronger message than she'd initially implied about her concerns about his unmarried state.

The woman greeted him more timidly than he could believe possible. This could not be the niece of his grandmother's friend—or perhaps she was. Perhaps her clothing was a ruse for a woman who was trying to hide her identity.

He realised he'd noticed another scent besides the beeswax. A flowery scent—lilac or lavender or honeysuckle, he wasn't sure which—was gently wafting into the air around him. He didn't know much about flowers, and until now one scent had smelled much the same to him as any other. This time, however, the floral scent captured his attention. It was fresh. Almost real. As if the blooms were in front of him.

He strummed a single harp string, the lonely tone resounding in the room.

'I'm pleased to finally meet you,' he said. He stepped away from the instrument, clasping his hands behind him, giving her the smile he used sparingly, and more with foes than friends.

Then he looked beyond the drab hair, the spectacles, the odd clothing, and without meaning too took another step closer.

Her skin was smooth. Apparently she hadn't laughed much in her life. Or she was much younger than he had initially assumed with a passing glance.

Letting the silence lengthen, he pushed all awareness of her as a young woman so far back in his mind that he hoped it might never resurface. He asked, 'How long are you planning to stay as our guest, Miss…?'

The niece's eyes locked on his face, and her chin lifted an inch. Her lips firmed, and he heard the soft inflow of her breath.

'Please call me Marie. And I have left any decisions about the length of our stay to your grandmother and my aunt. And you, of course.'

'Of course. You may call me Gabriel. Now, what do you know about a card game last night?'

Chapter Two

Marie hesitated before speaking. The man standing in front of her had the same look of the yeoman warders she'd seen guarding the Tower of London. Of course he didn't have a spear in his hand, nor a sword or any weapon. No, those were concealed behind his eyes…

Her aunt must have been drowning in liquor to have considered such a wager. They really didn't need to be making this man angry.

If she were a queen of yore, she could imagine choosing the Viscount to protect the crown jewels. He was sturdy enough… Plus he would be able to deflect any mischief with an emotionless blink—but one full of portent.

Shaking her head softly, she hoped her forced smile appeared unconcerned and pleasant. She touched the flounces on her dress before speaking.

'I daresay your grandmother and my aunt got carried away, drinking their punch. I completely release you of any obligation to anything that might have been agreed last night.' She clasped her hands together. 'I had no idea what was going on until I woke this morning.' She tilted her head, chancing a glance at his captivating eyes, and tried to give a dismissive shrug. 'I laughed it off and I hope you will do the same.'

She prayed he would. She'd never believed his grand-mother would tell him about the wager, and was mortified that her doing so had brought them to this moment.

'They entertain each other with the strangest games sometimes…'

There was not a flicker of relaxation from her host.

She used all her strength to remain upright and keep laughter in her expression, although worry had tightened her throat. Once again she found herself having to cajole someone into a better mood so she would be able to main-tain a roof over her head. She was proficient at it by now.

She forced herself not to ramble on. To choose her words carefully and control her tone. She bit the tiniest part of the inside of her lip.

'I hear there was a wager,' he said, raising his eyebrows in a display of unconcern that she would not bet a penny on. 'Do you know what it concerned…?'

Evasiveness wouldn't help. It would only make their conversation go on longer.

He moved to the floral settee beside which she now stood. 'Please…' He waved a hand, indicating that she make herself comfortable.

Well, she decided, easing herself onto the seat, it would give her a little more time to compose her words.

She picked again at the flounces on her dress, and ar-ranged her skirts as her insides churned. She didn't want to answer his question, but the silence in the room seemed to swallow her whole, and she knew she was going to have to be the one to end it.

She'd never seen him except from a distance before, but now he was so close she could reach out and pat his knee. As he perused her in much the same way a Tower guard might appraise a suspected spy, she kept herself from trembling and forced out words she knew would seem an admission of guilt. He held all the cards, so she might as well put hers on the table…face up.

'The wager stated that you would make me a proposal. But I assure you I would reject it.'

She bit the left side of her lip. The right side was getting overused.

His expression relaxed. 'You would reject it?' he asked softly, and he put just the right amount of amazement and hurt—maybe even a tiny bit of humour?—into his reply.

'Yes,' she said, careful with her tone. She knew better than to offend the man providing the roof over her head. 'I've never been the sharpest arrow in the quiver, but I know enough to realise it isn't right to force a man into proposing.'

A glimmer of amusement passed behind his eyes. 'Have you ever tried archery?'

'No,' she admitted, confused at this sudden change of topic.

'Well, you never know… You might be the very best arrow in the quiver,' he said, and his voice altered when he spoke the last part of the sentence, making it sound almost like a compliment.

She forced herself to act nonchalant, and only by staying perfectly still could she hide the happiness that wanted to force itself onto her face.

Let that be a lesson to her, she decided. Given that her insides had already warmed, just from that hint of a smile, she knew that if he ever directed a fully-fledged smile her way they might just combust. And she was too sensible to tumble into a trap like that. She'd seen women who had destroyed their lives because a man had portrayed himself as some Romeo or Bassano or Orlando but turned out to be an Iago.

She could not tell him that she and her aunt were one spoonful away from poverty and that they'd been given little choice. Lord Andrews had made it clear that Marie was to wed his nephew or leave for good. Aunt Agatha, who wasn't even really her aunt, had told her husband to have the carriage readied and they'd both marched out that same evening, heads high, jaws firm, with Marie's insides fluttering like a flag in a windstorm.

'I'll marry him,' she'd whispered to Agatha, not wanting her aunt to be homeless.

'The blazes you will,' her aunt had said. 'I won't have you repeating my mistakes. I married that first old goat to get a roof over my head, and then I wed Lord Drippy Nose. I had thought he might have a thimbleful of affection for me, but he quickly started treating me like a used sofa...complaining of the lumps but refusing to buy new upholstery. A man will treat a horse well if he buys it. He will treat a carriage well, no matter what it cost him. But a wife... No, I do not want that for you.'

The driver had opened the door for them and they'd ascended into the carriage and left for good.

Agatha had reassured Marie that her friend the Dowager Viscountess would understand their plight, and after a warm welcome things had progressed well between the two friends...until that potent punch had been introduced into their card game.

The night before, Agatha had wagered her pearls. The only valuables she had left. And she'd planned to blackmail the Viscount's grandmother—if you wished to call it that—with the letter of promise she had signed, using

it as ammunition to allow them to stay in the household.
The Viscount was never to hear of it, her aunt had told
her, when she'd stumbled into Marie's room to tell her the
details. She had promised she would not give the letter
to anyone, and she'd tucked it into her reticule for safety.

'But the servants may read it,' Marie had said.

'Well, I will keep my reticule close,' she'd replied, holding it high and weaving a little, before putting a hand over
her heart. 'And we can trust Myrtle. She has a heart of
gold…which she purchased at a good price! It's tiny, but
it does fit on a bracelet.'

She'd laughed at her own joke and then stumbled off
to bed.

But Aunt Agatha had played right into the Dowager
Viscountess's hands. Because Myrtle Arthur won either
way—either with a chance to pressure Gabriel into a marriage or a new set of pearls.

Marie knew she would eventually find a suitable way
to support herself and Agatha—she hoped to write a book
on botany—but she had to play her cards right while they
were in society, in order to position themselves in surroundings that would maintain her aunt's reputation. And
even Marie had to admit that having a bed with a feather
mattress and an uncracked washbasin in her room was
much to be preferred over the alternative.

They weren't homeless, exactly, but they were wobbling
at the edges of it—which was a feeling she was familiar
with. The woman whom her mother had paid to raise Marie
since birth had reminded her daily that her father had deserted her mother and she'd had to be hidden away—with
very little to her name, and certainly no paternal affection—so that no one ever knew. She'd loved reminding

Marie that the streets would be her home if the funds to maintain her didn't arrive.

When her real mother had died—a woman Marie had never even seen—her mother's companion, Agatha, had arrived in her life. At sixteen, Marie had shed the first and only tears she remembered shedding. She'd wept for so many different reasons and Agatha had reassured her, saying that from that point onwards, Marie would be her niece, and she'd continue to watch over her.

She'd kept her promise every day since, and had put Marie's needs over her own many times.

She took in a slow breath. 'Agatha is more than an aunt to me. She is the mother I never had. But we do differ in opinion on some things.'

Mostly their viewpoint about what was considered ethical. Marie never would have made the bet Agatha had in that card game.

Gabriel stepped towards the harp again, but he appeared unaware of it, his gaze still on Marie. His perusal of her face held a respect that seemed to say that no one in the world could be saying anything more important than what she was saying. Her thoughts—which had always clicked along like the inner workings of a timepiece, steady and with precision—reacted as if someone had wound them the wrong way, and she was aware of masculinity, and strength, and just how a woman could drown in the appearance of just the right man—or the wrong one.

And that irked her. He had to know that such gentleness would be dangerous to a female. He had to know that he had attributes that attracted women and caused their throats to dry and their hearts to beat faster. That his attentions would make it hard for them not to smile and simper and let all their fluttery feelings show.

Her anger grew. A man such as he could throw out charisma borne of generations of ancestors who had created the closed society that had forced her mother to keep her a secret.

Her life was precarious, and she was used to that. But his wasn't. He had the assurance of someone who'd never known a worry other than whether he should immediately purchase the best or wait for even better than the best to be procured for him.

She looked at her hands, rubbing her right hand over her left, stifling her irritation. When she met his eyes, she didn't waste any hesitation before speaking words fuelled in part by her anger. 'Your grandmother thought the card game a lark, and the wager a chance for her to get Aunt Agatha's pearls. They had both been drinking too much.'

She didn't believe she should tell him that her aunt had, in her foxed state, considered blackmail a good way to maintain their residence until they found another means of support.

But marrying was one thing Marie would not do.

Her aunt had already proved how marriage under less than ideal circumstances didn't ever lead to the happy ending one hoped for, and the woman she'd lived with in her youth had claimed harsh conditions made the soul stronger, and did much to improve one's fortitude. She supposed it had given her an invincible spirit—and now she had to use it to figure out how to put a roof over their heads.

'I don't know that it is a good idea to have someone in my house who considers a marriage wager a good idea,' he said calmly, peacefully, and much too easily for her liking.

Though two women had been involved in the game, she knew that this was not the time to ask him if he was speaking of his grandmother.

'I understand. Aunt Agatha knew she had a winning hand, and she wanted to wager something useful, she claimed. But you had no part in it, and...'

Perhaps her aunt had realised Gabriel wouldn't go along with it, but that haggling over the wager with his grandmother would keep her entertained until they could figure out something else.

She appraised Gabriel. He seemed to measure his responses, providing only just enough to keep her talking. And she had no choice but to do so—because he was the owner of the house she currently called home.

'I told her it was wrong but, as my aunt says, the biggest lie humankind believes is that we can change someone else's mind. Any attempt to change my aunt's mind is only going to make her even more determined to prove she has the best idea.'

He nodded. 'My grandmother is the same way...unfortunately.' A wisp of affection and warmth passed across his face. 'She's hard to corral, but we try.'

She had not been wrong when she'd first assessed him. He held a complexity behind his eyes that intrigued her. But she closed her mind to it, mentally backing away from him. Reminding herself he was a viscount. Reminding herself that the secret of her birth, and the society that he embraced, had deemed her someone who must remain in the background. It was only carefully constructed lies that made her welcome in his world.

She lowered her eyes briefly, and met his gaze when she lifted her head. 'I try to gently guide my aunt, but that requires changing an idea before it is set in her mind. Otherwise I seem to just make her more determined.' She touched the puckered hem on one of her sleeves. 'I barely slept last night,' she admitted, 'fearing the consequences of her evening's revelry.'

'I hope you barely slept because of the wager itself,' he said, glancing over her face. 'Not because I was the…shall we say prize?'

'Oh, no.' Her cheeks reddened.

'That would be a slap in the face, of a sort,' he said, his eyes a little too serious and his voice sounding almost… hurt.

Her mouth moved as she searched for a response. 'Er… um…'

He was jesting with her, she was certain of it, but nothing showed on his face.

She paused, studying that stone countenance. She peered at him. 'Out of curiosity, do you ever wager?'

'Of course.'

She closed her fingers into a fist and tapped her knuckles softly against her chin. Giving the lightest nibble to her lip before speaking, she asked, 'And do you ever…lose?'

His chin lowered just a bit. 'Not often.'

She could feel the air she breathed entering her body and warming her, caressing from the inside, just as that intractable stare relaxed enough to give her another glimpse of the real man. One she wanted to memorise—except she knew not to do so.

He bowed, just a bit, and she realised she was being dismissed. But she also comprehended that she was not being asked to leave his house—at least, not yet. Nor was she being held responsible for the wager.

The walls and the world around her turned softer.

For less than a heartbeat in time their eyes met—in a truce, or respect, or perhaps in the first heartbeats of friendship.

She left without saying goodbye. She didn't need to speak.

Without words, he had given her his approval to remain in his home for the time being—a kind of reassurance that made her think that perhaps she was staying in the most secure house she'd ever known…

Shaking his head, Gabriel exited past the butler, explaining that he would walk until he found a hackney. He didn't want to wait for a vehicle to be summoned and readied.

He'd only gone a few paces when his cousin's carriage rolled into view.

Pierce jumped out, leaving the door swinging, and grabbed Gabriel's shoulder to steady himself. 'You will not believe what Mother has said Grandmother and her friend Lady Andrews did last night!' He chortled.

'I might.'

Gabriel raised a brow and looked at Pierce, who laughed before punching Gabriel on the arm and stepping back.

'So, when's the wedding?' Pierce asked.

'February the thirty-first.'

'Fortunate for her. Who is the lucky woman?'

'Lady Agatha's niece… Marie.' Gabriel warned Pierce with a glower not to ask any additional questions.

'Ah, I've heard of her.' Pierce shuddered and signalled his driver to reverse the carriage. 'It's said that Lord Andrews' nephew finds her fetching—but he pants at every woman who crosses his path. I think even the lightskirts won't have him any more.'

Gabriel tensed while Pierce chuckled.

'She's pitiable,' Pierce said. 'My friend has said Marie would be improved only by standing behind a haystack, and he was surprised even Lord Andrews' nephew noticed her.'

'She is not pitiable,' Gabriel said.

'Well, I could get a look at her myself, if I wanted to, at Grandmother's soiree tonight. .' He leaned forward and his voice lowered. 'It sounds as if she's quite pathetic.'

'That's a lie.'

'No matter to me.' Pierce clasped the door handle. 'Just wanted to let you know why I'm going to be avoiding Grandmother's soiree tonight. Pressing business. I am planning to drink too much at White's, and I might not have enough time if I attend the soiree.' He paused, still holding the door. 'Want to join us?'

Gabriel shook his head, changing his plans in an instant. 'I will be attending Grandmother's event.'

'Oh, that should be *delightful*.' Pierce gave him a salute of farewell and stepped into his carriage.

Gabriel grabbed at the door and looked up at his cousin. 'Drop me at Aunt Susanna's house.' Then he stepped inside the carriage.

'Well, thank you for travelling with me,' Pierce said.

'You're welcome.'

He wanted to see what Pierce's mother knew about the two women living in his home, and he didn't trust Pierce's viewpoint where women were concerned.

Chapter Three

After returning home, Gabriel called for his valet. 'Were the servants able to keep the harp from being moved into the ballroom?'

'Of course,' Watson said. A look of nonchalance was chiselled into his face—which was not always a good omen. 'The musicians will be here, as you requested, and your grandmother does wish to dance. Lady Andrews is excited to be included in the event, along with her niece. The maids are hoping suitable attire arrives for the young lady before the event, but it doesn't appear to be expected. The niece is apparently steadily sewing away in her room.'

Gabriel stopped, noting the evening attire Watson held up for him. Watson was a valuable asset, who understood what went on in the rest of the house better than he ever could.

It perplexed him that the two women did not already have suitable attire. Lord Andrews was not impoverished—Gabriel was fairly certain of that, and would ask his man of affairs to verify that—but he also knew him to be a gruff, scowling man, always grumbling.

He knew Agatha was Andrews' second wife, and that his grandmother had known both women, calling the first 'a timid mouse' and Agatha 'more spirited'.

He continued his preparations for the event, feeling that for once his presence wasn't just to be an appearance to quieten his grandmother's antics. He wanted to find out more about Marie.

He'd agreed to let his grandmother have her soiree at his house, but their negotiations had been hammered out with him smiling graciously and his grandmother compromising where she needed to, in order to get the best deal she could. He'd made her promise keep the guest list circumspect, and the libations under control, but on food she could do as she wished. And he didn't have to worry about the event continuing overlong, as his grandmother would instruct the musicians to stop playing and the staff to start putting the refreshments away when she decided the time was right.

When he'd finished dressing, he trod his way to the ballroom and searched for Marie. She wasn't yet present.

As the musicians finished warming up their instruments and began their first tune, Marie stepped into the room. He found he was aware of her the moment she entered, even though she did nothing to bring attention to herself.

She'd been dressed plainly before, but now it was as if she had worked her hardest at appearing grandmotherly. Her dress was much like a puffball that had been gathered around her body, her gloves were too short and her shawl was an unsightly coil of clothing which reminded him of the rug in the entrance hall—only the rug was more fashionable.

Her hair was once again twisted painfully tight, and a feather hung crookedly from the band she wore around her head—which did not match her dress. It did match the shawl, however, which was a shame.

The only saving grace was the eyewear perched on her nose. The spectacles were cute. Impish. Framing eyes which, as she'd studied the room, were not cute or impish, but forbidding.

No wonder she did not have many suitors. In fact he would have said, based on her actions, her goal for the entire night was to be as discouraging as possible.

But her aunt was hooking a hand around her arm and dragging her off to speak with people.

An older male friend of his grandmother's—rotund enough to balance a drink on his stomach—approached Marie, handing her a glass of ratafia. The words of their conversation were well hidden by the murmuring voices around them, but it wasn't long before she pushed her spectacles up her nose, smiled, and put a foot behind her to retreat.

As the man leaned forward she kept moving away, creating an amusing picture.

Finally rid of the man, she went to speak with his grandmother.

'She is a beauty. Except I can't talk her out of wearing those spectacles,' Agatha said beside him.

The words gave him a start, because he'd been studying Marie so intently he hadn't realised anyone was near him. He could see Agatha's admiration for her niece in her face.

'And she is such a dear. Always watching after me most kindly. The daughter I never had.'

'Yes. She reminds me of a gem,' he said, appraising her. 'Uncut. Not in the correct setting. Easily overlooked. In plain sight, and yet hidden.'

Lady Andrews' eyes took on a new spark when she heard his words. 'Yes...' Her eyes were innocent, but her smile undermined the look. 'I would say that is an asset in a woman. I know I certainly do not like hearing tales of Rosalind Warton's many beaus, Rebecca Johnstone's unseemly behaviour in the Wilsons' fountain, Annabelle Logan's penchant for too many glasses of wine or Roberta Wiggins' inability to stop giggling...'

She stopped, smug with innocence. 'Have I forgotten anyone?'

'I believe you've covered every unmarried woman here.' He looked into her eyes. 'Except your niece, of course.'

At that moment Marie noticed them and her aunt beckoned her. The younger woman smiled, but didn't move nearer.

'She is a paragon of virtue.' Agatha gave a one-shouldered shrug. 'What can I say? She takes after the other side of her family.' She looked at him. 'You two have that in common, I suppose. We both know you don't take after your grandmother.'

'I don't know...' he said. 'Perhaps I just hide it better than she does.'

'I would hate your grandmother to be indebted to me... And the scandal sheets would so love to see our agreement...'

'You hide your participation in blackmail well. And it would hurt Marie more than anyone else.'

Agatha's expression changed again as she watched her niece. 'Yes, her chances to marry would likely be quashed. I know I can never use the contract, but I had to get your grandmother's agreement in writing. She's too conveniently forgetful—as we all are.'

'You should trust that your niece will find her own suitor if it is meant to be.'

'But she needs help in that area. No one truly notices her, and she does not seem inclined to put herself among people her own age. She doesn't know how to enjoy herself. And she thinks marriage is too much of a risk. She calls it "the guillotine of romance", and considers it a tragedy played out behind four walls.'

'Perhaps she is right.'

She waved away his words. 'I once thought that if we're both going to be miserable, we might as well be married and miserable together. But I can't see Marie marrying the man who asked her. One drippy nose in the family is enough.'

'A convincing argument for marriage.'

She grunted, then continued. 'My niece is upset with me for the wager. She thinks I went too far. But I think you'd make a good husband for her.'

She spoke the words so smugly Gabriel knew she expected him to feel complimented.

'I'm sure you have clean handkerchiefs…'

He disapproved of her words with a glance.

She frowned. 'Oh, well… I tried.' She patted her bun, puffed up her sleeves, gave him a mumble that relegated him to a lost cause, and then walked away to speak with another man.

Marie was a wallflower. And that was generous. She was avoiding everyone her own age and standing apart from the crowd, using the other guests as shields between herself and whomever might look at her.

But then, most of the attendees were his grandmother's friends, and the only younger people his grandmother had invited were potential marital prospects for him.

He watched Marie as another man approached her and

asked her for a dance. Moving closer, he was able to hear her rejection first-hand.

'I'm so sorry, my slipper is coming untied. I must go to the ladies' retiring room and see if I can fix it.' She darted away and disappeared into the corridor.

He realised she'd not danced at all, and when she returned she stayed on the perimeter again, talking with the older ladies and gentlemen. Hiding in plain sight as best she could. A part of society, and yet not really. One foot in and one foot outside of London's most elite, with her clothing placing her in some antiquarian setting not even suitable for dowagers.

He corrected himself. She only had one *toe* dipped in society, and even then was appearing to distance herself from that annoying appendage.

Some odd feeling stirred within him. Curiosity, he supposed. He certainly could not truly be attracted to such a beanpole of a woman, wearing more of an oversized dresser scarf than appropriate soiree attire.

He couldn't help but notice the parts of the dress that touched her body—a skill he'd acquired in his early teens which, at the time, had given him no end of frustration.

And now he felt a similar cauldron of desire igniting inside him.

Blasted celibacy was not doing him any favours.

He'd thought he'd left rushes of passion behind with his virginity, but apparently he was returning to virginhood and all the wretched longings that went with it.

He tried to focus on her spectacles, which drew his attention to her face and her eyes. He wondered if she truly needed them, or if they were a means of adding another layer to herself in a misguided attempt to keep people at a distance.

She was so different from the other eligible ladies of the *ton*.

He thought again of asking Rosalind to wed him. She could charm the buttons off a statue and was stunningly beautiful.

He turned in Rosalind's direction and was surprised when she scowled at him—until he realised she'd been watching him peruse Marie. He took a step towards Rosalind, feeling he needed to appease her. Rosalind was one of the few suitable brides for him, and it was time he sired an heir. Like some prize overpriced stallion...

He ground his teeth together.

But his second step stalled, and out of the corner of his eye he glanced at that vision of a woman hiding from society.

She pushed up her spectacles and somehow reminded him of one of those little bumblebees he'd dared to touch once. He had brushed a fingertip over its back, and instead of its hair feeling soft, as he'd expected, it had been rough. It hadn't stung him, but only because it had been happily staggering around on a thistle, covering itself in pollen.

Appearances could be misleading.

Curiosity kept rising and rising inside him—and then irritation slapped at him. Why was he paying attention to such a little mouse? Well, not a *little* mouse. She was tall, which made those blasted ruffly parts of her dress even more noticeable.

With a firm stance he moved to Rosalind and told her how lovely she looked—which was true. The man at her other side firmly agreed.

Gabriel asked Rosalind to save the waltz for him, and she apologised, saying she'd already promised her waltz to the Earl.

Gabriel hadn't known an earl could swoon, but the man almost did—right in front of him.

The Earl took Rosalind's arm and they strolled away.

Gabriel moved to speak to the musicians before catching sight of Marie again, and he kept his pace slow as he approached her, attempting to gauge where she would try to hide next.

He stepped nearer to her. 'I hope you are enjoying yourself?'

One really couldn't tell the host how miserable one was at his event.

'It's a beautiful night,' she ventured. Although she really wished to be relaxing in her room.

And now the Viscount had noticed her. She would likely offend him if she didn't speak glowingly, and she could not afford to offend him. Best she keep to herself. It was safer that way.

He raised his brows. 'You didn't answer the question. Are you enjoying yourself?'

She tried not to look at him, but she noticed that his voice was a rich caress to his words.

Studying the room, she said, 'The servants have worked hard to create a pleasant evening. The partridge was the best I have ever tasted. These musicians could play for any royal event. The guests all appear to be having a good time.'

'You are still not answering the question and that tells me a lot,' he said.

'I am having a…good time.' She put every ounce of acting that she could muster into her answer, trying hard to put truth into the words and feel happy.

'Then I'd hate to see you having a miserable one,' he said.

She tilted her chin down, crossed her arms, and words tumbled from her mouth, skipping her brain. 'It's not the event. It's just that I'd rather be alone in my room. Writing.'

He raised his glass, took a sip, and then asked, 'What was your aunt speaking with you about earlier?'

He'd seen those clipped comments. The instructive movements.

'Aunt was telling me about the men who are here tonight. The oldest ones. She told me of their flaws as she perceived them, and reminded me that she has not had the best fortune with men. Her first marriage was to an older man, and he died impoverished.' She clasped her hands in front of herself and spoke softly. 'She says the only thing that truly matters to a woman in marriage is coin, and that men prefer youth and beauty, but will sometimes settle for whatever is expedient.'

He could understand that perception. Men flocked around Rosalind. She was stunningly beautiful, and she knew it. As he saw the swooning Earl walk by and give him a superior glance, he decided she could dance with the Earl all night for all he cared.

'The older men invited tonight are friends of my grandmother,' he said, linking his hands behind his back.

'I know. But my aunt was afraid that one of your grandmother's friends might notice me, and I would be tempted because of…' She bristled a bit then, reminding him of a little cat when its tail was stepped on. 'She told me that if

I am to wed for funds, you should be my choice.' Her jaw jutted.

'Why?'

He hardly moved, more interested in her next response than he had been in the previous one, even though this wasn't the first time he'd heard of an older relative suggesting him as a mate for a young woman.

'Because you have a huge house and we'd never have to see each other.'

She peered at him as if she expected him to run from her presence.

'You have hardly spoken to anyone tonight. You might not need an estate in order to find solitude.'

Her jaw dropped.

'And I agree that if you court someone you don't want him to have grandchildren your age,' he said.

She gave the tiniest shrug. He wouldn't have spotted it if he'd not been watching closely. And when she glanced up at him he didn't see the fortress around her, but a glimpse of the somewhat uncertain young woman she was on the inside, evidenced by the way she was biting her lip.

'Your grandmother has not invited a lot of young men,' she said. 'She wants you to be the plum in the pudding. Evidently both she and my aunt believe in stacking the deck.'

'I would think,' he said softly, 'that my grandmother believes I could compete without assistance if I put my mind to it.'

'I did not mean to suggest otherwise,' she said. 'But you can see my point.'

'I can. And I understand you're not enjoying the event. Perhaps a dance will make it more tolerable. Shall we?'

Her eyes widened. 'Dance? Why are you asking me?'

'Because I want to.'

'You've not danced with anyone else here.'

'So you've noticed?' He spoke softly. 'I'm flattered.'

Her cheeks brightened.

'You're missing the point.' She whispered each word firmly. 'I do not want to dance.'

'Neither do I,' he said. 'But it's my house, and you're a guest, and these things seem to be expected.' He tightened the side of his mouth before relaxing it and speaking again. 'I think people sometimes pay attention to who dances with whom.'

'Yes, they do. And I don't want to offend anyone because they think I am overstepping my place. It's very kind of you to ask me, but I'm certain there is someone else who will take my place. Now, I must go to the ladies' retiring room. Please accept my apologies.'

'I will pass the time until you return in watching people.'

'But—'

'I hired the musicians. I have spoken with them. They will happily wait.'

'Very well.' She frowned, and pursed her lips again. 'I don't need to go to the retiring room after all. I'm not the best dancer, and I will likely tread on your boots, so please remember that I did my best to get out of it.'

'I've not been injured in a dance yet.' He nodded to the musicians. 'And you should perhaps drape your shawl over a chair before we dance. It will only get in the way.'

She studied the cloth and placed it down gently, as if she were bidding a friend who was going on a lengthy journey farewell.

A few notes of music signalled to everyone what to expect.

'I don't—' she said.

He questioned her with a raised brow.

'Very well,' she said.

As he put his hand on her waist her eyes widened, and she stumbled when he moved them into the dance. Then he took a step and had to practically pull her along, so he slowed, waiting to let her get into rhythm with him. She didn't have to make her reluctance so obvious.

They danced, unspeaking. He wanted to see if she'd break the silence, so he waited.

She danced on, her eyes looking into the distance, lips pursed. His grandmother appraised him, half glowering, and her aunt stood at the side, smiling, her body swaying along with the music.

'Your aunt appears happy,' he said.

She nodded, lips firm, and he could tell she didn't want to speak. Very well. He would give her the silence she wanted.

The feather on the band in her hair wafted as they danced, and it was the only thing about her that seemed happy with the movement—though it was a little off in its rhythm, just as she was. Her steps hardly constituted dancing.

As the music neared its end, he watched her still-silent, tense lips.

He supposed that was what he received for insisting she partner him. She knew how to get her revenge. By dancing like a rough-edged rock. She'd even trodden on his foot once, as he'd tightened his grip on her, moving her along.

He found he wanted to see a flash of that woman he'd glimpsed behind her carefully presented gaze. A spark of that happiness.

She continued to ignore him.

Miss Wallflower was likely to remain a wallflower for a very long time if this was how she acted when a man asked her to dance.

A flash of irritation unfurled in him. She could certainly have better manners…

The violins stopped and he led her to a deserted corner, which he knew she'd prefer, and let his hand slide from her waist, aware of the rustle of fabric beneath his fingertips. The feather gave one last flutter before it slid from the band, and he caught it and handed it to her.

But instead of rushing away, she let out a deep breath. She grasped the feather with both hands, and he saw happy, shining eyes gazing at him.

'That went beautifully,' she whispered. 'The dance was not nearly so bad as I feared. And I think I did rather well.' She twisted the feather. 'I did not know what to do when I stepped on your foot, and I so appreciate your righting me.'

'You're welcome,' he said, surprised at the emotion on her face.

'I am so relieved.' She bent her knees slightly, and bounced up, the feather bobbing as she gushed, 'My first true waltz and I don't think I mis-stepped much—except that once. I did have a bad beginning, but I caught up.'

'You have never danced a waltz before?' he asked.

Suddenly her happiness retreated.

'Of course I have.' She frowned. 'I misspoke.'

'Where and with whom?' he asked.

She sighed, and then answered softly, peering at him from under her lashes. 'My aunt instructed some of the servants to teach me. I danced with a footman, and the housekeeper hummed.' She shook her head. 'We did practise some reels, but they had work to do, and my uncle would have been upset to see them dancing instead of doing their duties. It would have been unthinkable for him to agree to my having a dancing teacher.'

'You did well.'

At least, well for someone who had never danced to music before.

'Thank you.' Her shoulders went back. 'It was frightening.' She peered around the ballroom. 'I tried to study the reels, and I think I could do one, but I'm not sure...' Her eyes widened. 'I might like it.'

The excitement in her face made him smile inwardly. Her enthusiasm was contagious, and he almost felt he had danced the first waltz of his life as well.

'You really didn't have a dance teacher or a governess? Someone who could teach you?'

He realised then he'd never seen her at any events. When Lord Andrews had been widowed he'd wed Agatha, but the couple had kept to themselves and the niece had not been mentioned much.

She put two fingers on the side of one spectacle lens, and pushed the glasses firmly. 'I didn't have any music in my younger life. Aunt has tried to expose me to dance it since I moved in with her, and others have helped, but it seems to just go in one foot and out through the other, to misquote Chaucer.'

Something about her eyes tugged at him, and he accepted the challenge inside himself.

'I have a challenge for you,' he said.

Her brows rose.

'To attend another event.' He studied her. That drab feather had been the most vibrant part of her attire. 'Perhaps a picnic. With no dancing.'

'I do appreciate the offer. And it would be pleasant. But I think my aunt needs me...'

He answered with the kind of stare that he would give a child covered in crumbs for saying she had no idea what had happened to the biscuits on the platter.

'Please... I am content in my room. Which is a very nice room. Very pleasant. An incredibly comfortable room. Thank you so much. The view is wonderful. The sun shines in so beau—'

'You needn't hide in it,' he interrupted.

He could see her evaluating his words.

'I can help you,' he told her.

If she truly hadn't danced a waltz before, and was so uncertain in social settings, perhaps he could help her feel more comfortable.

'Will you remain as a guest at my house for a while?'

The tension in her shoulders relaxed.

'Yes. Of course. I have nowhere— I mean, I am going to find a mirror.' She held up the feather. 'Thank you again for the lovely waltz.'

She scurried away so fast he was surprised she didn't leave a slipper behind.

Rosalind sauntered up beside him, and she had no trouble inserting herself in his line of vision and touching his arm. 'You know, I'm planning to wed soon...' she said. 'If the right person asks me.'

He smiled at her.

'The Earl is already dropping little hints,' she said.

'You would make him an admirable wife. A delightful countess.'

She levelled her eyes at him, then laughed before speaking. 'I will make the Earl an *incredible* countess.'

'I'm certain of it. You would make any man a stunning bride.'

'Thank you.'

Rosalind leaned against him, fluttering her lashes in a long goodbye, telling him that he did not know what he would be missing, and then she gave him a wave and sashayed away.

She would make a better wife for the Earl than for him, he decided. He studied the other women in the room, but noticed himself searching for someone else.

He thought of his other romances in the past—of how they always started with so much promise, and how within a few months his interest inevitably waned, and how within a year or so someone else caught his eye. If he was being honest, he had already lost interest in Rosalind—and she was the most beautiful woman in the room.

It was the way of passion—to burn, fizzle and fade. His father had once told him that no romance lasted more than two years, and that marriage was of little benefit to the male of the species aside from begetting heirs.

He decided to wait until the end of the event and see if Marie returned. But he knew it was futile.

The soiree was wrapped up quickly, with his grandmother practically walking everyone to the door *en masse*, and he stood sipping a drink, not wanting to go back to the silence of his rooms.

'Why are you still here?' his grandmother asked him after everyone had left. 'You never stay this long at my soirees.'

Then she answered for him.

'I saw you dance with Marie.' She waved her own mention of it away. 'That will make good on the wager, as far as I'm concerned. It was just a jest, and I let Agatha get the best of me. She'll have to forget about it now, because I'm letting her stay here, and they really don't have anywhere else to go unless they want to move back in with Lord Andrews. He's trying to force Marie to wed his nephew. I couldn't stand for that.' She puffed out her cheeks. 'I mean, it's fine for me to try to force *you* to wed. You're a viscount and my grandson.'

She waved her hands, emphasising the correctness of her own perspective.

'The niece doesn't have any other family?' he asked.

'Oh, don't get all soft-hearted. If she was any kind of niece at all, she'd try to find someone to wed and get a roof over their heads. But no, not her. She wants to find a way to support Agatha. She's trying to write a book on botany—as if that could help her. Next thing you know people won't be calling her a wall weed quietly any more, but loudly. Perhaps I should warn her...'

'Grandmother. Don't meddle in other people's lives. And don't be unkind to Marie.'

'I'm not,' she said, straightening her back and standing almost to his shoulder. 'I know she's unsightly. And she's much more fascinated by plants than people. Agatha loves her, though.'

'Like I love you?' he asked, patting her on the back.

'Much to your regret.' She beamed up at him. 'I have the best grandsons in the world. Sometimes they just need a little help in sorting out their lives.'

'Pierce might. But I don't.'

'Then why aren't you already married? It's your duty. Heirs and all.'

'I've thought about it.'

He had. And each time he had he'd discarded it. He'd heard from his mother the distress of being married to a man who could not remain committed to one woman. And he'd heard the rows of her parents, who were deeply committed to each other—and to disagreement.

Chapter Four

'Marie.'

No knock. No warning. Just her aunt's grey head poking around the doorway and an overly bright smile.

Marie wiped the sleep from her eyes and sat up. Her aunt moved to sit at her bedside, a soft vanilla scent following her. Then Gabriel's grandmother moved in behind her.

'Myrtle has a wonderful idea about how she can make good on her debt.'

'I know a publisher. For your book. Only it's not likely he will publish a book about plants...'

The wrinkles in Gabriel's grandmother's cheeks became prominent when she spoke, and she adjusted her ruby earrings while she talked.

'Sadly, I agree,' her aunt added. 'But you know how Myrtle and I had the duel? We were thinking you could write about that.'

'The duel?' Marie asked, straightening the covers around her waist. 'I can't imagine that will cover more than a few pages.'

'True...' Agatha said, putting a lone finger first on one cheek and then drawing it over her other cheek to rest there momentarily. 'True. But you know, I've had quite a life.'

'No. I don't know,' Marie said.

'And I did have an...um...adventure with Joseph Grimaldi, father of the clown, and he was quite a performer, if you know what I mean,' Gabriel's grandmother added.

'I don't want to guess,' Marie answered.

'You wouldn't have to. And since you're a virgin I could just add it in after you've finished.'

'She would,' Agatha added, nodding. 'And that will take more than just a few pages. A whole chapter, I'd say.'

'Plus, I did pretend to be a highwayman once, because I'd told my friends I was certain it wasn't that hard. But, well… It was. No one in that carriage realised that all I planned to do was take their handkerchiefs when I said, *"Stand and deliver."* I nearly ended up skewered, because even on horseback I am too short to make a ferocious thief.'

'Show her the scar,' Agatha said.

'Yes.' Myrtle lifted the hem of her dress and pointed to a small round welt on her leg. 'It went in here.' She moved her hand. 'And came out here. Luckily, the man's gun didn't go off, or it might not have ended so well, but he was prepared with his sword. I had the horse galloping like blazes, but the man was such a stalwart that he nicked me with the blade.'

'That's how she met her husband,' Agatha said. 'How fortunate that his was the carriage she stopped.'

'I thought he was the most handsome man I'd ever seen. I knew I just had to meet him again—if I lived. My parents were thrilled when I told them I'd met a viscount. I didn't tell them that I was stealing his handkerchief when I did so. You can imagine… They thought him a huge step up from Grimaldi, and would have paid any amount to impress him.'

'Her parents had already tried to interest Myrtle in a

titled husband,' her aunt added. 'She'd rebelled by having the liaison with Grimaldi. The next thing her parents knew, she was asking them if they could purchase the Viscount for her.'

'Is this true?' Marie clenched the bedcovers.

'Enough of it is,' Myrtle said. 'Some would say too much of it is.' She chuckled. 'My parents had not wedged their way into society at that point, and no one really knew me, but Father was making so much with his shipping endeavours and all his other investments... And I was getting enough pin money to purchase my chaperon's silence.' She looked heavenward. 'Those were the days...'

Marie slid her legs to the side of the bed, pulling her chemise properly into place, considering.

'So far it's all been rumours,' Myrtle said, 'and I have laughed it away. But now I'm getting older I would like to share my story with others.'

'What does Gabriel think of the idea?' Marie picked at the coverlet.

'Oh, I didn't ask him. He would likely be spitting fire.' She turned to her friend. 'Agatha, you will have to reconcile with your husband before this is published. I might need a place to live.'

'That's not likely to happen.'

'Don't worry. We'll just keep it a secret from Gabriel for the time being. No sense in upsetting him if we never finish it. His mother raised him to be a stickler. Which I appreciate.' She bit her upper lip before continuing. 'Did I tell you about the gunpowder experiment?'

'No...' Marie said warily.

'I'll show you a smaller version. Little bits of powder can make such a noise. You'll want to include the recipe in your book.' She held out her palm. 'About a fingernail's width in a clasped palm. I suppose the size of the person would change that somewhat, but then a bigger person would be able to run faster after lighting the fuse. We'll test the recipe now. And be sure to mention not to put it in a teacup. Those shards can sting...'

Gabriel was pleased that his grandmother had been so amazingly well-behaved at the soiree. A paragon, for her. She hadn't laughed too loudly or told any untoward jests. In fact, she'd been the kind of grandmother one would have hoped all grandmothers should be, and she'd not caused any problems in the past few days.

As soon as his hand touched the bell-pull to ring for breakfast, he heard female voices in the distance.

It was odd for his visitors to be about this early, but he stood, took a step to the window, looked out, and saw his grandmother, standing military-straight, with a lit torch in her hand. Lady Agatha was beside her. Marie was watching.

'No!' he shouted, palms on the windowpane.

'It's fine.' His grandmother raised her head, shouting back. 'I know what I'm doing this time.'

He lunged for the door and took the steps at jump.

Just as he made it out through the door, his grandmother was leaning over, lighting the fuse.

'No!' he shouted a second time.

She stopped moving at the sound of his voice, but the fuse was already lit.

Without a thought he jumped for Marie, grabbed her around the waist, and took several leaps with her in his arms, keeping his body between her and the mound of powder.

The explosion didn't even rattle the windows.

Marie stared at him, eyes wide.

He peered over his shoulder.

A big clump of grass had been removed, and the two elderly women were picking strands of grass and clods of earth from each other.

He kept a steadying arm around Marie and stamped out the last few embers from the torch his grandmother had dropped.

His grandmother stared at him. 'You could have started a fire, scaring us like that.' She practically sprouted a halo over the horns he sometimes imagined as she glared. 'You ruined a perfectly good demonstration.'

His voice matched the explosion in strength. 'I told you not to buy any more gunpowder.'

'I didn't. That was left over,' she said. 'Old. And it didn't seem to have its usual power. I don't know why you over-reacted.'

'What if something had gone wrong?' he asked.

'It did,' she said. 'You rushed out of the house and terrified us all.'

'I told you no more explosions.'

'I would not call this a *true* explosion—just a small movement in the air. No windows broken. Although I still say that last time that one was already cracked.'

She dusted a few specks of earth from her arm.

'I wanted to show Agatha and Marie how simple it is to make fireworks. I told them it's best not to leave drinks about, because the falling debris doesn't really add anything to the flavour.'

Suddenly he realised he still had a grip on Marie's waist and she was tight against him, surprising him with the delicate femininity hidden underneath the fabric of her clothes. A vibrant burst of scent, springtime and gunpowder, hit him—two scents he would never have imagined going so well together.

His grandmother turned to Agatha and raised her chin. She said, a little louder than necessary, 'I was being extremely careful. You should have seen what happened last time.' She looked down and shook her head. 'One little window. Again, it was likely defective to begin with, but of course I received the blame.'

Then she side-eyed him. 'I noticed you didn't clasp Agatha or me to save us from the impending blast.'

'Marie was closer,' he said.

'I don't think so,' his grandmother answered.

'She's more innocent,' he said, glowering.

His grandmother snorted. 'Well, you have us with that one. Come along, Agatha,' she said, summoning her friend. 'I'm his grandmother and he should have rescued me. My feelings are hurt.'

Then she glared at him again, and the two older women trotted into the house.

He realised he was *still* holding Marie and her heart was beating against his.

He had only been concerned for Marie's safety.

And now he was concerned for his own.

Marie knew what it felt like to be held by gunpowder. She felt it in his clasp and in the little sparks inside her.

'There's not another explosion planned,' she said, her feet barely touching the ground, so secure was she against him. 'You can… You can let me go.'

He released her, but his warmth stayed with her.

She dusted down her arms, even though nothing was there. 'You nearly scared the breath out of me.'

'My pardon. I didn't want Grandmother to get you hurt.'

She took off her spectacles and blew over the lenses. 'I had no idea such a small amount of gunpowder could make an explosion,' she said.

'I did.' He locked eyes with her. 'Promise me you will not let her do that again.'

She put the spectacles back on. 'Once was enough. But I almost missed it because you rushed out of the house. It was very dramatic.'

And it had been. She had been caught up by him. Clasped close. Then the explosion had sounded and he'd shielded her with his body. He'd started his discussion with his grandmother and she'd just kept silent, clasped like a little bird in a nest of male strength, surrounded by the scent of gunpowder, fresh earth and clean male.

Oh, she would never forget it.

'As mentioned, she broke a window once, when she was testing gunpowder. If a little of something pleases her, she will use four times as much the next time. I have no idea how much powder she used previously, but this time I can tell she did reduce it a lot.'

'She evidently doesn't think the broken window was entirely her fault.'

His eye-roll convinced her of his opinion, and her wry smile told him she agreed with him.

'Promise me you will not take part in any more of my grandmother's schemes.'

Probably best not to mention the memoir…

'I'm sure you have tried to tell her no on many things? She just doesn't seem to hear it.'

He frowned, his eyes locked on hers. 'See me if you need assistance with that. It's much better than dealing with the after-effects.' He took her hand lightly. 'You seem to have her spirit of dangerousness. Don't let her lead you astray.'

No one had ever said anything like that to her. Other people were adventurous. She was the stable one. The one who kept her head down and did as she was told.

She reached out, pointing to the dust on his shoulder, wanting to ease the tension between them. After all, he'd just tried to save her from an explosion.

'May I?' she asked.

He didn't react, so she dusted the specks from his shoulder.

He thanked her with a smile that lit a completely different kind of fuse inside her.

'When you are with Grandmother you must take care,' Gabriel said.

'Of course.'

But she knew it was not just his grandmother she should take care around. It was him as well. He was as flammable to her as the largest barrel of gunpowder.

She rubbed at her arms, sensing the true jeopardy to her heart.

'Do you know about their duel?' he asked.

'Yes. I have heard about it.'

Her aunt had claimed it was merely a lark that had grown a little out of hand.

'I am not happy any time gunpower or swords are involved.'

She stood, staring up at him, possibly the strongest man she'd ever seen before, and yet she could see the dilemma he had. A grandmother who sought attention and explosions. The Achilles' heel in his life.

'They laugh about the duel now,' she said.

'I am not at that point yet. I was hardly twenty years old, and having to relieve my grandmother of a sword because the two of them had felt that a duel was the best way to settle an argument. I don't think they were even angry until I arrived—and then they were upset that I was stopping their duel. The crowd enjoyed it.'

'Wouldn't it have been worse if they had been angry?'

'More understandable,' he said. 'Grandmother just wanted the theatre of the moment.' He walked over, kicking at the earth to cover the hole left behind by the explosion. 'No one I've ever seen loves to be the centre of attention more than Grandmother. She probably hoped your aunt would send that wager contract to the scandal sheets.'

'I'm sure not.' She paused, then whispered, 'I tried to get it from Aunt Agatha, but she keeps that reticule close. She has the signed agreement and the pearls in it.'

His stare indicated that he didn't want to be reminded.

'I must thank you for trying to save me—though it wasn't needed,' she said, trying to change the subject back to something safer. 'You added a bit of excitement to what would have otherwise been quite a dull explosion.'

Goodness, the man was studying her as if she'd just slapped him for no reason. And she'd given him a thank-you.

'A dull explosion?' He gave a strong stamp on the earth with his boot, and then another final one.

Somehow she felt she must explain to him. 'Your grandmother is a dear woman. And she is fascinating. You are fortunate to have her near.'

His eyes met hers while he picked up the remaining

pieces of the torch. 'Will you stay away from her fireworks in the future? No more letting her light fuses?'

'Sometimes she's hard to say no to.'

'I don't have any trouble with it,' he said. 'Again, come and find me if you need any help with that.'

She knew he meant every word, and that if she didn't go along with his plans he would be more formidable than his grandmother. Best to keep him in the dark about some things. And surely his grandmother would lose interest in the memoir...

Gabriel studied her, pleased at the thought that she might search him out, and then gave a wave to indicate they go back into the house.

'Your grandmother expected you would still be asleep and would not even hear it,' she said, scrambling to keep up with him.

He stopped and raised a brow. 'She will tell you whatever suits her purpose. It doesn't make me feel any better to hear that you are aware Grandmother is hiding her antics from me and you are assisting her.'

'Oh...' She cupped her chin in her hand and rested her thumb against her lips. 'Your grandmother said she had used gunpowder before and was experienced. Although she did claim the people who create the gunpowder sometimes vary the strength.'

'*She* varies the strength.' He lowered his voice and didn't move any muscle unnecessary for speaking. 'Experience doesn't always equal safety. Not where Grandmother is concerned.'

'I don't believe she would do anything dangerous...'

The short burst of air from his nostrils contradicted her.

'Perhaps she knows her boundaries,' Marie challenged.

'Her boundaries are the earth, the sky and whatever else she can reach.' He nodded towards the side of the house. 'That lower window is the one which had to be replaced, and not all things can be fixed so easily. She should leave explosives alone.'

'But nothing went wrong with the experiment. In fact, I found it exciting.'

Exciting? Her eyes were bright behind the spectacles. She didn't realise how badly she could have been injured.

'She has some tall tales... Do you think they are true?'

There was a question in her tone. Uncertainty in her gaze.

'Sadly, they aren't all tales, I suspect,' he said. 'And I also suspect she is a bad influence on you.'

'I like her.' She pursed her lips.

'You liked the explosives.'

'Yes...' She moved closer. 'You didn't need to save me, but it was a nice thought.'

'You were too close to danger.'

'Nothing bad happened. Except we interrupted your day.'

'That is not the problem,' he said. 'You need to stand firm against their schemes.'

'Ho!' she said. 'You have a veritable army of people behind you, and what I suspect are unlimited finances, and yet you cannot corral her as you wish. Why do you think I can?'

'She might listen to someone who isn't a relative.'

'When you find someone she listens to I would like to be introduced to them.'

Steady eyes challenged him and she moved forward, the flounces on her dress billowing as she opened the door and left him to stare at the wood and remember the blast of having her in his arms. The feel of his fear that she was going to be hurt. And the steadiness of her eyes when she dared him to find someone his grandmother would listen to.

She might be nervous at social events, but she was not evincing any such emotion when she was alone with him.

He remembered their dance and relived it, smiling at his misinterpretation and the memory of her happiness afterwards.

Opening the door, he called out her name.

She hesitated, then turned to him, and he spoke one sentence before they both went their separate ways.

'I suspect you are as explosive as anyone else in this house.'

Chapter Five

Gabriel woke early, knowing he needed to study the details of a new property lease. His grandfather had told him over and over that a viscount needed to be aware of what was going on within the estate and consider the details of all purchases and properties sold. Trust was for the poor, he'd said. A wealthy man couldn't afford it.

Normally he slept late, but it was as if memories of Marie had prodded him awake. He summoned his valet, who appeared without so much as a wrinkle in his clothing and in his usual good humour.

'What has the morning brought us?' Gabriel asked.

As the man gave a nod of greeting, he answered. 'Miss Marie is in the library, probably for a respite, and the two ladies are still discussing your rescuing her before them.'

Gabriel raised a brow.

'Maids on duty, sir. The housekeeper assigned the most talkative one to your grandmother's rooms yesterday. She thought it best…particularly after the explosion.'

Giving a nod of approval, Gabriel dressed quickly so he could speak with Marie.

'And one other thing I thought odd,' his valet continued, 'is your grandmother's new love of botany.'

'Botany?' Gabriel paused, his hands on his top waist-coat button.

'Yes. Apparently Miss Marie is writing a book on botany. When the maid walked into the library Miss Marie had a notepad and they were talking about roots and tubers and daffodils, or some such. The maid thought it a bit odd… as if they'd suddenly changed their conversation when she entered the room.'

'Probably trying to figure out which ones are most poisonous,' Gabriel said.

The valet nodded.

'I wonder if we should warn Lord Andrews.'

'I will let the housekeeper know that the maids are to immediately alert her and she is to tell me if any dangerous plans are mentioned.'

'Thank you.'

'And I will see what else I can find out,' he said.

Gabriel left the room, pulling the waistcoat into place, and took the short walk to the library. He would have thought he saw Lady Andrews sitting in front of the open window if the valet hadn't said it was Marie, and he still had to take a second look to reassure himself.

Once more she was wearing a dress not made for her, and she had that disreputable shawl around her shoulders. But today it appeared to have been tied so she could write comfortably. Her skirts billowed at her feet, and appeared full enough to trip her.

She always dressed in a form-swallowing gown that appeared a bit faded and forgotten, and he wasn't sure that she didn't wear the same few dresses, with a few different bows and ribbons placed upon them.

She wore her hair in a knot, pulled back and with no

extra twists or turns in it, just the minimum care possible. The same as the maids. Then it dawned on him. She dressed like a servant. Hiding in plain sight.

If she remade old clothing she wouldn't flatter herself. She used her sewing skills to conceal herself.

He tried to recall all he knew about her. But nothing came to mind. She had slid noiselessly into his world. If not for the wager, he probably would not ever have been truly aware she was living in his home.

She saw him and her pencil stopped in mid-air. The pages of her notebook fluttered as she flipped them closed with the barest crisp sound.

Her spectacles sparkled in the light. The morning sunshine floated over her. But she was so shaded by her clothing that it might as well have been cloudy.

'You are up early,' he said.

'Aunt and your grandmother were comparing notes on the dinner they attended at Mrs Smythe's,' she said, her eyes darting away. 'Really, it was a chance for more wagering than for a dinner. But this time the cards were in your grandmother's favour.'

She gathered up the book on the table beside her, and he could tell she planned to leave.

'Don't go on my account,' he said. 'You should continue to enjoy the morning.'

'It is getting a bit warm,' she said.

Then she seemed to think better of exiting, and returned her notebook to the table beside her. Removing the heavy shawl, she placed it over the arm of her chair.

'How long have you worn spectacles?' he asked.

'Several years. Aunt Agatha saw me peering too closely at things and decided something must be done. It hadn't occurred to me that I would ever have an opportunity to have something so fine.' She touched the rim of the glasses. 'They are the dearest thing I own, and I will always remember she gave me such a gift.'

With both hands she took them off for a moment, peered at him, and put them back on. 'If they bother other people I don't care. I could hardly believe it when I received them. Some days I take them off and look at things, and then put them back on for the joy of seeing how much clearer everything is with them.'

'They are lovely.'

Her long stare and the brief upsweep of her chin let him know she didn't believe him.

But it was true.

'Lord Andrews was upset that Aunt Agatha had wasted so many funds on something so frivolous and he complained, telling her they would likely ruin my eyesight completely. Then he left to go to his hunting box because he was so angry with her,' she said. 'Aunt Agatha decided to use what little funds she had left to hire a coach and go after him. She took me with her. I'd never been to the country before.'

Memories wafted across her face.

'I was sad that Aunt Agatha was distressed, but everything seemed so clear and beautiful that I couldn't keep from looking out of the window as we travelled. I'd never seen leaves high on a tree, really. They were just masses of green. I saw a bird Aunt Agatha told me was a linnet, and it didn't fly in a straight line, but moved up and down as it flew. Before, I'd never been aware of anything like that.'

Then she appraised him, but took a second too long.

'So, what do you see when you look at me?' he asked.

Instantly, he saw a shutter go across her eyes.

'A viscount,' she answered. 'From head to boots. A respected member of society. Assured. Quite distinguished.'

'And what do you see when you look in the mirror?'

Emotions fluttered on her face. He wasn't sure if he'd hurt or angered her, but she seemed uncaring, and answered, 'I am a poor relation. I'm only allowed to attend social events by the barest thread. I don't mind, though. If I weren't to be invited it wouldn't upset me much. But I feel my aunt relies on my presence to make her feel better, and I'm pleased I can do that. I owe her so much.'

'I would like to give you a chance to see something else in your mirror. I don't want you hiding away at any gathering, particularly for the picnic. You are a guest of my grandmother's and are every bit as welcome as your aunt is.'

Her eyes flashed at him.

'What you see as hiding away is simply my knowledge of my place. I am making my aunt more comfortable if I am at her side.'

'And at the soiree? Weren't you trying to avoid people, and not giving others a chance to get acquainted with you?'

'If they'd wished to speak with me, they could have.'

'Not when you graciously excused yourself.'

She shook her head. 'I know Aunt Agatha wishes me to converse, and get on well with people, and I understand that.' She turned away. 'I know I should make more of an effort, and I do try to make enough to please her. But I am not fond of nonsensical chatter with strangers.'

He knew that the Marie in front of him now was presenting more of her real self than the illusion she had created to conceal herself within her surroundings, surviving as best she could. He wanted to know more about this version of her—the true woman.

'Besides, I don't have the right clothing to be in society. It would only cause speculation and cold shoulders if I were to try to be a part of that world.'

'What if you did?' he asked.

No answer.

Rain had begun pattering down outside, and she studied the window. 'I suppose I should close that.'

'Only if you want to. The cooler air feels good.'

She stood and walked to the window, putting a hand near the rain. The drops changed the smell of the gardens, and changed the feeling inside the house.

Her hand reached out into the rain. Her eyes studied the drops landing on her skin.

'I almost wish everyone could experience what I did,' she said. 'Receiving these spectacles gave me a chance to appreciate how green everything was. How alive. And I realised that nature should be noticed. Before wearing my spectacles, I wasn't able to experience much unless I could walk right up to it. In truth, if I saw someone at a distance, I often couldn't tell who they were.'

She stretched her left arm wide, her body still safely inside the house.

'Getting my spectacles was like lifting the lid from a magic kettle and looking inside to see another world. One that had been there all along.'

He moved to stand beside her, and study the view she saw, but really, he savoured the moment of standing alone at the window with her.

A burst of wind and rain splattered them both, chilling the air even more. She tilted her head downwards and he saw a hint of displeasure on her face, her spectacle lenses becoming dotted by water drops.

She stared up at him, frowning, and he hoped it was merely because of the water.

'I suppose it is time to close the window,' she said, tugging it with her dry hand, and he reached out and helped the frame snap into place.

'These water spots on the lenses do give me grief.' She touched both hands to the sides of her spectacles. 'Even the widest brim on a bonnet doesn't always help with that.'

'I have a handkerchief.'

He retrieved the cloth from his pocket and she took off her spectacles, causing a few strands of hair to escape her bun. She stared at the water drops and rubbed at her lenses carefully, to dry the moisture, and he saw the longest eyelashes he'd ever seen. She studied him for half a beat before returning the handkerchief and putting the spectacles back on her face, working to get the earpieces set as regally as if she'd been adjusting a crown.

His heart thudded at the sight of her.

Behind the agreeable, amenable countenance rested a woman who would try to escape conflict until she couldn't do it any more. But she enchanted him.

'I must go. My aunt will be sending a maid for me soon, I'm sure. Or your grandmother will.'

'My grandmother?'

She lowered her voice and her eyes. 'I think she considers me a good audience.'

Now he understood why his grandmother had been less likely to cause any upset these last few weeks. Marie and her aunt were providing companionship.

'Grandmother prefers all eyes to be on her and all ears to be listening.'

'I would agree. She has lived with a sense of curiosity and adventure and has no trouble stating her opinions.'

She gazed at him, as if she could see into his soul.

'I do try to keep the peace between my aunt and your grandmother. I have a lot of practice in keeping as many people content as I can.'

'I have already seen that in you. It's a good skill to have.'

It had never been one of his. He employed people for that.

Then he noticed one of the books she had put on the table: *The Herball or Generall Historie of Plantes*.

Indicating the tome with a nod, he asked, 'You're interested in botany?'

'Yes. I have been trying to read all the books I can on it. I had thought…thought I might write a book on botany and that would give me a way to support my aunt and myself.' She studied the cover, eyes downcast. 'But it is impossible for me to discover all I need to know…'

He stared at it, a hideous volume, and lifted it with both hands. He opened it. 'It's a book about…plants?'

Perhaps he'd looked at it a few times, but he'd never really been interested.

'Botany,' she repeated, taking the book from him and putting the notebook on top of it.

'Are you reading it?' he asked, nodding towards the book.

'I was, but I'm putting it back now.'

'Perhaps you could write about something else. Something more…'

She studied him, eyes suddenly widening. 'I suppose that is an excellent idea. Excellent…'

In a whirl, she put the book into an empty spot on the shelf and turned to leave.

'You appear very learned,' he said.

'My friend Polly's mother taught me to read, thinking she could teach two more easily than one and we would help each other.'

Her words were rapid. She darted to the doorway.

'Wait, wait,' he called to her back, taking one stride to catch up with her and another stride to pass her. 'My apologies,' he offered, although he didn't really see that he'd done anything wrong.

'I heard a man once say to his son that no education is ever wasted,' she said, hugging the notepad close to herself. 'I'm not so sure of that, because I see people all around me with an education and it was only a chore to them. But it was a luxury I could not have. If they'd had to struggle for it they would have appreciated it more.'

She looked at her notebook. Her voice softened. 'Please forgive me. I forgot my—'

He knew what she was going to say. She had forgotten her *place*.

'When the weather is right, your "place" is overlooking the garden or on a garden bench,' he said, walking to her and taking the pencil from her fingers, using it to point beyond the window. 'Claim it.'

'It's not my place,' she said. 'It's yours. You were trained for the role you have in life, and I suppose I was for mine, too.'

'I worked hard at university. Sometimes...' A pause. 'When I wasn't watching the liquor diminish. Or listening to wild tales. Playing cards. I suppose it has done me well.'

'I assume you are quite proficient at revelry, then? Although it's not apparent.'

'I suppose so. But then, most of the other students worked on that skill equally, so we were well matched. I also learned a lot about history. About how other people think. And I met people from different areas.'

She clutched the notebook as if it might preserve her life. 'It must have been incredible to have such an opportunity.'

'It was. But I don't think I appreciated it until this moment. I just wanted it to be over so I could get on with my life.'

Her lips tightened and she didn't speak.

'Forgive me. I've been up all night, mostly,' he said, 'so I suppose my manners have nodded off. I did not mean to upset you.'

'I know. I suppose I am sensitive about…some things. Most things, possibly. Truth be told.'

'I suppose many people are sensitive about something.'

'And you?' she asked.

'Can't think of anything.'

'Nothing?'

'No. Don't think so.'

She studied him while the silence lingered, but it was a comfortable quiet, with the rain pattering down harder outside, adding a background music to their words.

She took the pencil from him and used it to point at his neckcloth. 'What if I said that your cravat has too many loops?'

He touched the fabric. 'Beau Brummel himself trained my valet.'

She shook her head. 'Perhaps you should have found someone else to teach him. Someone who liked smaller bows. Or none. One floppy knot or just a small knot can be quite attractive.'

He touched the linen and laughed. 'As opposed to what you think of this one now?'

Her eyes opened wider. 'A simple one can be impressive.'

'This is a costly neckcloth. The finest linen.'

'The cloth is magnificent,' she said, by way of appeasement.

He moved to the window, away from her, and unbuttoned the top buttons on his waistcoat, then he untied his cravat, put it into a simple knot and grimaced at it. Now he had too much length at the end of the fabric. He opened his waistcoat and folded the ends inside. In his opinion, he appeared rumpled.

He did up the buttons and stood for her perusal. 'Better?'

'Now you look unkempt.'

There was just the slightest dip of her head and a blush on her cheeks, plus a small smile of acknowledgement.

'See? The cravat my valet tied was better.'

'Different. Not necessarily better.'

'Perhaps I'll try a smaller knot at this picnic I'm planning to have. I want you to attend and not stay in the shadows. I will wager that you will capture attention and like it. And I will wear a cravat without style, though it may be difficult...'

'One without a dozen loops?' she asked. 'Or even ten?'

'For you, I will,' he said. 'And I hope you will consider staying out of the background. I'd like to help you with that.'

He saw the puzzled look on her face, but he didn't give

her a chance to question him before he stepped away, bowing slightly as a farewell.

'My man of affairs is arriving soon. When he leaves, I will talk with the butler and he will help with my plans.'

She hid her sigh, watching the doorway after he left. How wonderful to have someone in your employ who could help with everything in the household, and someone else whose job it was to make money for you.

All that would have corrupted many people, but it didn't appear to have tarnished one hair on Gabriel's head.

He'd not seemed to mind her spectacles, nor even that she liked botany and birds.

No wonder so many women were entranced by him. At least, according to his grandmother. Marie could believe it. She'd seen the women vying for his attention at the soiree. All of them beautiful, accomplished at dancing, and wearing beautiful gowns.

From the corner of her eye she'd even noticed a few spiteful eyes on her when she'd waltzed with him, and that had interrupted her concentration, causing her to misstep. He'd been so considerate, and kept her dancing correctly, and her heart had fluttered more than any bird's wings.

A woman might easily lose her heart to him.

Just as a woman might easily float into a disaster she couldn't recover from. It would be a tragedy to care for someone who might not return the affection.

As Marie had been growing up her guardian had constantly reminded her that men only stayed long enough to father a child or two and then went on their way. She'd told Marie time and time again that she must remain on her own path. She must be true to herself. It was better to live alone than to live with a woman-chaser—and she should know because she'd known plenty of them.

Even Polly's father had left his family. Aunt Agatha's first husband had died, and now the second had pushed her out of his house.

In fact, she couldn't think of a single male who'd remained constant to the woman in his life. Even when she'd been very young, and had had her only true, devoted suitor, she'd known her sweetheart hadn't considered marriage overly binding. That was why she'd called off the courtship—a blessing in disguise, in the end. The realisation of how close she'd been to a tragic fate resounded in her. He'd wed someone else and been a tyrant to his wife— she'd seen the woman's bruised cheek.

If Gabriel found out the truth of her past he'd not have any qualms about ridding himself of her. It would be horrible if he tossed them out, so she should not risk antagonising him.

She and her aunt had moved in—temporarily—with his grandmother because they really had nowhere else to go. Aunt Agatha claimed she was certain her husband would soon realise his mistake, and they'd be able to return to his mansion again. But eventually his nephew would inherit, and Marie wasn't sure what would happen to her then, except that she'd again be scrabbling for a place to live—possibly for both her and her aunt.

Better that Gabriel remain unenlightened than realise what dire straits she was in.

It wouldn't matter anyway. She was about to become part of an even bigger scandal.

She'd not considered the ramifications of writing his grandmother's memoirs until she'd put pen to paper and seen the words flowing. But Myrtle had made Marie promise to be certain not to tell Gabriel anything about the memoirs, as she thought it best he did not know until after they were published.

That promise hung over her now—a dark cloud that would do more than make drops on the outside of her glasses. It might lead to tears on the other side.

Marie returned to her room and looked over the notes she'd taken from his grandmother's reminiscences. She'd not realised how wealthy women could behave when doors were closed…

Chapter Six

She'd worked all evening on her notes, and Gabriel's grandmother had just given her another anecdote she'd recalled, and sent Marie to her room to write it up.

The house always seemed quiet, compared to the other places she'd lived. She and her aunt usually seemed able to keep Myrtle calm, and Marie didn't count the gunpowder as a true explosion.

Letting out a breath, she moved towards Myrtle's room—but then she heard robust footsteps. Gabriel. She stopped, and he turned a corner and almost collided with her.

She jumped away, then put up a hand to straighten her hair. 'I wasn't expecting you,' she said.

Just the top half of his body moved forward as he almost whispered the words, 'It's my house.'

'You are rarely on this side of the house, from what I have seen.'

'It's true I don't visit Grandmother much, but she often stops by my rooms if she hears a scandal she thinks I should know about.'

'She probably sees you often, then.'

He chuckled. 'Will you join me in the music room? This will only take a moment,' he said, holding out his arm.

With only the briefest hesitation, she took it, surrounding herself with the crisp, clean scent of him.

He led her towards the music room, opened the door, and indicated that she enter. 'I wanted you to know the picnic plans have been finalised. Except for the plan to do with you.'

The harp was in the centre of the room, with several chairs placed conspicuously around it for an audience. She and her aunt had sat in those chairs several times.

'A picnic sounds pleasant,' she said, hearing a small waver in her voice which she hoped he didn't notice.

It did sound pleasant, but only if there were few attending. Perhaps if he were the only guest it would be grand. But to be among all those society people would mean watching every step, and every word, and being on her most perfect behaviour. And she had nothing new to wear. Or really nothing old to wear…

'I have not requested any musicians.' His lips firmed for an instant. 'I will instead suggest Grandmother plays her harp, and that will appease her on not being consulted over the details.'

'I listen to her playing sometimes. It's enjoyable.'

His eyebrows tightened.

'It really is,' she said, suddenly needing to convince him that she told the truth. It was so much better than hearing someone having a row.

He led her to the chairs, but they didn't sit.

'You really do act more like someone of your aunt's age than your own,' he said. 'You even dress like her.'

'I know. I like more comfortable clothing.'

The dress she had on had used to belong to her aunt, so it didn't surprise her that he thought so. It was better for all concerned that she did not stand out, and this clothing would serve her well if she was able to obtain a position on a housekeeping staff. A light day dress would not.

She continued to be pleased to take the older dresses her aunt could no longer fit into. But, since sewing wasn't her strongest skill, the flounces and things she'd added to help them fit better hadn't really improved them much.

Funds had been a struggle all her life. And now she and her aunt depended on Lord Andrews, and he was a penny-hoarding, miserly man. But still, he had provided a home for them, for a time, and she had appreciated it. Living with Aunt Agatha had been the best years of her life.

She saw Gabriel's eyes glance over her hair and she touched it defensively. She always pulled it back primly. It was the easiest, quickest way to style it, and suitable for someone in her station.

'Perhaps you could speak with my grandmother about a shopping trip? She dearly loves shopping trips.'

'I don't know,' she said. 'I'll think about it.'

She did, and dismissed it.

'Grandmother could help you. It would give her something to do other than wager on me or meddle in my life.'

'I don't know that a shopping trip is the answer.'

It wouldn't be for her. She could not buy anything to wear for a picnic. She wore shawls sometimes, to cover her clothing better, but feared they didn't help much.

'Today my valet tied my cravat with less loops.' He touched the flowing burst of fabric at his neck.

'I can't tell.' She pursed her lips. 'It appears your neck-cloth is so tightly wrapped around your collar that if you dropped something you would have to bend at the waist to look down.'

He tugged at the silk, but didn't reduce its neatness. 'I have to give an appearance of maturity in order to be successful in conducting business.'

'You certainly do. But is it really necessary at your age?'

'My age?' he asked, eyes narrowing. 'It's not rare for someone my age to have inherited an estate.'

She studied him. 'How old are you?'

'Twenty-seven. Last month.'

'Oh.' Her mouth remained open. She studied his face. Peered at his hair.

'It's not thinning,' he said, his eyes giving her a straight glare. 'Or greying. At least, not noticeably. And anyway, I have been told it will make me look even more distinguished.'

She nodded. 'Your clothes work very well at giving you an air of maturity. I thought you were much older.'

'Appearing responsible is important to me.'

'You succeed.'

She hesitated, studying him right down to the last tiny wrinkle at his eye, imperceptible from any distance. She'd never have noticed it without the spectacles' help to her vision.

'I don't think either of us likes the clothing of the other very well,' she said, changing the subject from age.

A look of whimsy in his gaze told her he recognised what she was doing.

'If I wear a more simple cravat, would you consider dressing for a younger age?' he asked.

She didn't really know if that was a possibility. 'I would like to remain in what I'm comfortable wearing.' She crossed her arms. 'It is what is on the inside that counts.'

'Said the lady who has critiqued my neckcloth.'

'I thought it needed to be said and that you would not mind. It's such a simple thing to alter.'

He let out a whoosh of breath. 'Not where my valet is concerned.'

'Then I apologise for even mentioning it. It was entirely wrong of me, and I beg your forgiveness.'

'You're apologising for mentioning it, but you don't say you've changed your mind.'

Her teeth were almost gritted behind her smile, and she forced truth into her words. 'The neckcloth looks amazing. Mature. Respectful. Perfect for business.'

There—she hadn't lied. Still too many loops, though.

His smile told her he was reading her mind.

'Not all people look closely enough to see the inside,' he said, giving a tug on his cravat to increase the size of the loops. 'And the outside is considered a reflection of it. If you are considering suitors, the first thing you see is his outside. I see your dated attire, just as you see my impressive cravat.'

'I am not considering suitors,' she said. 'And I'll have you know that this dress was made with very expensive fabric...once upon a time.'

She couldn't tell him how strained her aunt's finances were, nor how new clothing had never been a consideration for Marie. A new dress was out of the question. Aunt Agatha had tried to keep their dire financial situation a secret, but his grandmother now knew all the details.

She took in a breath, seeing the image of something she'd never had right at her fingertips, tempting her beyond anything else. 'Perhaps a new frock would be nice, but I'm completely happy with my appearance.'

'As I said, my grandmother could assist you. She is always leaving fashion plates lying around, and she gets fraught if a servant moves them. She would help.'

His grandmother definitely wore the latest fashions. 'I am not sure what she would think of that offer. I shall have to decline.'

That hurt. The image of a new dress so possible and yet so far from her. She didn't think she'd ever had a completely new frock, but she'd been happy each time one was passed down to her. No one could have been happier to get a useable dress than she.

They walked a few more steps and she peered at him from the corner of her eye.

'Changing your cravat would be so easy for you, though. Just use fewer folds. It would take less fabric and save on funds.'

His eyebrow twitched.

She firmed her jaw.

Now both his brows nearly met in the middle.

'You would be impressive still with a plain cravat, a black waistcoat and coat and boots.'

'You wish me to vanish into the woodwork?'

'No. You'd never disappear into your surroundings. You claim them. You need no extra help. In fact, I think the opposite. I think you would appear more powerful in the plainest of clothing. And that is a compliment, and the truth.'

She wasn't speaking flattery. His movement was always purposeful. Intent. He never ambled, or meandered, or sauntered. She didn't think he planned his steps, but they were as strong as if he'd drawn up careful plans and moved precisely into them.

'I will happily wear plainer clothing if you will give

simpler gowns a chance, and at the picnic we can both see how we like the change in our appearance.'

He stepped away, so that her hand slid from his arm. 'The picnic is a week from today—surely a dressmaker can have a gown whipped together by then?'

'That's a short time,' she said, not willing to admit it had taken almost a month for her aunt to receive the last gown she'd purchased. 'My aunt's seamstress could never work that fast. I don't think it's possible.'

Particularly not with her limited funds.

'Grandmother could handle all of that for you. Her seamstress is skilled and quick. And I am sure she would make it a gift to you after the risk of your lighting the fuse for her.'

'Please don't speak with your grandmother about a dress for me. It would not be wise.'

She knew his grandmother might read more into such a simple idea than just the spirit of generosity, and would likely ask a hundred questions, determined to put a barrier between Marie and Gabriel. Recently the older woman had been talking about Rosalind as the perfect wife for him.

Marie imagined herself deflecting bolts of lightning-strong attention from his grandmother. If the slightest thing went wrong—such as anyone finding out she wasn't using her real name—both she and her aunt could be homeless.

'My dresses are fine. Just not elaborate.' She made a decision. 'I must thank you, but I cannot see me having a new frock at your expense.'

She touched the sleeve of her dress, running her fingers over the embroidery stitches she'd added. The stitches helped cover up the places where she'd made a mistake in

taking in the garment and puckered it. She was no seamstress, but she could get the job done. Just not perfectly.

'Do as you wish,' he said. 'But if my grandmother sug-
gests it, will you consider it?'

She pursed her lips and didn't answer. Oh, it would be
magnificent to have new clothing, but she did prefer to
stay in the shadows. It deflected so much unpleasantness.

Nothing changed in his face, and perhaps that was what
alerted her to the fact that she'd irritated him. He was used
to others going along with his suggestions.

'I will go ahead with my plans,' he said, and reached
into his pocket and held out a folded piece of paper with
her aunt's name and hers written on it. 'My man of affairs
has taken care of the invitations.'

Taking the paper, she perused the script for a moment,
and then opened it up to read the date of the picnic.

She lowered her gaze and told herself not to be regret-
ful. It was only a picnic and a dress…though a picnic with
a written invitation.

His voice interrupted her thoughts.

'I have also come to see you this morning because the
gardener is working,' he said, 'and I thought he could tell
you about the plants while I check to see what changes I
want made for the picnic.'

He held out his arm for her to hold, and something in his
eyes dared her to take it. She gave him an answering blink,
and he smiled.

That blasted smile was her undoing.

'Would you walk with me in the gardens?' he asked.

She put the invitation on a chair and took his arm. 'Since
you ask… I was thinking of going that way.'

She couldn't hear his chuckle, but she felt it.

Together they walked outside.

A man was trimming plants with shears, and he had a scythe propped against a tree.

Gabriel walked over to look at the ropes coiled at the edge of the garden, and a wooden chair that had no legs. 'Excellent work on the swing,' Gabriel called out to the man.

The man gave Gabriel a nod and a smile.

'I wanted more activity than people just milling around having lemonade,' he told her, taking her to stand closer to the man. 'Henry has tended plants all his life,' Gabriel said, 'and he can answer any questions you have about the garden.'

'Could you tell me what kind of foliage that is?' she asked, pointing.

The gardener unleashed a torrent of information, telling her not only what was planted where, but also when, what had previously been tended there, how he worked the manure into the soil so it wouldn't burn the plants, and various other facts about the vegetation.

'It's no wonder this garden is so beautiful,' she said to Gabriel afterwards. 'He knows more about gardening than I can even ask about.'

'He constantly surprises me with the planting, and he is also an excellent carpenter,' Gabriel added, stepping aside. 'I sketched a drawing of the swing for him, and you will hardly believe how he has improved it. I'll fetch it to show you.'

Chapter Seven

But he had another reason for going inside. In addition to giving Marie a chance to learn more about the plants, he also had a question to ask his grandmother.

Detouring to his grandmother's room, he knocked on the door and entered after she called out, pleased to find that she was alone.

'Grandmother. I'm planning a picnic, and my staff is taking care of the invitations.'

'Are you inviting Marie?'

'Yes.'

'Well, don't have a romance with her. She's not right for marriage.'

'You wagered me as her potential groom.'

She dropped her head to one side. 'I know, but I was positive I'd win. I had the cards put by.' She pressed her fingertips to her neck. 'I wanted those pearls. They're lovely. Agatha keeps them in that reticule and hardly lets it out of her grasp.' She puffed out her cheeks.

'Does she not trust you?' he asked.

'Of course she does.' His grandmother rolled her eyes. 'At least at a picnic there won't be dancing,' she said. 'I saw Marie nearly trample you.'

'She hasn't danced much.'

'I can see why. That pathetic little wall weed has not blossomed as I hoped.'

'Why—…?' He paused. 'Why do you call her pathetic?'

His grandmother grimaced. 'I saw her at the soiree. She didn't even take off her spectacles for the night. Don't let yourself become attracted to her. She doesn't have any idea about how to comport herself correctly. She can spell, I suppose, but she's nothing like Rosalind, or the other ladies who attended.'

'What is different about her? How is she not more than equal to Rosalind?'

'Can't you see?' she asked. 'I mean, she's a pleasant young woman, and I know she says she's twenty-four, but I don't believe it's possible she's that young. And really, that's too old for you. Also, she doesn't have any true skills. Not like Rebecca, who plays the piano wonderfully. Or Rosalind, who has all the men asking her for a dance.'

She strode over and slapped his arm.

'Don't be a dolt. Even you must see what a disaster Marie is in society. It was a little embarrassing for people to see I had invited someone who dresses so abominably to my soiree.' She shook her head. 'That is what I get for trying to help a friend.'

'I suppose she'll arrive at the picnic in a worn dress,' he said.

His grandmother gave a low grumble, much like an unhappy cat.

'Her dress at the soiree wasn't that bad,' he added. 'But it wasn't in the same category as anything your seamstress can make.'

'True,' she acknowledged.

'Why don't you have your seamstress make new frocks

for Agatha and Marie? Perhaps as a gesture of kindness and a form of repayment as I didn't make good on your wager.' He shrugged.

'I really do like Agatha… Almost as much as those pearls she has.'

'Be magnanimous.'

'Very well.' She put a hand to her temple. 'I must do the right thing sometimes, and I'll not raise a fuss. Just watch out for the wall weed. She would not be an asset to the family.'

'Yes, she does have a habit of letting people lead her astray with explosions.'

She shook her head. 'I know. I know… The girl is a little too amiable for her own good. That's another thing about her I don't like. She is so agreeable. Hard to get a cross word out of her. Never know what she's really thinking.'

His grandmother's lips and pupils were barely visible because she scowled so deeply. She waved him away.

'Oh, go ahead and invite Agatha and Marie if you wish. The jest is on you. The other ladies will make her look dreadful by comparison. And even if you put a new dress on a turnip, it's still a turnip. I'll see that they dress appropriately, if it is possible. Just because they're my friends.' Her eyes looked decidedly unpleasant as she closed one. 'But if I go along with your clothing ideas, you must have my harp put out at the picnic.'

He sighed. 'If you insist.'

'It's really not fair to her,' she said.

'The harp?' he asked, stopping.

'No,' she snapped. 'Your noticing Marie. You're not one to keep the same woman on your arm for long.'

'The picnic isn't about Marie. It is simply an occasion to invite my friends.'

'If you say so,' his grandmother said. She let out a cross between a sigh and a curse. 'You've always been a protector. Always. Now you're trying to protect Marie and… Well, I'm certain you don't know everything about her.'

'Are you going to tell me what it is you know that I don't?'

She pressed her teeth together for a moment. 'At some point I'll probably tell you everything.'

'You should keep some secrets, Grandmother.'

'We'll see.'

His grandmother was partially right, he thought as he left the room, but only partially. He had tried courting many lovely women, and could often be utterly fascinated by one, and then his attention waned.

The one time he had seriously considered marriage it had been to Rosalind, who was perfect at all social functions. She'd been groomed to be the bride of someone in society, and he'd sat at many dinners listening to tales of what her newest niece had done, or a new horse that had been added to her stables, or how wonderfully delicious the pheasant tasted—or the soup, or the duck, or the wine, or the potatoes. But no matter how 'truly wonderfully delicious' everything tasted, boredom had been the main course on his menu.

Marie was almost the exact opposite of Rosalind, and he wondered if that was what had caused him to notice her. She had been unfamiliar with attending a soiree. Uncomfortable.

He didn't want another occasion where she would not

fit in. He wanted her to feel at ease during the picnic. He would make certain she did.

In his room, he found the drawing he'd left Marie in order to fetch, and put it in his coat pocket. It was little more than a few lines of a sketch, but the swing Henry had created would be a nice addition to the garden.

Just as Marie was a nice addition, he thought, when he stepped outside and saw her talking intently with the gardener.

When she spotted him, and returned to his side, he showed her the picture, and watched as she compared it to the finished swing and complimented the gardener.

Then he took her back towards the house.

'Will you let my grandmother's maid arrange your hair on the day of the picnic?' he asked.

'I could not.' She touched the escaping wisps. 'I'm sure she keeps her servants very busy before any event.'

'Grandmother will be distracted by her harp. She likes it placed just so, and I will instruct the servants to have plenty of problems that will keep her occupied.'

He barely paused in speaking, not giving her time for a rebuttal.

'We should all try new things from time to time, I suppose. I will be having some new clothing made. Including a shorter cravat.'

He gave a bow, and then left before he could get into a disagreement.

'Wait,' he heard her call out.

When he turned he saw she'd stepped into the corridor, pulling the door shut behind her. They were alone.

'I wanted to thank you. It's very kind of you to let us stay. To watch over us. But please don't be disappointed if

I am not at ease among your guests. I am not accomplished at the finer points of conversation.'

'You don't have to be. This is a picnic. A chance to enjoy the day, the sunshine and the life at our fingertips.'

He took her hand, clasping it, and it seemed he felt the sun's rays shine upon him from within her eyes.

'You don't have to say or do anything—just relax and enjoy yourself.' He held her hand between them. 'Just this once, take in the day and see what it feels like to have fun in life. When you look in the mirror before the picnic begins I want you to see someone comfortable in society smiling back at you.'

'No matter what I wear, I'll still be the same Marie,' she said.

'Just as I'm the same man without the loops in my cravat? It might not be as hard as you think to change old habits,' he said. He placed a soft kiss on her knuckles before releasing her hand. 'And it can be worth it.'

He told himself he was doing this for Marie, because he'd seen the joy in her face after the waltz and wanted to give her a chance to have the same attention that the other ladies did. To see what it was like not to hide away.

But he wasn't sure he was telling himself the whole truth.

Chapter Eight

Something felt off to him. But it wasn't the game.

He put his cards on the table in front of him. Pierce had inherited their grandmother's love for gambling and had won this hand, but overall Gabriel had done well.

The clock struck midnight—a signal to the other men that it was time to end the game. They pushed back their chairs, bade Gabriel and Pierce goodbye, and left, clapping each other on the back and jesting about their wins and losses as they moved out through the door.

Gabriel didn't rise, but interlaced his fingers, put them on the back of his neck, and stretched. His carriage driver would have returned to collect him, but he wasn't ready to leave. The house would be so quiet upon his return. Perfect for sleeping. But too quiet.

'Getting older, old man?' Pierce asked.

Gabriel peered through half-open eyes. 'Yes. By the way, you're invited to my house for a picnic Saturday next. In fact, I insist you attend.'

'Is Grandmother going to play her harp?'

'Of course.'

He purposely didn't tell Pierce that she had ordered a toga, because she was going to present her compositions dedicated to Ancient Greece.

Pierce appeared to have swallowed something bitter. 'Oh.' But then he smiled. 'I'm sure you'll have a lot of marriageable ladies present.'

'Probably not.'

'What?' Pierce said. 'What is the use of having an event if you do not provide the best decorations?'

'The ladies are not decorations, and I'm not going to invite the usual set.'

'Well, Grandmother won't like that. She already thinks you are neglectful in your marriage duties. She blames your mother for that.' He fought a smile, but it emerged with a chuckle. 'Has she given you the names yet?'

'I know the ladies she has decided I am to choose from.'

'Not those names.' Pierce snorted in laughter. 'She's thinking of names for your future children. Thinks it is too important to be left until the last moment.'

'I'm too tired to kick the legs out from under your chair,' Gabriel told him.

'And I'm just tired enough that I'd fall.' Pierce sighed, collecting the cards, shuffling them, and straightening the edges, tapping them carefully into place after he put the deck on the table.

'Everyone has left earlier than you, which is unusual,' Pierce said. 'Nor did as many people show up for the card game as I expected. Did you notice...?'

'That it didn't seem the same without Robertson and Egleston?' Gabriel completed the sentence for him. 'Yes.'

Robertson was on his wedding trip and Egleston was so deeply besotted with his new beloved that he was most likely with her.

'Better them than us,' Pierce said, but he glanced up

with hesitation in his eyes. Then he yawned, and gave a half-laugh. 'So damn hard to feel sorry for them right now.'

'Give yourself a good night's sleep,' Gabriel said.

Pierce patted his waistcoat, a smile appearing and fading. 'I hate it that my friends are missing out on all the enjoyment.'

'I have said you're welcome to come to the picnic.'

Pierce snorted. 'I'm not sure I'm ready to settle into the tedium of picnics.' Then his eyes shone, and he leaned back in his chair, bouncing the front two legs off the floor. 'But if I'm awake I might stop by.'

'Oh, don't bother,' Gabriel said. 'It will just be harp music, lemon drinks in the garden. And maybe an archery contest.'

Pierce coughed, and the legs of his chair thumped down again. 'You are making this sound entirely too dreary. I may drop by just to see what you're up to.'

Gabriel laughed, rose, and strode out through the door.

The fresh night air hit his face as he stepped outside and his groom hopped down to open the carriage door,

Gabriel leaped inside the carriage, getting comfortable while the groom returned to his perch.

Card games were not the excitement that they'd used to be, but perhaps that was because his friends had aged and the tales of their tomfoolery had tamed somewhat—or he'd just became so used to them that they weren't fresh any more.

He pulled down the shade, crossed his arms, leaned into the corner of the carriage so he could stretch his legs to the opposite side, and closed his eyes.

He tried to sleep but he couldn't. He could only think

of Marie. Her spectacles and smile. The woman he saw beneath the severe exterior.

And suddenly he didn't want to sleep any more. He wanted to stay awake and think of her. And he wanted to rush home. To her. Only he wasn't rushing to her, but to his own bed. Alone.

The carriage stopped and he jumped from the steps, seeing his house loom before him, the same towering expanse he'd seen his whole life.

He looked up to the windows of the room his parents had once shared before his mother had decided that her parents needed her more. She'd left a long time before his father died, and nothing had really changed except his father had been home less. He'd had no reason to pretend he believed himself married any more.

True, his mother and father had come together for important events, but that had been dramatic. He'd grown to hate them being together. Separately, his father had been genial, charming and charismatic. Alone, his mother was thoughtful, discerning and caring.

Together, each had been capable of smiling while they struck out at each other with soft-spoken jabs designed to draw blood. Marriage had turned them into gladiators, fighting to the mental death.

Marie sat in the chair, biting her bottom lip, afraid that Gabriel's grandmother would return from checking on her harp and become upset that her maid was brushing Marie's hair.

She didn't like anyone else arranging her hair because the woman who'd taken care of her while she was growing up had always used it as an excuse to pull it. When

the woman had decided it was time for Marie to wear her
hair up, she'd grabbed her by the braids, sat her in a chair,
undone the braids and pulled her hair up into a knot above
Marie's head, given it a few tight twists that had nearly
lifted her out of the chair, and stuck pins almost through
her skin, telling Marie that this was how she'd best wear
it from now on.

Agatha had appeared from time to time, bringing with
her a much softer touch. She'd been sent by her employer
so the woman's husband would not know about the child
his wife had secretly borne long before they'd wed. Supposedly Marie's true father had died before even knowing
she was on the way, and his parents had called her mother a
liar. Her mother's parents had been equally unkind, according to Agatha, so Agatha had helped conceal Marie and
had become a friend to her as she grew. Agatha might not
be her true aunt, but she'd cared for Marie as if she were.

This time, however, the process didn't seem to take very
long, and it didn't hurt. In only seconds the maid had put up
a loose knot—so loose that Marie wasn't certain it would
stay in place. Then she gave a few snips to the hair she'd
left free, and fashioned some curls to frame Marie's face.
The woman added some delicately scented pomade, and
then stood back to let Marie look in the mirror.

'Oh, she's not finished yet,' Aunt Agatha said, stopping Marie from seeing her reflection and presenting her
with a tiny case.

She looked inside to find some cosmetics. The maid
whisked the case from her aunt's hands and insisted she
would be best to apply it.

Marie looked at her aunt. 'You shouldn't have.'

Instantly, she knew when her aunt had purchased it—

while Myrtle's seamstress had been fussing over her she'd left them.

She met her aunt's eyes and frowned. 'You *really* shouldn't have.'

Her aunt shrugged and looked away. 'That's your opinion. I spoke with Gabriel and asked if his grandmother would mind if I added a few incidentals to the cost of the dresses, and he said most certainly not. I told him our wager was paid in full.'

Marie looked at her hands, clasped in her lap. She didn't want the wager to be fulfilled. It connected her to Gabriel and united them against the two older ladies' machinations. It wasn't that she'd expected him to honour the terms of the wager, but she would remember that waltz for ever. Perhaps it hadn't been perfect, but it would be perfect in her memory.

When the maid had finished, Marie studied herself in the mirror. A stranger stared at her—albeit one wearing her spectacles. She was a society woman with a beaming aunt looking on.

She didn't recognise herself.

She could not become accustomed to this. She was going to have to make her own way in the world, and the woman she saw looking back at her now would never be hired to work for others. She would provoke unwanted attention from the men of the household.

She forced herself not to run for her old clothing. For just this one day she could pretend. One day. She would enjoy the picnic.

Marie wanted to discover Gabriel's opinion of the changes in her, but she refused to search him out.

Chapter Nine

A few tables had been collected from the house and were now spread under the shade of the trees. The gardens appeared just as Gabriel wanted. The swing was sturdy, and his grandmother was sitting on it, using her feet just enough to give it a side-to-side movement. Her toga flowed gracefully, and the matching band around her head sported a few dangling jewels. Her harp had been given a small platform where it rested serenely, unaware of the beating it was about to receive.

His grandmother didn't care if the harp was considered something relegated to the lower classes. She enjoyed any opportunity to play it, and woe to anyone who might take a seat at the strings.

The soft scent of the rose bushes filled the air, mixing with a hint of smoke from the kitchen chimney. On the side away from the house a coiled rope target was in place, along with the quivers of arrows he and Pierce used to practice.

An older couple walked over to speak with his grandmother, and two of the men he'd made sure would arrive early stood by the table, its cloth billowing softly.

Pierce walked up to him. 'I'm not late this time. But where are Rosalind, Rebecca, Annabelle and Roberta?'

'My butler took care of the invitations. Not Grand-mother.'

Pierce scowled. 'I should have known something was awry. For you any leisure activities are not about enjoyment, but results. You hardly care about gambling—you just want to keep abreast of other people's views.'

'If you are called away early I will survive,' Gabriel said. 'I only invited you because I had a momentary lapse in sense and was afraid I'd ordered too much food.'

'It appears you've provided enough for me, but are the others going to have anything?' Pierce indicated the relaxed group milling about, then gave a low whistle. 'Who is that?' he asked.

From the corner of his eye, Gabriel saw Pierce straightening his cravat.

'It is nice to see a new face. Who *is* that lovely woman?'

Gabriel turned to the woman and hesitated for a moment.

Marie.

Warring emotions battled within him.

Only it wasn't her. It was as if a society beauty had taken her place, and he found he was angry that this woman was there in her stead. He had caused the change, yet he found he wanted to see the old Marie.

Behind her spectacles he could still glimpse her, but he missed the way she'd looked before.

He spoke her name softly as she walked towards them. 'Marie… I would like you to meet my cousin Pierce.'

'Marie?' Pierce gasped her name loudly, and Gabriel turned in time to see her smile.

Pierce moved ahead, his vision locked on Marie.

'Gabriel did tell me I would not want to miss this picnic,

and I can see why,' Pierce said, before giving an elegant sweep of his free arm to indicate the refreshments. 'I'll fetch a glass of lemonade for you.'

Gabriel didn't hide the warning in his voice. 'Best be good, cousin.'

'Always.' Pierce gave an apologetic glance at Marie and shrugged his shoulders. He bowed his head and used his fingertips to rub his temple. 'Sadly, it's when I can't be good that I'm at my best.'

Gabriel groaned, and Pierce smiled before walking with her to the refreshment table.

Gabriel decided it had been a mistake to invite his cousin.

Then Lord Epperson and Foster Elway arrived and greeted him, and in the same instant he saw them both notice Marie.

'Who's that?' Epperson asked.

'Miss Marie,' Gabriel answered, seeing the wheels turning behind Epperson's eyes. 'Lady Andrews' niece.'

'We must make certain Pierce doesn't monopolise her,' Elway said.

'Epperson… Elway…' his grandmother said, walking up to them. 'Help me see if the harp is in tune.'

They both walked away, although neither looked where he was going, both sets of eyes still firmly on Marie.

Someone else stopped at his side, and he turned to see Agatha smiling at him.

'That was wonderful planning,' she whispered. 'I didn't grasp what you were thinking when you suggested these changes for Marie, but now I see that you are making sure she receives notice. How thoughtful of you.'

'Thank you.' He clamped his jaw.

'And you have invited Elway and Lord Epperson. It will

be wonderful to see what they think of Marie, as they are of marriageable age and mind.'

He'd not been thinking properly. He'd wanted Marie to be flattered, not devoured, and now the poor woman would probably be overwhelmed by all the attention.

'Epperson's low on funds, and Elway thinks himself much better than he is.'

'Thank you for reminding me—as I reminded you of the flaws in the ladies your grandmother invited to her soiree. But they're both kind men, and Marie would make a wonderful match for either of them.'

Agatha squeezed his arm, beaming at him.

'Marie will be receiving more than one invitation to go on a carriage ride, perhaps to the theatre.'

Gabriel smiled, and extracted himself from her grasp. 'I'm sure she will receive a lot of notice today.'

'Oh, and your sweet cousin is watching over her.' She studied him. 'I think Marie has met him several times, when he and my husband's nephew were traipsing here and there. I wonder if something is developing between them?'

'That's just his *modus operandi*.'

'That's Latin, isn't it?' she asked.

'Yes. It means he's always developing something somewhere with some woman.'

'Of course Marie is such a doting niece that I would hate to lose her to marriage. But if Pierce asked, I would understand. Because he is...' She shut her eyes briefly, smiled, and took in a deep breath. 'Not entirely unsuitable.'

'Yes. He has a winning smile, a way with words and a good tailor.'

Still dreamy-eyed, she answered, 'You do understand?'

'Marie would be better off with the tailor,' he mumbled under his breath.

Marie's aunt laughed. 'I didn't know you were such a jester.'

He didn't answer, but walked with her to Marie's side, where Pierce was talking, raising his hands, laughing, and commanding everyone's attention.

Then he heard the plink-plink-plink of several harp strings, and a few discordant notes as his grandmother tested her strength.

'And a glass for you, Lady Andrews.' Pierce gave Agatha the glass of wine a servant had poured, and then collected two more, for Gabriel and himself.

'It's a beautiful day,' Pierce said, staring at Marie.

'Isn't it?' her aunt said, trying to pull Gabriel away with her when she took a step.

He didn't budge.

Lady Andrews nudged him. 'We should go and see what your grandmother is going to play for us.'

He gave a warning glance at Pierce, and then followed Lady Andrews to his grandmother.

He spoke with them both, sharing idle chatter, but as he did, he turned slightly so that he could keep his eye on Pierce. Not that Pierce would try anything inappropriate or do anything questionable, but it wouldn't hurt to keep his attention on his cousin.

But then he realised he was lying to himself. It wasn't Pierce he was watching. It was Marie.

Then the music started and the conversation slowed, but the eyes on Marie didn't. He stood close enough to hear Pierce's comments to her during the pauses in the music.

So much praise for everything—from the beautiful harp to the lovely tendrils of her hair.

Gabriel smiled on the outside and cursed on the inside. He should never have considered suggesting his grandmother's maid help Marie with her preparations for the picnic, nor involved his grandmother in providing a seamstress for her.

Gone were the old-fashioned bits of cloth that had overwhelmed and swallowed her. This simple but perfect dress suited her, and made her appear anything but plain.

Epperson and Elway did not leave Marie's side, which he'd expected, but he'd not foreseen how it would irritate him.

The music stopped, and Pierce complimented his grandmother, then he saw Elway and Lord Epperson argue over who would get Marie her next refreshment.

Marie didn't have to worry about her conversational skills. She only had to stand there, nod, sip and smile. All the men were competing over who could garner her attention.

'Do you like archery?' Pierce asked her after she'd finished her drink. He bowed over the empty glass as he took it from her.

'I've never tried it,' she said.

In unison, all three men gave different responses.

'A shame.'

'You simply must.'

'I can't believe it.'

'We will be happy to assist you. I'm sure you're a natural,' Pierce suggested.

With the three men egging her on, Marie had no choice but to go with them to the bows and arrows. An umbrella stand had been taken from the house to use as a holder for the quivers, and three bows leaned against the target.

Pierce took one bow to Marie, another for himself, and Epperson grabbed the last one.

All three men were more than happy to assist Marie with her aim. It was indeed fortunate he'd invited men so interested in archery and so courteous, Gabriel thought wryly.

She took aim and shot, and her arrow hit the target but didn't get close to the centre. The men cheered. No one had ever got so much praise for such an errant arrow. Twice more she shot, the arrows once again going over the target, and they all commiserated, telling her that they had also had similar bad luck when they were learning.

Gabriel hadn't created a monster but he had unleashed one inside him—jealousy. The picnic had lost its lustre. And so had all the changes he'd instigated. He touched the one loop of his cravat and tried not to watch all the attention that was being showered upon Marie.

It irritated him that these men likely wouldn't even have noticed her in the ugly dresses. Although perhaps they would have. He wasn't sure…

Marie had taken a step back, and now Epperson was standing entirely too close to her for Gabriel's liking.

In a few quick strides Gabriel had closed the distance between them and inserted himself ever so slightly between her and Epperson, taking the archery bow from his friend.

Epperson stepped away.

Gabriel had not meant to put himself in the game, but once he'd seen Epperson so close to her, his feet had taken over.

'Care to shoot against me?' Gabriel asked her, taking an arrow from the quiver.

'You only say that because you have seen how untrained I am.'

Elway gave her an arrow and a warning. 'Gabriel's as good as Pierce. Their mothers started them with archery early, though she had to train them separately as soon as they realised they could injure each other with the arrows.'

'Perhaps you will be fortunate,' Gabriel said.

'It will not be a challenge for you,' she answered.

'Let's make a wager,' he said.

Her head tilted and her smile was whimsical. 'You saw how badly I am aiming.'

He nocked his arrow, placed his feet, and looked at her. 'If I hit the centre, consider it a marriage proposal.'

'Whoa...' Pierce said, stepping back. 'Gabriel has upped the ante.'

He pulled back the string, and no one moved but him. He let the arrow fly.

It was a little off the mark, but not much.

'If I were you, Marie, I'd take it as a complete miss,' Pierce said, and propped the end of his bow on the ground while he peered at the target.

'Let me try,' Epperson said, but Gabriel would not release the bow.

Marie stared at the arrowhead. So close to the centre. She turned to him, questioning him, wondering if he had missed by accident or on purpose.

She could tell nothing from his expression.

'If you hit closer to the centre than I, we will take it as a yes to my proposal. Or anywhere in the first two coils, let's say.'

Gabriel looked as if he were doing nothing more important than making an observation on the weather.

'Anywhere else is a no.'

'Anyone can have a lucky shot and hit the middle.' She bit her lips, studied the target. 'But you're on.'

She aimed, took a breath, and paused. She wondered how serious Gabriel was, and if she should sincerely try to hit the centre. But it didn't matter. She knew her chances of hitting the target were low—and even if she could do it, marriage was a farce. She didn't want to go through anything like that.

Still, she couldn't help rising to his challenge. She aimed for the centre, steadied herself, pursed her lips, and released the string. The arrow thumped into the last coil.

'I was right,' he said. 'You are hiding a great skill.'

'You could see the terror in her eyes,' Pierce said. 'She was afraid she'd hit the centre.'

'Try again,' Pierce said. 'I'm still proposing. And if you hit the target at all, we'll be married by Special Licence.'

She nocked her arrow, and this time tilted the bow. The arrow whooshed past the target and hit the ground behind it. She could not risk getting closer.

'Whoo!' Pierce said, jumping back. 'Who's next?'

'Not risking that,' Elway said. 'If she doesn't get us with the arrow, she might get us with the bow.'

The men chuckled.

Gabriel retrieved her arrow from behind the target, his from near the centre, and then hers from the last coil.

His lips turned up as he saluted her, tapping the wood of the bow against his forehead.

'That's all for me,' Gabriel said, handing his bow and

two of the arrows to Elway. 'I've been unfortunate enough for one day.'

'And I don't think I should risk hitting one of the guests,' she said, giving her own bow and arrow to Epperson.

Pierce looked at Epperson and Elway. 'Drinks next time at White's are on the loser. You men ready for a challenge?'

Gabriel left them to their game, and Marie followed him.

'I am getting more attention than I have ever received before,' she said. 'You certainly know how to manoeuvre a picnic.'

He glanced over at her, letting her eyes catch his, and bumped up his brows in agreement before he returned his eyes to the harp, even though awareness of her consumed his thoughts.

'You're the one who has made this an event,' he said. 'You're stunning.'

It was true, and yet he found the words took all his breath.

'Thank you very much. But this is just for one time,' she said.

The wistfulness in her voice threw an arrow shaft into him.

'And I don't know that the men would be so fascinated if not for the changes.' She touched the frames of her glasses. 'They've each said that it's my spectacles that intrigue them. I've never heard that before.' She took them off and stared at the lenses. 'I'd hate to think that they would not be so fascinated with me if not for—'

'Everyone wants to be attractive.'

'"Attractive" is in the eye of the beholder, and I haven't changed that much. I'm me—just with more costly clothing and cosmetics.' She fluffed the curls framing her face. 'I do like my hair, though. And I thank you so very much for the new dress.' Then she twirled around. 'But this is more *not* me than it is me.' She ran her fingers over the line of the bodice. 'I don't know what it is, exactly, but this is not how I see myself. It's confining.'

'Do you see yourself in those older, worn dresses?'

'They suit me more than this. I have to walk carefully in this gown. Small, ladylike steps. And if I am in a hurry I have to pull up the skirt to make more room for my legs, and it feels improper.'

'Not one of the men here would complain,' he said.

'Because they're courteous,' she said. 'I'm a person who needs to have more cloth. The seamstress promised me that I would like it, and I didn't have the heart to tell her it doesn't suit me. Do not get me wrong—I do like it. In fact, I adore it. But I could not sit about on a bench for hours in it. Or traipse through a woodland.'

'It suits you. Ask any of the men here.'

She looked at her feet, then at him. 'Are you playing matchmaker?' she asked, putting a hand over her heart, blinking her eyes as if to hold back tears.

'Perhaps I was at first,' he said. 'But not one of those men deserves you.'

Her face relaxed. 'They're all very kind. It doesn't matter, though. I'm not myself today. I do feel like I belong,' she continued, 'but the men are only giving me attention because I'm the only woman here near their age.'

'That's not the reason they're admiring you. I dare you to look in the cheval mirror in my grandmother's room and not note how beautiful you appear.'

She shrugged away his words. 'I would have expected

you to invite Rosalind. Your grandmother has told me the two of you are practically betrothed.'

'I'll let you in on a secret. *She* is practically betrothed—but not to me.'

'Why haven't you wed? Are you not anxious to produce heirs and so on?'

'It's a tough step to take,' he said. 'Marriage causes so much upheaval, and it can turn even the most well-ordered house into a shambles within. I know it's past time for me to provide an heir, and I'd really thought to ask Rosalind, but when I had to decide I knew I would not be marrying her.'

Rosalind would have been the perfect woman to be his wife. To produce heirs. She came from the right kind of family. Had the right manners. And he liked the way she sometimes wore a little flower tucked in her hair. But still...

He remembered when they were children, and Rosalind had carefully minded her steps around even the smallest puddle. Solemnly walking precisely behind her father, never rushing to catch up after avoiding a puddle, but calling out softly, 'Please wait...' when a particularly large area of mud was in front of her.

'Can't you walk closer to me?' her father had always asked.

'But your boots might splash me, dearest Father,' she'd answered, peering up, a smile in her voice.

'And we can't have that', he'd replied, tapping the carefully secured plait that had been set upon her head like a royal crown.

And with shoulders and chin high she'd continued on. Years later, she hadn't changed, and she was perfect for marriage. Perfect, but she took too damn long crossing a road.

'I keep giving myself excuses as to why I haven't wed, and I know time is forcing me into it,' he said. 'But when I knew I had to make a choice between marriage or letting Rosalind go I found I wasn't willing to take that step,' he said. 'It all boils down to the fact that marriage causes either boredom or upheaval. I would be bored because the woman has no mind of her own, or I would be upset because she does have a mind of her own.'

'Your grandmother describes your mother as having bored your father, and herself as never boring anyone.'

'True. But perhaps Grandmother is settling down now that she's getting older.'

Marie gave a tiny shiver.

'You should have a wrap. I can send someone for your shawl.'

She frowned. 'My shawl doesn't match this dress at all. But it's so warm and cosy.'

He imagined her, snug in it, with a happy smile on her face. Comforted. Alluring in her own way.

He raised a hand to summon a servant. 'I'll send someone—'

'No,' she whispered, and he dropped his arm.

He found he wanted to see her wrapped in it—because she was cold, he told himself. Not because he hoped it might discourage the other men at the picnic.

Perhaps he would fetch it for her later and they could sit on his sofa, talking as the day turned into night and the night turned into morning...

Blast! He knew he should not be giving her so much notice. He'd invited these men in an attempt to garner attention for her, and perhaps somewhat to play matchmaker so as to reduce the risk to himself.

He'd never been one to have mindless dalliances. He'd been faithful to each woman he'd had a romance with. And yet, no matter how much promise each one had started with, the romance had always turned sour before entering its second year.

He remembered a most polite but vitriolic carriage ride with his parents, during which they'd had a conversation as if he weren't there. His father had stated to his mother that he didn't understand why she was complaining because he'd never kept any woman in his life—except her—for more than a year. And then his mother had enumerated the many ways in which that made him a failure as a man.

He'd not believed it—his mother arguing with his father and taking him to task over how short-lived his romances were.

He had to acknowledge now that she had had a point.

When Gabriel had matured, he'd noticed his own attentions had wavered just as his father's had. But he'd made certain not to bring a wife into the equation. He refused to make any woman as unhappy as his father had made his mother.

Sitting in a carriage with Marie and realising his attention had waned would be unforgivable, and he would not do that to her.

He tensed. His thoughts had taken a gallop, running astray, and he felt as though he'd been bucked to the ground and trodden upon.

'That is what my aunt said. I could hardly believe my ears. What do you think?'

He'd been lost. Completely. 'I believe I think exactly as you do on that.'

Her face lit with happiness. 'Thank you. That's very kind.'

'Any time.' He didn't care much what he'd agreed to, because the happiness on her face put the same feeling inside him.

Then she studied him. 'As I suspected, you're still elegant, even without the extra flourishes on your cravat.' She smiled. 'It makes you look younger, as well. Dare I say boyish?' she asked.

Plain words—and yet they did make him feel like a youth. 'Thank you.'

'I wouldn't say it if it weren't true.'

Then Elway walked up to them and asked if she would be so kind as to go with him on a carriage ride the next day. Within seconds, they were surrounded by Epperson and Pierce.

Epperson challenged her to another test of her archery skills and Gabriel noticed something flicker in her gaze. He hoped it was a little dismay.

'Of course,' she said.

Afterwards, she wandered to a tree, inspecting a nest with all three men. Pierce commented loudly on the beauty of the birds.

His grandmother walked up to him. 'Stop looking at her,' she mumbled under her breath. 'I don't know what has happened. She doesn't look like a wall weed now.'

'Please lower your voice,' Gabriel said. 'I'm making sure Pierce behaves.'

'She's not so pathetic as I thought,' she grumbled. 'But I still say she's at least twenty-five. Still, she might make a good wife for Pierce. He needs a woman to settle him.'

Gabriel's head jerked sideways and he stared at his grandmother. She was studying Pierce, with a hawk's determination in her stare. Then she gave a slow blink, ready to swoop. 'I'll invite him to tea tomorrow.'

'She's going on a carriage ride with Elway.'

'Blast,' she said. 'Well, he'll have to stop by after that.' She crossed her arms, hands tight. 'I think I'll chaperon on that ride with Elway. I'd best not let Agatha know. I'll just invite myself after Elway arrives.' She chortled. 'There's more than one way to be a good grandmother.'

Off she went, with a compassionate, gentle smile on her face, and she moved straight to Marie, inserting herself into the group so that the only man standing close to Marie was Pierce. When Elway and Epperson moved, so did his grandmother.

Marie didn't seem to know what was happening, but she appeared radiant.

He'd known there was a beauty hiding under the tight knot of hair, the hideous dresses and the decrepit shawl.

Sometimes it didn't pay to be correct.

Chapter Ten

He now understood why his grandmother put away the libations and sent her friends on their way at the end of her gatherings. Pierce, Elway and Epperson could not seem to tear themselves from Marie, even though everyone else except for her aunt, his grandmother and a few servants had already left.

Finally, his grandmother managed to wrap one hand around Elway's arm and one around Epperson's and lead them towards their carriages. It appeared to him that she would have tugged them each by the ear if they'd resisted.

Gabriel strolled next to Marie, giving her a respite from Pierce's ramblings about the beauty of swans and how Marie reminded him of one.

Gabriel stared at his swan-sotted cousin. 'It appears that everyone is leaving.'

Pierce would likely want to spend the night if he found out Marie and her aunt were staying with his grandmother.

'Ah, yes.' Pierce's head swivelled around. 'I was enjoying speaking with Marie so much I didn't notice.'

Then he spotted her aunt. 'Would you two lovely ladies like a ride home in my carriage?' Pierce asked.

'We're—'

'That's already taken care of,' Gabriel said.

'I'm sure,' Pierce said, his eyes meeting Gabriel's.

Finally, Pierce gave her a longing glance, bade them all farewell and said he hoped to see them again soon. Of course, Gabriel noted, he was gazing directly at Marie when he said that.

'Oh, it's been so nice since your grandmother invited us to stay here,' Lady Agatha said. 'You will find us on the side of the house where she has her own entrance.'

'Wonderful,' Pierce said, straightening his cravat. 'How fortuitous that I'd been planning to visit Grandmother more.'

'Yes.' His grandmother stepped up beside him. 'He is so devoted to me… I don't know what I would do without him.'

Pierce took his grandmother's hand and gave her a caring glance. 'I'll visit again tomorrow, Grandmother dear.'

'I'll look forward to seeing you,' his grandmother answered, 'as you always brighten my day. I'm so fortunate to have a grandson like you. And I do like it when you stop by the confectionery shop on the way here…'

'Of course.' Pierce winked at her and then strolled away, all but twirling his hat.

'Ah…' Lady Andrews smiled. 'Such a nice young man.'

'Perfect,' his grandmother answered. 'Mostly…' she added more softly. 'And he would make such a good… um…husband for the right woman.'

'Or an even better one for the wrong woman,' Gabriel said. 'If his actions are to be taken into consideration.'

'The right woman.'

His grandmother corrected him with a stare. Then her lids rose, as if a thought had just occurred to her, although to Gabriel's eye she overacted a bit.

'Someone like Marie.'

'Oh, they would be perfect together,' Lady Agatha said.

Gabriel could almost feel it when Marie's eyes darted to him, but he kept his face devoid of expression. Something must have leaked through, however, because Marie smiled.

'Please don't accept him on my behalf,' Marie said to her aunt.

'Of course not. You can do that yourself,' Lady Agatha said, as she watched Pierce's carriage roll by and they exchanged waves.

Her aunt reached out, patting Gabriel's arm after the vehicle disappeared from view.

'Our debt is more than paid in full. A picnic today. Tomorrow a carriage ride. And a visit from your cousin also. Instead of a proposal from you, perhaps there will be one to be accepted from your cousin. Indeed, you have made good on the wager many times over.'

She gave him a pat on the back of the hand as the group moved towards the archery field.

Gabriel's brows lifted, and his lips rose as well, in just the smallest acknowledgement. Then he went to the quiver and heard the arrows rustle inside.

Gabriel took one and put it in Marie's hand. 'A memento.'

'You should have been listening before, Aunt,' Marie said. 'Gabriel proposed. In front of the others.'

'He proposed?' His grandmother's voice went up two octaves. 'Gabriel?'

'Yes,' she said, 'and I refused politely.'

Her aunt squawked. Eyes open wide. 'She didn't shoot at you afterwards, did she?' She turned to her niece. 'Oh, Marie. Say you didn't.'

'I didn't,' Marie said, laughter in her eyes.

'She refused quite emphatically, though it was charming.' Gabriel put a hand over his heart. 'My first proposal. Shot down.'

Before she could chastise him, his grandmother's attention was caught on the harp being moved.

'Oh. Oh. Oh!' She ran to the servants, directing them. 'Small steps. Small steps. Be careful.'

'It would be horrible if such a beautiful instrument were broken,' Lady Agatha said, and then followed her friend into the house. 'Never to hear those melodious strains again…and again…and again.'

After the two women had left, Marie patted the arrow. 'Apparently you like to wager as much as your grandmother.'

He shrugged, turning up his palms. 'Sometimes wagers are just too tempting to ignore.'

'The picnic was enjoyable,' Marie said.

'The parts with you in it were. Elway, Epperson and Pierce, on the other hand…' He let his face tell her what he thought of them.

'They were kind,' she said, tapping the fletched end of the arrow on his shoulder.

'I tell it as I see it. By the way, Grandmother plans to be your chaperon tomorrow.'

She studied him. 'Do you think your grandmother is going to try to further a romance between Elway and myself?'

'I don't think so.'

She sighed. 'He is a nice man…'

Frowning, he held out his hand, palm down, and then tilted it back and forth several times. 'Hmm…'

'I don't think two chaperons would be a good idea.'

'Not for Elway, at least.'

He knew that would be his grandmother's plan. To disrupt any chance of a romance between Marie and her suitor so that she might become more aware of Pierce.

He studied the puffs of clouds overhead. He hated to say what he was about to say next. 'I suggest you send a note to Elway and tell him you wish to leave an hour earlier than planned. Then take a maid or your aunt with you and sneak out. I really don't think you'd want my grandmother chaperoning you.'

Marie nodded. 'She has a lot of stories to tell.'

'My earliest memory of Grandmother is when she wrapped herself up in my bedclothes and pretended to be a ghost. She jumped out to frighten me one night. She claimed she was trying to make me brave.'

'That is an unkind thing to do to a child.'

'My dog went after the ghost, which stumbled, and I attacked it with a candlestick. Luckily my father heard the uproar and saved her. He thought it was hilarious, but I'd actually hurt my grandmother. She said she'd just been playing a game with me.' He paused. 'I wasn't afraid of ghosts, but someone hiding in my bedclothes was certainly a threat. It was rough to see her black eye. She sported it for weeks. Mother wanted it added to Grandmother's portrait.'

Marie brushed her fingertips against his arm. 'I did not hear any family stories when I was growing up,' she said. 'Nor live them. At least not stories of my own family. I have little knowledge of my past.'

'What do you remember of your family?' he asked.

Marie could easily answer that honestly. 'Very little. I remember Aunt Agatha would arrive and sometimes recount to me a story about my mother.'

After she'd given funds to the lady who had cared for Marie.

'But I was too young to realise the import of that. I was more concerned with any treats she might have secreted away for me.' She ran her fingertips over the feathers on the arrow, smoothing them. 'I had to content myself with only her short visits. I couldn't live with Aunt Agatha as long as she was employed as a companion.'

Because Agatha hadn't been able to take Marie into her mother's house.

Agatha had told her later that Marie had probably been better off not living with her mother, who had been Agatha's distant cousin. She'd also once said that Lord Andrews probably wouldn't have been so cantankerous if she'd married him first. Apparently his initial marriage had thrived on conflict and made him the man he was when he entered his second union.

'When Aunt Agatha married she finally had a place for me, and she took me in.'

Marie peered over her shoulder, seeing the target, the swing, and the maids gathering up the remaining refreshments and the tablecloth. Two male servants were at hand, to whisk the tables back inside.

'I've had such good fortune,' she said, remembering the endless hours of laundry and errands she'd done for the woman who'd cared for her, knowing that not every orphan had someone to shelter them.

She'd been able to meet her aunt's society friends after moving in with Agatha—not a docile one in the group, but none as cantankerous as Gabriel's grandmother. But then Aunt Agatha's husband had complained about Marie living in his house when she should be married, and a huge disagreement had erupted—particularly because his nephew needed a wife and Marie refused to take on the job.

So Aunt Agatha had turned to her old friend Myrtle and asked for a respite until things were sorted, mentioning to her that her marriage was not the happiest.

Marie had expected her aunt's husband to come searching for them the next morning and demand they return, but he'd been quiet. That had incensed her aunt, and she'd determined to return home immediately, but Gabriel's grandmother had told her that would be playing right into his hands. That she must stay and make her point.

They'd had a fifteen-hour discussion on strategies with husbands, during which Marie had ended up feeling more empathy for her uncle than anyone else.

Her aunt had noticed how Gabriel stayed on his side of the house, and didn't seem inclined to berate the women around him, and had wondered aloud if he might make Marie a good husband.

A few days later the women had been drinking too much punch, and late that night her aunt had burst into her room to tell her the details of the winning wager.

Marie had been incensed, but she loved her aunt so much that she'd kept her ire to herself and tried to maintain her composure, knowing she would not accept any such proposal or go along with the wager in any way.

'I'm thankful that your grandmother invited us to stay,' she said now.

'I am too,' Gabriel responded.

She raised her eyes to his, surprised at the sincerity in his voice. 'Because my aunt and I keep your grandmother entertained?'

They paused while a servant went past them with the

umbrella stand and the quivers, and Marie stepped forward and put the arrow away. Then more servants bustled by, with the remainder of the picnic supplies, and they were left alone, with only a soft breeze and the scent of a neighbour's cook baking drifting over them.

'If you wish to think that, then yes.'

'I'm pleased that you've given us respite from my uncle.'

'Your uncle must surely have noticed his wife is no longer in residence.'

'I'm sure he has.'

She hoped he had not injured himself in his celebration dance.

'He should show understanding for his wife.' His voice hardened. 'It isn't that I mind your living here,' he said, 'but your aunt should be in her own house, with her own husband.'

'So she won't be experimenting with more explosions in your garden with your grandmother?' she asked.

'Explosions are never good.' He scrutinised the trees overhead, from where a shower of leaves was descending. 'Except maybe this kind.'

She reached out, dusting some flecks from his sleeve, and he stopped examining the leaves and watched her. She captured the cloth of his coat and tried to pull him closer, but instead she stumbled into his shoulder and he turned, catching her with both hands.

'Were you drinking the lemonade or the wine?' he asked.

'I was drinking in the sight of your manly cravat.'

He released her arms. 'Well, I suppose my valet will have to get used to it.' He tugged at the single loop.

'Perhaps you should continue wearing all those coils when you are out and about.'

'I've been enjoying staying at home recently, and I have just figured out the reason for that.'

'Explosions?'

'You could say that,' he said. 'But now the problem is that Pierce will be visiting more. I should not have let him know about the picnic.'

She heard all the different inflections in his tone. When he mentioned her staying it was warm, but it iced over when he spoke of Pierce. That pleased her more than she would have expected.

Having a place for her aunt to stay was important, but what made her happiest was the fact that Gabriel didn't seem to mind having them in residence.

'Your grandmother has been so gracious…and she's fascinating.'

One brow went up and he challenged her with an innocent blink of his eyes. 'Gunpowder?'

'I didn't see how such a small amount could cause such a large bang.' She ducked her head. 'It was louder and stronger than I expected.'

'That's Grandmother.'

'She's fascinating.'

'Yes. Like gunpowder.'

'True…'

'Those men were doing a terrible job when they were showing you how to shoot arrows,' he said. 'They were so busy vying for your attention that they hardly had any time to teach you how to do more than hold one. Preening peacocks.'

She laughed, and waved away his words. 'It might not have been just them. I truly am not interested in the hobby. I am much more interested in just being outdoors and in the garden.'

Standing near him emboldened her senses. Every breeze caused strands of her hair to brush her skin, and she even felt taller. Not as tall as Gabriel, but close. And he stood there so relaxed. Perfectly dressed.

In that moment she was happy that she'd worn the new dress and looked similar to society ladies. She doubted the men would have noticed her otherwise—not like Gabriel. He'd been aware of her even in the dowdy clothing.

He'd wanted to change her, though, and now she was dressed exactly as he'd planned. She suddenly didn't feel proud of herself because she'd altered her appearance.

'I appreciate the efforts you have made, and the results, but I like my old clothes and they make me how I wish to be.'

'You didn't enjoy all the attention at the picnic?'

Quiet words this time. Studied.

'It was more enjoyable than I expected, and I did have a grand time. But I like solitude even better. Routine moments.'

Every man *had* noticed her, she knew. And she'd wondered if it was because they were seeing her or just someone new.

'I like my hair freer, though,' she said, reaching up and fluffing the curls around her face. 'I do. But the clothing is more restricting.'

This experiment in her appearance was a success for her, and a learning experience in many ways.

'I would do it again, but I don't really need all the notice. I mean…' She shrugged. 'It doesn't change anything about me. I suspect it is the kind of thing that is important to others. Much more important than it is to me.'

'You are entrancing either way. A sweet nose. Big eyes behind the glasses. Long lashes. An elfin smile.'

'I've never seen an elf,' she said. 'So I am not sure if I should take that as a compliment.'

'You should. And even if I were never to compliment a thing about your appearance, your mirror should smile back at you every morning for the opportunity to see your face.'

'Silver-tongued,' she said, 'with no additional help.'

If one could be rough-edged and silver-tongued, he was. And when he chuckled softly the sound filled her with something she'd not felt ever before. She didn't dare look at him. He might be able to read her expression.

'If you enjoy gardens,' he said, 'then come with me. My neighbour's gardener is just as knowledgeable as mine, and he has different plantings. He's always working, and he can talk for hours about plants.'

She looked into his eyes and felt as if she was about to take a grand adventure, even though it was nothing more than a walk at his side. But maybe it was more than that. She had a feeling it would change her life…

She strode forward and ignored the little wound that felt like an arrow in her heart. Gabriel had been trying to find a husband for her from among his friends. That was so… Unpleasant.

He had walked on ahead of her and she put it out of her mind, hurrying to his side. He was just a friend, and his heart was in the right place. He didn't mean anything by it, and she didn't have to wed anyone anyway. Especially if these memoirs went as well as she hoped.

Chapter Eleven

'You're right,' she said, strolling with Gabriel back to his home, sniffing the small rose that his neighbour's gardener had given her. 'Between him and your gardener, they know everything there is to know about the plants they tend.'

She shook her head. When she measured herself, she realised she truly knew nothing about botany. She had thought she'd scented lilacs, or honeysuckle, but then she'd noticed huge mounds of flowering roses.

She did love nature. All the vibrancy of seeing green burst out after the rain, the feel of raindrops cooling the air in the heat of summer, and those days with her aunt at the hunting lodge had been beautiful.

'I told you about my dream of writing a book about botany,' she said, 'and you suggested I might try writing about something else. I've now decided to take your advice and give up the subject of botany. I don't know enough.'

'That doesn't mean you have to give up your love of nature.'

'True…' she muttered, watching a butterfly land on the hedge.

She didn't dare ruin the afternoon and tell him she was writing his grandmother's memoirs.

But apparently her conflicting emotions showed.

'A book about botany is surely not your only option,' he insisted, trying to reassure her. 'Perhaps a fictional story?'

'I really don't like the darkness in some of the stories everyone is reading these days,' she said. 'I suppose it has its place, but not for me.'

'Grandmother knows a publisher,' he said. 'More or less. She once threatened him with his life if he mentioned a word about the size of her derriere.' He paused. 'That might not be a route to take, though. He might bear a grudge.'

'I have made it my vow to take care of my aunt, and I will. She still has the pearls, and if we sell them it could help us get by.'

'Just don't jump into a marriage with Elway.'

She laughed. 'We're only going on a carriage ride. And he and Epperson were both nice to me. I appreciated that. You didn't tell them to do it, did you?'

'Absolutely not.' His eyes narrowed. 'I would never invite a guest whom I had to tell to be nice to someone.'

'So did you stack the deck, so to speak?' She lifted her brows. 'With marriage-minded men?'

'My cousin Pierce is not in that category.'

She shrugged. 'What about Elway and Epperson?'

'It was only an opportunity to show you how much attention you could get if you wished it.'

'I am completely happy with my plain ways and with not being noticed. This dress—' she held out the skirt with her left hand '—is nice for parties, but it isn't practical. I feel a bit like a flower in it, and I suspect the other gardener wouldn't have been so kind as to give me a rose if...' She paused. 'No. He was nice. He would have happily given me a rose even if I'd approached him wearing my serviceable clothing.'

'I'm sure he would.'

'But I don't know that Elway would have invited me on a carriage ride. And although I know Pierce somewhat, he's never noticed me as he did today. He didn't seem to remember me at all, and yet I'm certain we've talked before.'

'Maybe that only proves he's not the sharpest arrow in the quiver,' Gabriel said, emphasising the words and moving closer to her, sharing the jest.

Gabriel knew without any question that Pierce would return to see her, and that Elway would pursue her. And he knew without a doubt that Elway would propose if she gave him half a chance. He'd never been wrong when he had a feeling as strong as this. Never.

And he only had himself to thank. At least Elway was a mostly reputable man. He would not be the best husband in the world, but he would not be the worst, either. He would show off Marie on his arm. Happily welcome their children. Provide for Marie's aunt. She would have a respectable and comfortable place in society, and she would probably be happy.

In fact, he'd done an admirable job of being a matchmaker. Only he wished he'd left it alone.

'Elway can be sullen from time to time,' he said, by way of warning.

She laughed. 'I was raised by one of the most sullen women I've ever known. I didn't try to cheer her out of her moods—I only tried not to worsen them. I don't think Elway's moods will concern me on our carriage ride.'

'I wasn't thinking about tomorrow's carriage ride but the next one, and the next one and the next one.'

'Your imagination is running amok.'

'Amok?' he said, leaning closer. 'No one has ever said anything like that to me.'

'Ah…' she said, resting the rose briefly on his sleeve. 'Perhaps it's time they did.'

He took the flower from her hand, sniffed it, and lightly ran the petals down her cheek. 'Amok…' he said. 'Perhaps it is because of you.' He returned the rose to her.

'You're jesting.'

'I wouldn't make light of something so serious.'

She turned, leading the way into the house.

His heart was taking over, and he didn't know if he would ever be the same. And he didn't know why he had so foolishly made certain to introduce Marie to eligible men.

Then she hesitated and turned back, approaching him with timid steps.

'Thank you for giving us a place to stay while we consider our future,' she said. 'Uncle has written Aunt Agatha a very hateful letter, and she was crying last night because she'd never expected him to become so vicious. He never treated his first wife this way, and Aunt Agatha can't believe he has turned against her so much.'

'I'm happy to have you here.'

He'd never had a guest like her. Someone he wanted to search out and encourage, see flourish. In the short time he'd known her she appeared to have become stronger. More self-assured. A different person from the woman he'd first seen.

'Perhaps Grandmother can give you some ideas for a story,' he said. 'She was, after all, once imaginative enough to put the bedclothes over her head and jump out at me.'

Dismay flickered behind her eyes, and he hoped hearing of his grandmother's antics didn't upset her too much.

'Just take care around Grandmother. As you know—given that she talked you into lighting that fuse—she can be persuasive,' he said. 'She causes people to do things they would not ordinarily do.'

Just as Marie had done to him. He had planned a picnic with her in mind and invited potential suitors. Only to regret it. But he didn't regret seeing Marie carefree and coveted. He was happy for her that she'd received the attention, even though jealousy simmered inside him.

He wasn't used to that. In fact, he'd never felt it before meeting Marie. At least, that was what he thought he felt. He wasn't sure. Perhaps the sun had affected him. Or the harp music. Or the reflection glinting from her spectacles.

Her stunning spectacles.

And that rose scent.

He'd never smelled a rose so beautiful. Or seen such a beautiful day.

He stood for a moment, savouring the scents, the sun and the nature around him.

The world had never seemed so alive.

After Marie had returned to her room, a maid knocked on her door, saying that Gabriel's grandmother and Marie's aunt requested her presence. They were curious to know which suitor she'd preferred.

Both women refused to believe that Marie wasn't interested in Epperson, Elway or Pierce.

'What of Gabriel?' Marie asked.

'Oh, he went to such an effort to see that other men noticed you,' Aunt Agatha said.

'True,' Myrtle added. 'He dearly cares for me—even if he hides it well. He planned for me to play for everyone, and he invited eligible bachelors. And during our discussion of the event we spoke of Rosalind. I know he didn't invite her because there were so many unwed men there.'

'True,' Aunt Agatha said. 'If he were really interested in Marie he wouldn't have invited Pierce. That man is decidedly more handsome than Gabriel.'

Pierce was decidedly *not* better looking than Gabriel. If her aunt hadn't been so dear to her, Marie would have offered her the spectacles.

'I know,' his grandmother added. 'Gabriel is the steady one. Pierce… Well, he just makes hearts flutter.'

She studied both women's faces. They were not saying this to gauge her reaction. They truly believed such nonsense.

'I would say Gabriel is better-looking than Pierce,' she ventured.

His grandmother raised her brows and then looked at Agatha. 'Does she need new spectacles?' she asked. 'I will certainly be happy to make sure she has them.'

'Oh, thank you,' Agatha said, patting her hands together. 'That would be wonderful.'

'I do not need new spectacles. I can see perfectly well with these.' She touched the frames.

Both women glanced at each other, and their mouths thinned. Then his grandmother started telling tales of her own rómantic pursuits, and recalled the great number of men who'd pursued her—although she was certain her dowry had had a lot to do with that.

Her aunt chimed in occasionally, to remind Gabriel's grandmother of a suitor she'd forgotten to mention, and then the woman would be off on another tear.

Perhaps Gabriel wouldn't mind that she was writing his

grandmother's memoirs, Marie thought. She looked at her notebook, took out her pencil, and started writing notes on the stories. His grandmother wasn't only interested in lighting fuses on small amounts of gunpowder, apparently. She preferred, figuratively, to light the whole keg. Or several.

She knew she would have to tone down the tales, because no one would ever believe them. In truth, the ribald stories had shocked her, and she wondered how the older woman had acquired such an imagination. Not that she would ask. When his grandmother had started telling her about the explosion Marie had doubted it aloud, claiming it wasn't possible to do such a thing, and that had led to the demonstration. She couldn't risk that happening again.

Myrtle had been telling the truth, and if she always told the truth then she must have been a trial for Gabriel, his father and her husband.

She took a few notes and tried not to think of Gabriel. Or his reaction when he learned about the memoirs…

Chapter Twelve

'Grandmother said I'd find you here.' Gabriel walked into the room of his house in which the maids stored items no one wanted.

He'd known when Elway had arrived. Known when he'd left. And had waited, wanting to see Marie again. Particularly when he knew Pierce would likely be there in the evening.

When Gabriel hadn't been able to resist any longer, he'd searched her out.

He'd known which room to find her in when his grandmother had said she'd sent her to 'the Battle Room'. Unartistic paintings of Roman centurions adorned the walls, along with a few garish battle scenes which were mainly splotches of colour, and one costly but useless sword was propped in a corner.

Other than that, the room was furnished with two trunks, a nightstand and a crate, and various other household items.

Marie peered up from the book she was studying while sitting on the overturned crate. She was dressed in her serviceable clothing again, but her hair was still wisping around her face. The window's light shone on her, bathing her in a way that made her appear innocent—except for her eyes, which contained a whimsy he'd never seen as she peered at him from behind the spectacles.

He navigated through the doorway into the room—which must surely have only been created because of an architect's mistake.

'What are you reading?' he asked.

She held the book out to him and he opened it in the middle, revealing blank pages that smelled of dust and old paper.

'It's an abandoned journal. Your grandmother's.' She took it back and put it aside on the floor where she now knelt, dismissing it, obviously more impressed by the trunk and its odd collection of contents than by the journal. 'She sent me to look for it.'

'Blank,' he said. 'Nothing like her life.'

She reached into the trunk again. 'Interesting things inside this trunk, though. A treasure trove.'

He walked closer, his gait relaxed, wanting to stand near her. 'This is my least favourite room in the house. I always try to relegate Pierce to it when he visits, and he laughs and takes another.'

'It feels…preserved. As if no one has seen it in a long time.' She rummaged in the trunk again and held up a wooden toy. 'A little carved horse. Amazing…'

'I remember that,' he said, taking the smooth wooden toy. 'Didn't know what had happened to it. But I never played with it much. I had real ones to ride.'

'You started riding early?'

'Of course. Our country estate has stables.'

'What if you had fallen off?'

'I did. And Old Joe stepped over me. It hurt when I hit the ground, but I learned that way. Grandmother always said, "Fortunate you didn't hurt the horse." But she picked me up, dusted me off and sat me back in the saddle. Old Joe stared at me as if he couldn't believe I'd fallen off. Every time I tried to saddle him after that, he would swat at me with his tail while he moved away, or he'd place his hoof over my foot—not putting all his weight on it—as if he didn't know what he was doing. But he knew.'

'Your grandmother always said that she was glad you hadn't hurt the horse?'

'Yes. But, as I said, she always ran out, picked me up and checked me for injuries, all the while saying that a good horse couldn't be replaced, but I could. As the "spare", Pierce could get away with anything, and he spent his days and nights in revelry. Whereas I had to learn to manage the estate and could not be so rash.'

'But I know that you sometimes go out wagering with him and arrive home in the early hours.'

'Sometimes… Not long ago, while most of my friends were at the card table, I slipped away for a conversation with the Earl of Westcott. He was a good friend of my father's, and it was pleasant to hear his memories. To talk with him. Discuss views. He even told me some stories about my grandfather I didn't know.'

'That must have been so pleasant,' she said. 'All those family memories and that heritage. And learning about it.'

'Yes. Grandfather was a good man, and I have fond memories of him. He was gruff sometimes. And he hated his valet shaving him. I remember his white whiskers, always showing on his chin. His clothes had all seen better days. Except for when he went to Parliament. He might have been mistaken for a tenant on his days in the country—unless you looked into his eyes. His eyes could have carved through stone without a chisel. He was a wealthy peer and he knew it, and he made sure everyone around him did as well.'

Gabriel must have inherited his grandfather's eyes, Marie thought. She would wager on that.

He returned the toy horse to her and she carefully placed the little wooden creature back into the trunk, keeping her eye on it. And then she closed the lid, putting the latch in place and running a finger over it to remove a speck of dust.

'I haven't heard many stories of my parents,' she said. 'Aunt Agatha wasn't overly fond of my mother, even though she was her companion for years, but she has shared a few good memories. She told me about the duel with your grandmother. Is that the sword?' She pointed to the golden hilt.

'Yes. The infamous sword from the infamous duel. It's been in my family for generations. Grandmother achieved what the swordsmen of the past had kept from happening and made certain it would never again be used in combat. She nicked the blade and gave it the curve it now has.'

He lifted the sword, his hand hardly fitting under the knuckle-protecting hilt, and gave it to her.

'It's beautifully crafted,' she said.

As she touched the gold, her fingers brushed his. '

'This was the only sword in our family, and Grandmother decided she needed it.'

'I've never met anyone like her...'

He wanted to tell her that while his grandmother was truly amazing, he preferred to be with someone like her. Someone who didn't crave attention or too many wild adventures. Who liked a simpler life. A calm presence.

'I do care for her, but not for everything she does.'

'She loves talking about her adventures.'

'Far more than I enjoy finding out about them.'

He remembered his friends often raising a glass to his grandmother's antics. He'd laughed it off, because after all they were cheering her. But he'd been mortified that his grandmother relished attention so much, and could seemingly find endless ways to attract notice.

He put the sword back into the corner. He reached out a hand and Marie took it, and he lifted her to her feet. She didn't take her hand from his clasp, comforting him in his memories of all the unsettling adventures of his family's past.

'Sometimes it is best you don't have to hear the exploits of your family,' he said. 'Cherish that. The knowledge that you are making the chronicle of your own life.'

She squeezed his hand. 'You are fortunate to have a family. So much heritage. When your grandmother told me I'd find her journal here, I expected a volume filled with all the adventures she's mentioned, but it only has two entries. One is *Today I started a journal.* The other is a statement saying that she hopes whoever reads it is visited by the plague. She didn't tell me that when she sent me to fetch it.'

It seemed natural to keep standing there with her hand in his, the room surrounding them like a cloak.

'I do appreciate my heritage,' he said, but at this moment he felt more than the antiquity of his past. He could see the possibility of a future he'd not really imagined before. A partner at his side. Someone to share his life with.

He didn't think he'd ever just stood in a quiet room, holding someone's hand and feeling so connected with them. They were alone together, and that made him wonder how long the attraction would last. Perhaps she was someone with whom he might feel an attraction beyond a year.

His concept of marriage as nothing more than the union of two separate individuals who had meals and children together as they continued on with life wavered just a bit. Probably because of the silence around them.

He moved a hair's breadth closer. 'I'm sorry for the misfortune that brought you here, but I'm pleased to have you staying.'

'That is kind of you to say.'

'Not kind. Simply true.'

She squeezed his hands and leaned closer, putting the tiniest kiss on his cheek. It was as if that rose petal had brushed him again, and the softness reached deep into his heart, robbing him of speech.

'Forgive me for being forward,' she said.

He stepped away, his fingers sliding from hers. He didn't want to be close to her when next he spoke. He wanted her to understand, and to take his words lightly.

'Miss Marie.' He stood by the door and gave her a slight bow. 'You can be forward with me any time you want. I assure you I will let you know in the kindest way if I ever think you are stepping into impropriety.' Then he paused. 'It will probably be in the next day or so, but I'll let you know.' He hesitated. 'Possibly…'

He stepped to the other side of the door, closed it softly. Waiting, he examined his thoughts. He seemed to be carrying a bit of her spirit inside him. A calmness that he'd not felt before. A peacefulness.

He opened the door again. She was touching her lips, looking pensively out of the window.

'If I overstep, you must let me know as well,' he said.

Her reverie ended and she smiled. But then it faded and she swallowed, and her gaze darted downward.

'Of course.'

'What's wrong?' he asked.

'Nothing,' she said. 'I do wish to thank you for being so kind.'

She took in a deep breath, and then a deeper one. She held on to the trunk latch, her knuckles turning white.

'I want you to know that your grandmother has said she has made amends with the publisher she had the fracas with,' she said. 'She has been telling me story after story about her past, and I am writing her memoirs.'

His mouth refused to speak. And perhaps it was best that it didn't.

The wonderful feelings she'd engendered swirled into a maelstrom, spinning out of control, surrounding him and pummelling him into another kind of awareness.

He gathered his resources, giving himself a chance to consider carefully what she'd said and weigh his response even more cautiously.

Story after story about Grandmother's past? Oh, he knew full well some of the things his grandmother spoke of behind closed doors—he'd heard plenty of whispers—and it would certainly get other doors slammed if she spoke about them publicly.

To hear rumours was one thing. To see her misdeeds listed one after another in print would be damning.

The family name would be ruined.

His financial partnerships might flounder.

His mother's new beau would be offended, and the beau had a young daughter who would learn of it.

His maternal grandparents were frail, and did not need to know the sordid details of his grandmother's life.

He forced his jaw to unclench. Surely he'd misunderstood. He stepped back, his entire awareness on her face. He enunciated his words with precision.

'You are doing what?'

'Writing a book. About her experiences. Your grandmother thinks it is a grand idea. She's anticipating the chance to complete her memoirs and I am helping her.'

She bit her lip.

He heard someone in the distance. A servant moving about? Or the ghost of his father laughing?

He could not let anyone overhear this. He softened his voice.

'You cannot write about my family,' he said.

'I already am.' Her words were measured. 'Besides, it was almost your idea. You told me to write about something else.'

'Not my family.' His voice wavered in its intensity. 'Not my grandmother's life.'

The room was silent.

'I only plan to tell the exact stories your grandmother gives me.' Her voice was all innocence and light.

Oh, he could imagine that. 'I forbid it.'

She put a hand to her chest. 'You cannot do that. You will be destroying my chance of supporting my aunt and myself. My future.'

'And if you publish that book you will be destroying my family heritage. My life. I know what tales Grandmother has to tell. Other people in society will have their secrets revealed, and they will never be able to forgive that. Grandmother is already half a pariah.'

Gabriel reined himself in. He had managed to keep so many things from being discussed. His title had value, and he had power. But now she stared at him with determination.

'You can't ruin my family name,' he said softly. 'You have overstepped.'

With that, he shut the door softly.

Outside, he made two long strides towards his grandmother's room before he heard the door he'd just shut opening and pattering footsteps behind him.

She darted around him and stopped. 'Please don't be angry,' she said.

'Oh, I left anger behind quite some time ago.'

Soulful eyes studied him.

'My mother felt she had to move from Town because of Father's unfaithfulness and Grandmother's way of bringing unpleasant attention to the family,' he said. 'To have my grandmother's memoirs published will destroy my mother. She'll never feel able to come to London again. She has tried hard to shield her family from the whispers and tales, but if you write this book it won't be whispers, but fresh shouts.'

A horse neighed in the distance, the sound carrying through the open window, and a muffled command followed. Gabriel went to the window and slammed it, uncaring if he broke the glass. His hands remained clenched on the wood.

'I thought Grandmother would be a bad influence on *you*, but now I am not sure the reverse is not true.' He stared out through the window.

'I am not a bad influence on anyone. I can't be. I am always the least important person in a room. Even the maids have more say in where they go or stay and what they do in their free time. I have no employment, and I must always fit my needs with those around me. I love Aunt Agatha dearly, and I am thankful for her every day of my life. I must help her survive now.'

He released the window, relaxed his jaw, and turned to her. 'You are learning to mix your own form of gunpowder—and this is more volatile to my family than you could imagine.'

His mother and grandmother already barely tolerated each other. To bring the past into the open—a past that he had tried to protect the family from—was unthinkable. He could imagine the flare-up between his mother and his grandmother. His maternal grandparents would be aghast. And his grandmother's stories were always slanted. More like half-truths. Leaving out the parts that didn't portray her in the light she wanted.

Marie would be emphasising events that he had spent his life trying to diminish.

He calmed himself. Drew fresh air into his lungs.

He was approaching this all wrong. He needed a chance to gather his resources and consider the path to take. Besides, his grandmother had a short attention span. Short except when she was the subject of conversation.

'You must understand. I need a way to support my aunt,' Marie repeated. 'I do not want to have to depend on my uncle's largesse, and now it is as if he is waiting my aunt out. Refusing to help her financially and expecting us to return to his house and put up with his wastrel nephew destroying everything he touches.'

'Wait,' he said. He needed to tread carefully. 'I was hasty. I would not want you and your aunt to be without refuge. You are a guest of my grandmother's and that has been good for her.'

Or it had been until the blasted memoir idea had surfaced.

The eyes that stared at him were not reticent. His grandmother's influence was corrupting her. He wasn't sure he knew this woman. This Marie.

'You are keeping Grandmother mostly calm and quiet,' he said. 'She's not been asking for gambling funds. She restrained the last explosion to our gardens. The sword has stayed in its hilt...'

'I talk them both out of most of their newer ideas.'

'Don't unleash the secrets of my family's past, nor fabricated tales which will be taken as the truth.'

She responded quickly. 'I suspect you have heard most of them before.'

Oh, he suspected he had not. His friends had often asked if certain rumours were true, and it always pleased him to say he'd never heard of them before.

His words were soft, but they couldn't have been more direct. 'Have you already put pen to paper?'

Her eyes darted down and to one side too quickly. He didn't need a verbal answer.

'Will you let me read what you've written?'

'I don't know that it would be a good idea.' She went to the doorway. 'But come with me and I'll show you something I've started. You should know it anyway. It's about you.'

Gabriel wasn't smiling.

She took him into her room, and handed him the sheaf of papers on her desk.

He read of a young grandson who was almost standing on the back of the horse, letting it gallop over a stack of hay. A magnificent feat.

'She's talking about Pierce,' he said, returning the papers to her. 'Can I see the others?'

He motioned to those she hadn't given to him.

'Certainly.'

They were just a few pages of notes telling of his grand-father's proposal, and the dilemma it had caused when she would not accept or reject it. In part, because his grand-father had believed he loved someone else. She had also believed she loved someone else…but she could be a vis-countess. The one thing his grandparents had agreed upon was that they wouldn't let love for others stand in the way of their union if they both decided it was in their best interests.

He read a little. Then looked at her. 'This is not true. My grandparents had a good marriage. Tumultuous, some-times. But one with love.'

She looked at the desk, then sat down and dipped her pen, and drew a small heart on the top corner of the blank page in front of her. 'She told this to me as the truth, and she did say the marriage was wonderful.'

'You're describing him as mercenary and her as a woman only after a title. You have the facts wrong.' He held out the papers, half crumpled in his grip.

'She says this is the truth, and I believe her.'

He shook his head. 'I've not heard this before. She's embellishing.'

She stood, taking the papers back, straightening them. 'Let's ask her.'

He opened the door for her and she moved by him, sud-denly aware of the masculine shaving soap he must have used, the crispness of his clothing, and the irritation on his face. Walking beside him in the corridor, she could feel his intensity, and hear it in the distinct steps he took.

After a quick rap on his grandmother's door, they went inside.

His grandmother had a small pencil in her hand. She dropped it when she saw Gabriel, and gave an overly innocent blink.

'Grandmother, Marie has told me about the memoirs.'

'Well…um…good,' she said, but she gave a quick glare to Marie. 'I have a few more things I want to cover with her.' She touched the handkerchief on her desk. 'I have just remembered a disagreement I had with my husband the morning before we were wed… We had such a row.' She laughed, lifting the handkerchief and dotting it to her eye. 'I'd just found out he didn't intend to go through with the vows, and it set me off something fierce. Particularly as we had just spent an intense night together.'

Gabriel cleared his throat. 'Grandmother. Marie is writing about you meeting Grandfather and claiming he wanted only your dowry and you the title of viscountess.'

'It's true,' she said, standing, her laughter fading.

'You've never said such a thing before.'

'Well, it's good that I'm getting it out in the open now.' She crossed her arms.

'Is it fact?' Marie asked her.

The older woman's eyes opened wide. 'Of course.' She uncrossed her arms, studied her left hand, fingers folded, and used her thumb to flick at her wedding ring. 'I fell deeply in love with the way he looked and his title. Then I fell in love with the man attached. He was in love with the nice amount he would receive from my parents, and he fell in love with the woman attached.' She studied Gabriel. 'A man doesn't find out his true worth until he is married.'

'Grandmother, that's mercenary.'

'It's not a perfect world.' She examined him. 'But you're already settled. You don't need a wife except for an heir.' She pulled a face. 'Let's not speak of that. I wouldn't want to see this conversation in my book.'

Her gaze locked on Marie.

'But Pierce does need a wife. You're much more presentable than I thought. Pierce will fall in love with you faster than a hat pin can fall to the ground. I could have everything ready for your vows just as fast. Think about it. Maids of your own. Footmen. A butler. A carriage.'

'I don't need you trying to marry me off,' Marie said, with a tiny shudder hidden in her words. 'And I don't need that kind of excitement. From what I've heard, your marriage was considered good—up to and including the time you had your husband locked in a tower with you to prove to him that the two of you were truly meant to be together.'

'What?' Gabriel's voice broke the calm.

His grandmother rolled her eyes. 'Don't act so shocked. I've not told you everything about myself. If you think back, I've hardly told you anything. You've listened to others instead, and they don't know what went on in the privacy of my home.'

'At least not yet,' Gabriel said.

'I have no secrets,' his grandmother said, scrutinising her pencil. 'Just things I've not yet mentioned. And I need a little excitement. My life has been dull lately, and having these memoirs published will give me something to talk about at social events.'

Gabriel peered heavenward and muttered something before turning to Marie.

'You cannot aid my grandmother,' he told her. 'Let her write the memoirs herself if she is so inclined. Don't put pen to paper against my family.'

'It is your grandmother's wish. And it is her story to tell.'

Gabriel's eyes narrowed, and she saw the rebuttal in them.

There was a brief knock, and Pierce opened the door and walked in. 'Grandmother… Miss Marie,' he said, giving a deep bow. Then he turned. 'Oh, Gabe. My valet is moving all my things into my room here. He saw a spider at home, and I didn't want him to live in fear, so we have come here for safety. I knew you'd be thrilled.'

Gabriel took in a deep breath.

'So, what has everyone been up to?' Pierce asked.

'Marie is writing my memoirs,' his grandmother said. 'Isn't that thoughtful of her?'

'And the pages are not bursting into flames?' Pierce asked, walking forward to bend and give his grandmother a kiss on the knot of grey hair.

'No,' Myrtle answered. 'But I wouldn't stand too close to your cousin just now. He's in a bad mood.'

'Well, that's fine. I really came to see Marie.'

Gabriel thought he heard the sound of an explosion again, but didn't say a word as left the room.

Chapter Thirteen

The house was so quiet he would have thought himself alone, but the butler would have alerted him if anyone had left.

He had to let Marie know that he had enough power in society to prevent his grandmother's story from being printed. It was unfair to let her invest time in a project that she expected to benefit from financially and would not.

According to a maid, she was were playing cards in his grandmother's rooms. Leaving his desk, he walked to the other side of the house.

Within a few moments he'd rapped on his grandmother's door and entered after she called him to come in. He wanted to see Marie, and there she was, sitting apart from everyone else, studying a piece of paper in front of her. Pierce and her aunt were playing cards with his grandmother.

A quiet, contented little domestic scene.

Marie appeared unaware that anyone had stepped into the room, so intently were her eyes focused on the paper, but he knew she was conscious of him. The pencil wavered. Then her teeth touched her bottom lip.

'It's too late for you to join us, and I know it's probably too boisterous for you,' his grandmother said, holding a hand of cards, the box for them open beside her. 'We shall stop playing.'

'It's only half past eight,' he said, standing behind his grandmother so that he could see her cards. They were dismal. No wonder she wanted to end the game.

'That's late for some of us. Particularly if we get up at first light.' She snapped her teeth together, tapped the cards, and put them face-down on the table.

Her aunt yawned, gave everyone a little wave, and then rushed from the room.

Pierce stood, pulling his coat from the back of his chair. 'I've had my carriage readied and I have pressing business to attend to.' He winked at Marie. 'I hope you can use some of the tales I've told you.' He waved, and headed for the door. 'Goodnight, all. I should return about first light.'

Gabriel forced himself to concentrate on his grandmother, the table and the room, but in truth he only saw Marie.

If he continued to tell his grandmother he didn't want Marie writing the memoirs, both women would become more determined. His grandfather had told him more than once that the quickest way to get his wife interested in something was to speak against it.

His grandmother studied him. 'Time to sleep. Goodnight, everyone.'

Gabriel gave her a nod and spoke to Marie. 'Can I have a moment of your time?'

'Blast!' his grandmother said. 'Don't worry her. It's not a good idea to get on a bad footing with her, because Pierce is going to fall in love with her and they'll probably wed—and you know how I want everyone in the family to get along.'

'I'm not going to wed Pierce,' she said.

'You will break his heart,' his grandmother said, standing. She yawned wildly and raised her arms high, then pressed a hand against her lower back. 'Oof… That was a stretch. Pleasant dreams,' she said, closing the door to her bedroom behind her.

'Would you like to continue the game?' he asked.

'The card game?' Her brow flicked up. 'I wasn't playing.'

'Perhaps you are playing. With more explosive materials than a simple fuse and gunpowder.'

She reached for the deck, but he put his hand between hers and the cards. 'Let's find a more private place.' His eyes indicated the door. 'I can assure you it's highly unlikely any conversation here will be ignored.'

He moved his hands away from the cards.

She lifted the deck and spoke softly. 'Your sitting room?'

Nodding, he stood.

He didn't speak as they walked down the corridor, forcing his mind to remain detached.

Inside his sitting room, he led Marie to a chair and helped her to be seated. He was shocked at the emotion the simple action unleashed inside him. Other than family or cousins or close friends, he'd always welcomed guests into the main sitting room. Never in his private quarters. But she didn't seem the least aware of this departure from his normal routine.

Marie reached out, took up the cards as if they were strangers to her, and shuffled, biting her lip.

'What shall we wager on?' he asked.

'Perhaps we could just play a few games for the joy of winning?' she said. Then she fumbled the cards.

He put the back of his chair against the table and straddled it. 'Deal. I know the game, and I play with viscount's rules—which means no handkerchiefs, no reticules, no hats, no mirrors, no feigned illnesses or other surprises that might alter the course of the game.' He paused. 'Did I leave anything out?'

She shuffled again, pursing her lips. 'You do make it more challenging.'

So did she. Lamplight shone around her, and although she wore one of the older, frayed dresses, it somehow merely accentuated the contrast between her beauty and the garment's dowdiness.

She didn't deal the cards as smoothly as he would have expected. It was more like the way she danced. Hesitant. Stumbling.

But she paused for a moment, raised her brows, and said, 'I feel the cards are in your favour.'

'Are they?'

'I would think so.'

And then she fumbled them again, almost dropping them onto the table.

No one had ever captured his attention with a card shuffle and a flick of the wrist the way she did. She passed out their cards slowly, deliberately, as if it were her first time.

He looked at the faces of his cards. Four aces.

'You probably should have wagered,' she said.

He examined the cards a second time, and then looked into her amused eyes. 'You're good.'

She laughed, and reached out, taking his cards and shuffling again. 'I suppose you would like a more traditional game. With the usual cards in disarray.' She turned them face-up and spread them on the table. 'When I was younger, and the stakes were high, I learned that I needed to win if I wanted to eat, so I found a way to increase my odds. I made the cards my friends. Then, after I moved in with Aunt Agatha, instead of embroidery or music or dance, we used the cards to amuse ourselves. Her husband was upset, but it was an inexpensive way to spend our time.'

Gathering the cards again, she shuffled.

'Do I need to cut the deck?' he asked.

'You don't. But I'm going to request that you do so,' she said. 'And you may shuffle every time.'

'You trust me?'

'You've apparently not played cards a large amount, and your grandmother said that she tried to teach you a few tricks and you were incensed.'

'True. Wagering usually bores me. I only play cards because otherwise I will not see my friends.'

'Perhaps the wagers aren't right for you.'

As the night lengthened their games seemed to more slowly, and became more of an afterthought to their companionship.

Finally, after a win on her part, she put the cards on the table, grabbed her pencil, and tallied the score—or tried to. He found he didn't want to see her stand, stretch, and yawn, say that she must be going. He wanted her to remain with him.

'I'm so tired I can't seem to count,' she said. 'I stayed up late last night writing, and your grandmother woke me early. You might need to check these totals.'

He moved to her side briefly and checked her figures. Except for a few scratchings-out, she'd made the correct sums.

They were tied. 'One last game?' she asked.

'No,' he said. 'I would like us to end evenly.'

'That sounds so final.'

He didn't speak at first, but then he saw the waif-like sadness in her eyes.

'Would you like to take a walk?' he asked. 'Now? In the moonlight?'

He peered out through the window. Under the stars, perhaps he could explain to her again how much it meant to him not to have his grandmother's life in print, and she'd understand and agree.

He studied her, willing her with his eyes to walk with him, to comprehend how important it was for him to remain above idle chatter and to move beyond his grandmother's misadventures.

In answer to his unasked question she leaned across the table, stopping only a fraction from his lips. He moved forward. Just enough. Their lips brushed. It was a small kiss, but it blasted through his body, giving him the feeling of being enveloped in something stronger than he was.

'We should say goodnight now,' she said. 'It's late and I'm sure you're—'

'I can fetch some wine and cheese and we can sit under the stars.' He stilled, eyes locked on her.

A fanciful smile. 'I'll be waiting. Perhaps sleeping, but I'll still be here.'

'The sofa is yours,' he said. 'And I can always wake you.'

'With a kiss?' she asked.

'If you're asleep when I return…'

He didn't want to ring for a maid, so he slipped downstairs and gathered what he needed. Talking to someone might ruin the wonderment of the night.

After he'd gathered the items, he made it back up the stairs two at a time.

Opening the door softly, he found her with her arm propped up on the sofa and her head resting back, eyes shut. Her glasses were still perched on her nose. She didn't move.

He wanted to kiss her, but he didn't want to wake her.

Quietly, he put the bottle of wine on the table, and the cheese. Then he poured himself some wine and sat, finishing the drink. Perhaps he should let her sleep for a few moments. He stayed in the chair across from her, relaxed and stretched back.

Such a delicate woman…and someone who could ruin his family name.

He propped his elbow on the arm of the chair and his cheek on his fist. He stretched a little more and shut his eyes. It was as if he was in the middle of a dream. A dream with sunshine, and a laughing Marie dealing cards from the bottom of the deck, all of them winning ones for him.

'Gabriel.'

He looked up. He'd not heard her move from the sofa nor felt her nudge his arm.

'We can put off the walk until another time,' she said. 'Pleasant dreams.'

'Wait,' he said, standing. 'I don't want to put it off.'

Somehow he knew that if he did, he might never again get a chance to be with her like this.

He went to his dressing room, pulled out a coat and returned, wrapping it around her shoulders, taking his time, enjoying the slumbery scent of her. The sight of her with his coat draped against her and her hair more tousled than he'd ever seen any woman's arrested him.

'This is better than my shawl,' she said, running her fingertips up the lapel. 'Thank you.'

The kiss she gave him was more than a brush of lips. It was a soft, moist moment that he shared with her, ending on a promise of more.

'Do you think we need a lamp outdoors?' she asked.

'No. I know the way.'

He led her outside and they sat in the middle of the garden. He spread the food between them and then lay back, interlacing his fingers and using them to cradle his head. His back was against the ground and his eyes faced the stars.

'Do you do this often?' she whispered, taking a bite of the cheese.

'Usually just once or twice a year. It's harder to find perfect nights than I would have imagined. But they exist. Like tonight.'

She finished eating and picked up a twig from the ground. She used it to scratch at the earth a few times, even jabbing the stick into a dried leaf and lifting it.

'You're not eating or drinking?'

'I brought it for you.'

She tossed away the stick, propped up her knees, and pulled his coat closer as she looked overhead.

'On a cloudless clear night, in the summer,' he whispered, his voice a low rumble, 'if you listen closely you can hear the sounds of the night.'

'Owls?' she asked.

'Mr Glenn next door. Snoring. At least, I think it is him. Who knows? It could be Mrs Glenn or a servant. But I think it is him, because once I heard her shout out that she wished he would stop that awful noise.'

'Do you snore?' she asked.

'The neighbours have never complained.'

'They would not dare.'

'You don't know Mrs Glenn. Our families have been neighbours for decades. And across the way is the Earl and Countess of Bennington's home, which has been in their family for generations.'

'I cannot imagine such history.'

'My heritage is important to me. And if you put Grandmother's memories and moral lapses and buffoonery into written form, then it will be alongside that heritage for ever. A long reminder. Write something else. I'll even speak with the publisher and make sure you have all you need to be published.'

'I promised your grandmother. And besides, I don't like secrets.' She pushed herself to her feet.

'Are you going in?' he asked.

'If you are only here to try and talk me out of writing the memoirs, then yes.'

He stretched out his arm and put his hand over his heart. Being with her at that moment was more important than anything else. 'I will not mention it again until that little cloud gets past the moon.'

He saw the toss of her head, and knew it meant she was staying.

'I can't believe you lie out here like this,' she said. 'On the ground. With nothing between you and the earth.'

'You should try it.'

'My dress will get dirty.'

'It's just a few blades of grass.'

She didn't respond.

'It's warmer here, beside me,' he added.

She stepped to his side, tapped her slipper against his boot. 'Are you inviting me to lie beside you?'

He rose from his reclining position. 'The outdoors is plenty big enough for two.'

She sat beside him, their shoulders touching. 'I'm surprised you don't lie on a bench.'

'Too narrow. Too short.'

He put an arm around her, and suddenly the night wasn't cold any more.

The clouds moved over the moon, and he watched them, but he was more aware of her at his side. 'I've always watched the sky alone. Never had a night like this before.'

The kiss happened without his expecting it, and warmth filled him from head to toe. Her hand was on his chest. The night air was changing from cool to tinglingly comfortable. He felt the crush of their clothes joining.

She pulled away. 'I...'

'Let's not talk about it,' he said. 'Things happen without people meaning them to.'

He stood and put out a hand to help her rise. She seemed to fall into him.

'Things happen,' she said. 'My aunt has told me that. Over and over. But...'

He could tell she was lost in her thoughts when she lowered her eyes and studied the ground that was all darkness.

Like the memoirs. Like aloneness.

Marie stood unmoving. She should leave. One kiss might lead to two, and she was fairly certain she'd surprised him. That kiss wasn't something she'd expected to do.

She stepped away, hugging his coat close and surrounding herself in the scent of him. Leather, shaving soap, and delicious maleness.

He kissed her forehead. 'You've made this night one I will never forget.'

He lifted the bottle and glasses from the ground. The soft clinking sound was like a cymbal, signalling the end of their time together. She didn't want it to end.

'That's true for me also,' Marie said.

It was. She felt she could say anything she wanted to him.

Then he put his arm around her, the bottle and glasses still in his hand, and the tenderness of his lips surprised her. Tender and bold at the same time. He held her with one arm more securely than anyone else could with two.

She rested her hands against his chest, not ready to move away. But he didn't seem to have the same reluctance. He let her go, led her to the door. She supposed she could have put herself back into his arms, but she didn't.

'I'll be watching the sky tomorrow night,' he said. 'If you wish to join me.'

'I will,' she said.

'You could give up the memoirs,' he said, 'and stay here while you work on another topic. Let me know what you truly wish to do tomorrow night.'

'And if my viewpoint doesn't change—as it won't—will you still want to see me?'

'Of course.'

Chapter Fourteen

All day Marie had taken careful notes of his grandmother's tales, and she was determined to tell Gabriel that she wasn't going to give up on Myrtle's story.

The funds from publishing such a book would give her and her aunt some security. Besides, his grandmother had had a truly amazing life, and had not let the boundaries of society define her. She'd been her own woman and fulfilled her own wishes, sometimes at risk to herself and at risk to her happiness at home—but her husband had always forgiven her, she'd claimed.

And Marie hated secrets. Like the secret of her birth. Perhaps if people did not keep things so hidden, she would know her ancestral history.

She had grown up without parents. Without anything like the little toy horse Gabriel had taken for granted. The closest she'd come was when Polly's mother had made Polly a rag doll, and then a second smaller one from the scraps for Marie. Her first toy. The first thing she'd ever really owned. The woman who'd cared for her had burned it. She'd never reacted, but it had felt good when she'd been able to leave her house in the carriage, and had heard the woman had had to wed for money.

She almost felt bad about that. Almost. And she was

going to do all she could to keep the same thing from happening to her.

Marie had decided that if Gabriel was going to insist she give up the memoir, she must get as much information as possible before he cut off her access.

But even as she wrote Gabriel stayed in the recesses of her mind. She could hardly wait until the sun set and she would see him.

The temperature was perfect. The night was still and dark when she stepped out. But she could navigate her way into the garden easily.

Gabriel waited on the bench.

'I only plan to stay for a moment,' she said, having decided to go back in to work on the manuscript.

'Why?' he asked.

It would be best to tell him now. Best that he truly believed she wouldn't abandon her dream of being able to support herself. And writing a book such as the story of his grandmother's life would help tremendously.

Her place in society might be damaged, of course. She wasn't sure. Perhaps she could publish it anonymously? No, she wouldn't do that. She wanted to live a life without secrets.

'Perhaps I will stay out a little longer,' she said, absorbing the delight at having him at her side. 'I think I will.'

He took her hand. 'I'm pleased you have decided not to go in.'

'It is a magnificent night.'

He was responsible for that in so many ways. He had the garden and he understood her wish to enjoy the outdoors around her.

His hand covered hers, and even though the touch was innocent, it felt as though he was holding her in his arms.

She checked. 'Only one loop on your cravat again?'

He tugged at the small knot. 'Yes. My valet is deeply concerned, as I am taking so little care with my appearance, but in time I expect him to grow used to it.'

She hesitated. Leaving his home would be hard, because she would be putting him in her past. She liked being in Gabriel's house—not only because of him, but also because there was less friction here than anywhere she'd ever lived. Her aunt had taken her in without hesitation, but Agatha's husband had raged at her. Most often about Marie. About keeping secrets. Making his life a lie.

Her stomach had lurched when she'd realised the whole story. She doubted she would have ever moved in with Agatha if she'd known it in advance. Oh, she knew she wouldn't have. That explosion in the gardens had been minor compared with the fury unleashed by Lord Andrews. And, truly, she didn't blame him.

When Lord Andrews had told them Marie needed to marry his nephew or leave he'd known what he was doing. But Gabriel's grandmother had taken them in, and she seemed to like Marie well enough. She didn't really see her, though.

She didn't think Gabriel had truly seen her either. She was merely there—someone who would easily fall in with his plans. When she didn't fall in with people's plans they did what he had done—acted crushed, bereft, as if she'd turned into a beast and attacked them with no cause.

Only Agatha had ever really seen her, sacrificed for her. In fact, she'd supported Marie's decision twice when she hadn't wanted to wed. She'd claimed it untenable that

Marie take such a risk to try and improve her circumstances. She'd also claimed Gabriel's grandmother was the only woman she knew who had actually mourned her husband.

'Did you know your grandfather well?' she asked now.

She hoped Gabriel wouldn't get upset when he discovered that a few of his grandfather's errors were included in the memoirs. Gabriel's grandmother had told her that her husband had been a rake before they'd wed. In fact, he had claimed that men were not supposed to be faithful, but to be discreet. She'd responded by telling him he'd best keep his 'sword' put away, because she didn't want it to be sporting scars. She'd not been jesting.

She had also admitted, sadly, that she'd been so concerned with keeping her husband faithful that she'd not had a lot of time for her son, and she worried that Gabriel seemed to be following in his father's footsteps. At least where his heart was concerned...

'I remember him as a man who didn't take things too seriously,' he answered. 'I watched him shoe a wild horse once. A farrier had dared him that he couldn't do it and my grandfather accepted the challenge. You should have seen it when he let the horse go. He wasn't happy, and was intent on biting Grandfather's ear off. Or his nose.'

'Probably why your grandfather didn't live a long life?'

'He was already in his seventies when that happened, but he didn't act a day over sixteen most of the time. We had some good adventures. Grandmother was a lot younger than him, but they were well suited.'

'She told me she had to keep an eye on him.'

'She was the one more likely to cause a rumpus just because the calm bored her. Mother hated that. She's now watching over my other grandparents, who are gentle-minded people. Both frail. Living just outside London. I have several aunts and uncles, and their families are scattered about as well.'

'I didn't know either of my parents,' Marie said. 'I find it odd that you have so many family members.'

Listening to his grandmother's tales had made her feel better. She wasn't the only one with a secret, and her parents hadn't been the only ones who didn't adhere to propriety.

'But you have your Aunt Agatha. And Grandmother has mentioned that Agatha has some sisters…also some distant cousins in the peerage.'

'Well, yes.' She touched her bottom lip. 'But I suppose it's that I don't have any stories of my family that I took part in. The stories are all about other people. None with me involved. It's similar to seeing a play. You watch the characters, and at the end everyone goes their own way.'

Marie would have liked to know her parents, but she supposed it would never have been possible. Supposedly her father had died without knowing about her, and her mother had refused to acknowledge her other than by paying a woman to take care of her. Which she'd resented, Agatha had said, and was why she'd sometimes neglected to send the woman funds if she wanted something new for herself that was costly.

During her childhood she'd imagined her parents were travelling together somewhere, and one day the lady who'd cared for her had discovered that, and laughed so hard she'd cried.

'Do you believe your parents were content in their marriage?' she asked Gabriel.

There was a too-long pause.

'No. I don't know that my parents even spent much time in the same room. I did see Father furious with one of his sweethearts once. He had apparently ended their meetings and she hadn't taken it well. She wrote Mother a letter. Mother delivered the letter to him, after she had written notations on it and added her own viewpoints. I was with him when he came home and found the letter on his desk. Father was furious and Mother, strangely enough, was smug.' He touched his forehead. 'I learned all I ever wanted to know about their marriage that day.'

He'd had a whole plethora of family members growing up. A mother, a father and both sets of grandparents. So much more than she'd had.

And yet she still thought that she'd been so very fortunate. The woman who'd been paid to care for her might not have been kind, or loving, but other than a few times she'd not been outright cruel. Of course Agatha had told her that the funds would stop if Marie was mistreated. That might or might not have been true, but it had helped.

That was how she remembered her childhood. That and the cold winters. Putting on all the clothing she owned in order to stay warm. Gloves that didn't match and were beyond mending . Water freezing in the pitcher on the nightstand.

She couldn't complain about the woman being unkind on that measure, because they'd lived in the same house and she'd been sparing with her coal to save a few pence. They'd eaten together, and frozen together, and scrubbed their clothing together.

After Marie had moved in with her aunt, Agatha had kept on giving the woman funds, and Marie hoped the woman was doing well. But she and Agatha might have to resort to selling a frock or some stockings if Marie didn't manage to find a way to earn some money soon. She did not want Aunt Agatha to sell her pearls until she could get a top price for them.

In the darkness, Marie's voice floated across the night, more melodious than the most beautiful songbird, and Gabriel wondered what his grandmother had said to her about his father, or about his other grandparents, whom she disdained. They were tedious and wearisome, she'd told him, and had thanked him for taking after her instead.

His mother had admitted to him once, while throwing up her hands in consternation, that she'd been blinded by his father's smile, his title and his funds. She said he'd had the most attractive smile she'd ever seen. No one else had even come close, in her opinion, but sometimes she'd wondered if he might have been a better person if some woman's husband had dislodged a few of his teeth.

She'd told him privately that she'd thought his father had had the wrong mother. She'd never given her mother-in-law more than the weakest of upside-down compliments, saying she didn't want to say anything if she couldn't say something nice.

'She has nice ears,' had become her usual statement. 'Yes. She has beautiful ears.'

Otherwise, whenever his grandmother was mentioned, her lips would tighten and she'd reach up and tug her earlobe.

After his father had died he'd been surprised when the rest of the world had seemed more peaceful and to go more smoothly. Everything had been relatively quiet. Oh, he'd had to rein in his grandmother, but sometimes she'd seemed to have lost interest in creating a stir. She'd stopped staying out all night, and other than purchasing some rodents from the docks, in order to release them into the carriage of an enemy, she'd been happy to confine herself to creating more minor upheavals.

Marie took his hand. 'What are you thinking of?'

He rubbed a thumb over her knuckles, aware of the softness of her skin and the delicateness in her features. 'Taking on the duties of a viscount was easier than I expected after all Father's concerns. I had been raised to do it.'

'Your grandmother says that you are magnificent in the role.' She squeezed his hand. 'And she has admitted that you are not afraid of the dark, or even ghosts.'

He laughed, giving her hand a tug 'No. Grandfather always warned me that anything scary usually has a person attached.'

'I wasn't afraid of the dark when I was a child,' she admitted. 'But it is easier to trip over things, especially if you don't see well. The room I have now has such a lovely window, which prevents that from happening.'

'It does?'

He knew that he had the best rooms, and his grandmother had the biggest, in the opposite wing of the house. His mother had a set of rooms reserved for her visits, and Pierce always stayed on the side closer to Gabriel's rooms.

Lady Agatha had one of the nicer rooms, from what he could discern, with the fireplace that served both his grandmother's bedroom and hers, and Marie had a usually unused room near it.

'I thought the room you are in was mostly bare,' he said.

'Your grandmother has let me move things about. I can

show you how comfortable it is,' she said, pulling him up and leading him back into the house.

Once inside, she went towards his grandmother's rooms, but stopped at a bedroom he'd always considered little more than a storage room.

'There are much better rooms,' he said.

'I'm a guest, and this is closest to my aunt. I like it. If you always take the smallest space you are less likely to be displaced,' she said, laughing.

He frowned. 'You must move into another one.'

'No,' she said, opening the door. 'It's cosy.'

He walked in behind her. She'd left a lamp glowing, and it showed a dim room. He remembered the lumpy sofa from his grandfather's smoking room. The small desk had a chair snug against it, with a rip in the arm. If he remembered rightly, the chair had been the subject of an argument over which colour upholstery should be used for mending it, and the discussion had never been solved.

'You're comfortable here?' he asked, but he could see the answer in her eyes.

'This is my favourite room. The best I've ever had. Aunt's rooms are elegant and fine, but this one is so comfortable for me.'

'That sofa…?'

'Sit,' she said. 'But not there.' She pointed to a spot with a spring poking through.

'This should be mended,' he said. 'Or burned.'

'It's wonderful.'

She nudged him to the other end. He did sit, and it was comfortable enough. She sat beside him, turned towards him, her arm along the back of the sofa and her knee perched between them, almost as if she were alone, and suddenly everything about the room became cosier.

'See? It is relaxing and pleasant.' She turned. 'The chair has seen better days, but both are so comforting. I know the rest of the house is more elaborate, but this feels perfect for me. Everything is a little mismatched. And if something does need a new patch, it's not a concern.' Her eyes lit. 'Like a home. Not so much a mansion or an estate or a palace. But comfortable and a little well-worn.'

He heard the truth in her words and saw it in her expression. Time seemed to wrap around the look in her eyes, and it took everything else from his thoughts.

The silence connected them, and it seemed to be telling him all about her. He felt he had known her all her life. All his life. Even before they were born.

Then she put both her feet on the floor and moved closer, snuggling against his side so that he had her in the curve of his arm. Her head fell to rest against his chest, tickling his skin in a way that infused his body with awareness of her.

'I should go,' he said, and at those words she seemed to pull him closer.

'But this is nice. Maybe even nicer than lying on the ground looking up at the stars. Although on that night they'd never seemed so vibrant to me.'

They'd never been that vivid before for him either. They'd dazzled the sky.

And all because she had been with him.

She didn't want him to leave. She didn't. He'd been so kind, and he had let both her and her aunt stay in his house, and now she had invited him in to tell him the truth about her plans with his grandmother.

'I can't count on your kindness for ever,' she said. 'I have to make my own way.'

He took her fisted hand in his and studied it, holding just the fingertips and rubbing his forefinger over her smallest finger. 'Sometimes you have to trust someone.'

'I don't want to have to trust anyone.' She put her palm over his knuckles.

'I understand.'

He moved only a hair's width. Or that was what it seemed to her. And she relaxed against him. Or perhaps she slipped, as if she'd been standing on ice and the sun had touched them both and she'd no longer been able to remain upright.

She didn't even know the moment he stopped holding her hand and touched her chin, but the whisper of his lips against hers caused her to cling to him, amazed that another person could cause such a revitalising sensation in her. He'd taken the night and turned it into a sunrise.

She touched his cheek, feeling the strength in his jawline, the masculinity under her grasp. Stubble that should have been uncomfortable was blasting a wonder.

'You... I thought... When we kissed before, I thought it amazing.'

She stumbled over the words. Her mouth didn't want to speak. It only wanted to caress him.

'It was. It still is.' His lips touched hers as he spoke. 'Only more so.'

Then she remembered what she'd wanted to know. She'd not planned to ask him, but the words formed.

'Will you remember me? After I leave?' she asked.

'I will remember you. Never doubt that.'

After kissing her fingertips, he held her face in both

his hands, and she didn't feel confined but adored, as if she basked in his presence. She'd never felt so revered before. So cherished.

She removed her glasses and led him to her bed. She knew she could never wed him, because he didn't truly know who she was, but she could have the memory of these moments with Gabriel, which she would treasure for the rest of her life.

He ran his hands down her face and the strength inside him seemed transferred into her, as if she could feel not only his hands, but his entire body behind them. But then she realised it wasn't strength she was feeling from his touch, but from his eyes.

His lips, feather-light, belying the strength she'd felt, brushed hers, and then he moved away, just enough to take one more lingering look before returning to the kiss, softly and only enough to connect them. Until she wrapped herself around him, pulling herself closer. She could not be near enough to him. Not just his lips and his hands, but all of him. The distance was too far. She needed more.

His body pressed against hers, and their clothing was a wall between them, creating friction but not satisfying her, leaving her bereft.

She held herself away to touch his cravat, her fingers tangling in the fabric as she tried to untie it but only made a knot.

He paused, removed the cravat and slipped it and his coat away, tossing them to the floor so they landed with a soft fluttering sound. The fabric of his sleeves billowed out, and she realised she'd never noticed the true width of his shoulders before.

Long fingers undid each of the seemingly endless buttons of his waistcoat, and the adoration in his eyes for her appeared just as infinite as the fastenings.

Then he clasped her shoulders, lowering his head to kiss the pulse at her neck, and she heard him whisper her name.

She clutched his chest, her fingers gripping his shirt to hold herself erect, and when his arms went around her they enclosed her in a masculine scent that she would happily have lost herself in. She didn't need to hold herself upright. He did that for her with no effort.

A breath later he had touched the clasps of her dress and slid it from her shoulders. Then he placed it over the chair at the foot of her bed, moving delicately.

He stopped for a moment, his eyes changing, heating and melting at the same time. 'You remind me of a fragile figurine,' he said. 'Something too delicate to even be on display.'

She turned, letting him undo her laces, and when the corset dropped to the floor she fell into his arms, her chemise blending with his shirt, and her body feeling the thinness of their clothing. She wanted to be beyond that fabric. Closer to him. Wrapped in the sensation that she knew only he could give her.

She reached for the ties of his shirt, quickly undoing it. She asked him with her eyes, and he nodded, and she slipped the shirt over his head, amazed to see continuing evidence of his strength, and the difference in the planes of his body compared to hers.

Tentatively, she touched his sides, amazed at the vibrancy that flowed through her as her senses adjusted to the sensation of his masculinity, and then she ran her hand over his chest, following the small path of hair that contrasted with the smoothness of the spot where the dark stubble ended at the base of his chin. She slipped her hands around him and rested her cheek on his shoulder, savouring the feel of him.

His breath touched her ear, causing her to clasp him closer, and she felt the trail of his kisses and tongue and put her head back, so he could find her lips before moving away again.

He pulled the bedcovers back and she ran her hand down his arm, pressed the hair under her fingertips, and then she clutched his hand before slipping between the coverlet and the sheet.

'Lovely,' he whispered, studying her face while he removed his breeches and joined her in the bed.

She tugged at her chemise and he helped her pull it over her head. And then she could pull herself against him completely, feel his hardness between them, waiting for her.

He kissed her shoulder, the bristles of his beard caressing her skin, causing the intensity inside her to spiral. And then they joined together, feeling heartbeats and desire, and finally reached a place where they could be sated.

She lay on his arm, not exactly basking in the glow of lovemaking but thinking about what she'd done. She'd let her passions overwhelm her. The same thing that she'd inwardly criticised her mother and father for. She'd been weak.

She rolled away from him.

'What's wrong?' he asked, putting his hand on her arm, moving closer to hold her and put a kiss on her hair.

'I've not been truthful with you,' she said.

She didn't want to tell him, but she also didn't want to hide her past. She knew he would turn his back on her for her deceit. She would have her belated integrity, but she would not have him.

It was a risk she had to take.

'What do you mean?'

'I've not been honest.' She held the covers to her chest and moved so that their eyes locked.

'About what?'

She took in a breath, slowly exhaled. 'About…about my past.'

'Have I asked you to tell me?'

'Our lovemaking. It is a commitment to honesty.'

'I'm not sure that's written in stone. Or even in sand.' He gave her a kiss on the shoulder and lay back in bed. 'I almost wed once, but it would have been a mistake for both of us.'

'You?' she gasped, his revelation derailing her planned confession.

'Yes. Jane Brock. What could go wrong? I thought. I wasn't particularly ready to wed, but she was a peer's daughter, and I knew she was a respectable woman. A good person. But then one day we were sitting in her house, and our chaperon fell asleep. Jane and I were at a loss for what to say to each other. We laughed about it, thinking the chaperon must be having a better time than either of us.'

'What did you do?'

'We parted as friends and I wished her well.'

'Did you intend to wait and wed for love?'

'I thought I was in something close to love with Jane.'

He sat up, propped himself on one arm, and looked at her. The light was dim, but his words were so direct that it seemed she could see into his soul when he answered.

'Jane was a nice person, and at first I assumed we would

eventually fall passionately in love. But I doubt we would have. I enjoyed talking with the chaperon more than with Jane.'

Marie rose from the bed and put on enough clothing to be decent, but not enough to go out in public.

She stood by the bedside, and at first he seemed unwilling to break the silence.

He half smiled. 'Don't look so upset.'

'I'm not. Just assessing things.'

And understanding more than she had before.

Then she remembered her aunt's husband, tossing them out, and how Agatha had made her promise never to wed if her husband didn't truly love her. *Never.*

'But surely Uncle does love you? We're leaving in his carriage,' she'd told her aunt. 'Not on foot.'

Agatha had crossed her arms. 'And if I don't have the courage to step away I might as well be throwing my body underneath the vehicle. That's how it will be every day until he respects me. Either he takes me back on my terms or we risk starvation. You'll be able to find respectable work, and I'm completely happy being a beggar on a street corner. Better than being a beggar under my husband's roof.'

The words reverberated in Marie's mind now.

Gabriel would always be a peer. He could court so easily, and all the women would fall in love with him—as she now realised she had. She had no guarantee he would not become like his father...like all the other men she had seen. Chasing from one woman to the next. She could not live with that. She could not be a beggar under her husband's roof.

Gabriel's grandmother had said that had been the root of the problem between Gabriel's parents. His father had thought his mother a lesser person, and that she would have no choice but to put up with his straying. Which was true.

She had seen women so happy with their new husbands, thrilled to be gifted with so much love, and then it had all changed, leaving those women scrabbling about for a meal, or a new roof over her head.

It would be better for her to leave with parts of her heart intact, rather than stay with him and have her spirit bashed into a thousand pieces. They had made love, and she would have that happy memory for ever. But now she must walk away—or risk being pulled into the mire, where she would be an unwelcome addition to the household.

She paused, and then formed her words carefully. 'There's something you should know. About me.'

'I already know,' he said.

'You know?'

'Grandmother told me. No one really knows who your parents were.'

She deliberated for a moment. That was for the best, she supposed. She didn't want to cause Agatha and Lord Andrews—Drippy Nose—more distress.

She lowered her chin, and her gaze, and bit her lip.

'It doesn't matter.' He caressed her face. 'It doesn't change one lovely hair on your head. One flutter of your lashes.'

After seeing the upsets between Agatha and the husband who had claimed to love her aunt so very much before they wed, she was wary of marrying for love. Love was less dependable than anything else. It seemed too fragile to withstand day-to-day nearness. Or even week-to-week.

* * *

Gabriel left the bed and gathered his clothing, donning his shirt, waistcoat and breeches quickly. He lifted the cravat, studied it a moment and smiled, then tossed it to her.

She grabbed it from the air and held it in her hand, then she brought the neckcloth closer to her body, looking beyond the fabric. Her eyes were searching and she appeared dazed, lost in thought.

He almost hated himself. He should have been stronger. He shouldn't have made love to her. He'd not meant to. He'd not planned it. And now...

He didn't want to leave, but knew he should. And he would.

But only after he asked her again to forget about the memoirs.

'Will you stop collaborating with my grandmother?'

She shook her head.

'Why don't you write a fictional story in which you disguise the incidents about my family so much that no one will know who you are writing of?'

She touched the fabric of his cravat. 'I want to pay homage to your grandmother's strength and force of will. She is a strong and admirable woman.'

He snorted. 'She is a rebel.'

'Well, yes,' she said softly, raising her head. 'She rebelled against society and did as she pleased and thrived. She's a Boudicca with a happy ending and without the terribly bad parts.'

'To me, it's an embarrassment. She is my grandmother. You cannot take advantage of her like that. She deserves to be respected in her later years.'

He spoke softly, wanting her to understand. Wishing

they could stop talking about his family and crawl back into bed and spend the night together.

'Take advantage of her?' She shook her head. 'I respect her for her courage. Her honesty. She has told me she calls me a wall weed.'

He wouldn't even have thought his grandmother would be so rude to Marie as to let her know of the nickname.

'A wall weed,' she said. 'And it fits me. I imagine myself a climbing plant, moving up the walls and towards the light, holding close to whatever I can to make my way.'

'It was wrong for her to tell you such a thing. You can see how her judgement is clouded.'

'It's not her judgement. She has little of that. But she says if we write this book together I will turn from a wall weed into a warrior woman, with a home of my own. I will be making my own way for my aunt and myself. Aunt Agatha agrees. She will sell the pearls and get a house in my name, so her husband cannot take it. The money from the book will put food on the table. And your grandmother assures me that if we put enough fascinating stories in the first volume, we can hold out enough to make a second volume.'

'*Two* books?' The embarrassment would go on for ever. 'You do not have to put your energies into that,' he said.

The columns holding up his mental truths concerning her were slowly crumbling into dust. She'd worn the new dress, but she'd quickly returned to the frumpy dresses that were from the past and didn't suit her. He'd thought she was hiding behind them, but perhaps she was staking her place in her world by saying that she would wear the clothes she wished to wear.

'I suppose you mean I could wed? Instead of making my

own way?' she said. 'I don't want that. And I wasn't impressed to find that you were trying to find suitors for me just as your grandmother is trying to find suitors for you.'

He didn't regret showing people how beautiful she could be. Showing *her*. He'd wanted her to know that she could shine in the middle of a social event. That she didn't need to hide.

'You'd prefer to write a book that will destroy my heritage?' he asked. 'Bring to light—for ever—the things in my grandmother's past that I have worked hard to get beyond? Hurt my grandparents? My mother?'

He could not believe she seemed so caring of everyone but him and his family.

Gabriel fell asleep in his own bed and woke to the scent of springtime, though he wasn't sure if it was real or if it was caused by the memory of Marie. Then he realised he had been awakened by the valet opening the door.

'You have a guest in your sitting room,' his valet said, his voice disapproving.

Gabriel moved only his eyes.

'Your cousin. He is propping his boots on the furniture.'

'Kick him out of the house.'

'I have tried. Gently. But I suspect you will have to do it. I also think the butler will be happy to help. The three of us can make it more memorable for him.'

The butler was not soon to forgive Pierce for the mud tracks he always left in the entrance hall, and thought his personal habits caused too much demand on the staff.

Gabriel finished dressing and went to his sitting room, where Pierce was sprawled. Asleep. How could his cousin have fallen asleep in the time it took him to sit?

Gabriel walked over, and with the toe of his boot moved Pierce's leg. 'You know you're supposed to be staying in your own rooms when you're visiting.'

Pierce sat up, hair rumpled, clothes rumpled and expression unrumpled. 'Yes. But your sofa happened to be closer, and I didn't feel like taking another step.'

'I am sure the butler would have been gracious enough to put you in a wheelbarrow.'

'Straight out to dump me in the garden. I don't think your staff enjoy my being here.'

'They don't.'

'You should speak to them about that.'

'I'm fine with it. You need to be neater—and not demand things at odd hours of the night.'

Pierce ran a hand through his hair, smoothing it. Then he tugged his cravat into place. 'Since you mention it, I think I should stay for a while longer. I'm not getting any younger and I miss Grandmother.' Pierce winked. 'And there's something intriguing about Marie. The spectacles, I suppose. I keep thinking about her. Her aunt is married to Lord Andrews, so she has a viable connection to society. I'm feeling courtship-minded.' He leaned forward, hands on his knees. 'Unless, of course, you two are having a romance. Which would explain why she is living in your house.'

'Marie and I are friends, and you are not to mention her.'

Piece jumped up, walked over, and gave his cousin a punch on the shoulder. 'I should have known when she was at the picnic, looking so lovely. Keeping the best beauties for yourself.' He frowned. 'Because she has spectacles it will make it easier for you to court her. She can take them off and pretend you're handsome.'

'Do you plan to go down the stairs feet first or face first?' Gabriel asked.

Pierce gave his cousin another half-hearted punch, before tugging on the bell-pull. 'Romance is in the air! Gabe has a new romance with a reputable woman. He's all aflutter. I can tell by the way his teeth grind when I mention her.'

'You're about to lose the ability to grind your teeth if you don't watch what you say.'

Pierce clasped a hand over his heart. 'I will be silent. Quiet as a mouse. Not even a hungry mouse. They make too much noise.'

He lifted his boot and gave it a polish with his hand. 'Why did you invite Elway and Epperson to the picnic? That wasn't very well thought-out, now, was it?'

Gabriel kept silent.

Pierce moved to lift the glass beside the decanter. 'Grandmother's memoirs should turn the whole of Town on its ear. So I can understand your being irritable—not that it's any great change.' He took in a deep breath. 'Every little stumble and crash of our family splashed out for all to see… I'll revel in it, but it will kill you. And it will upend your mother and her family. I don't envy you that.'

A maid rapped on the door and Pierce opened it. 'Please have a meal brought to my room.'

'You can eat in the dining room,' Gabriel said. 'You don't need to be making extra work for the servants.'

'Fine.' Pierce peered over his shoulder. 'I forgot to tell you that I saw your mother last night. We were at the same event—imagine that. I did let it slip that Grandmother had been gambling, using you as a wager, and she didn't see the humour. Expect her to visit, as she said she would be here today. She fears you need help with Grandmother, and she wants to see the person she lost you to.' He grinned. 'Don't worry. I didn't tell your mother about Grandmother's memoirs. I'm saving that.'

A man could be a viscount. He could be a duke. He could be a king. He could control countries. But a man could not control his family.

Chapter Fifteen

He didn't like eating in the formal dining room, but he had to attend so he could make sure his mother and grandmother didn't brawl.

His mother had arrived just before dinner, giving him two lectures on being wary of people who did not have his best interests at heart. Then she'd glared as she tugged at her ear.

She'd also asked what was going on under his roof, and then told him to please spare her the details and get straight to the part about his grandmother's gambling.

He had reassured her that all was well, and she told him that she shouldn't have taught him not to speak badly about family members. And although she hadn't torn her earlobe off after speaking, it wouldn't have taken much more effort.

She'd said she would be at dinner and expected his grandmother to be in attendance, and that she would assure that would happen by telling her former mother-in-law she hoped to have a quiet conversation with Gabriel.

He was leading her to the table when his grandmother strolled in, lacking all but royal robes and a sceptre to go along with her commanding arrival. She was never the tallest woman in a room, but she acted as if she were.

His grandmother and mother greeted each other with

perfunctory almost-kisses on the cheek, and then his mother stepped away—much in the same way two boxers would eye their opponents.

'Don't look so glum, Flora,' his grandmother said. 'I've been having a wonderful time with Gabriel, and he's so happy to have me staying with him—although I doubt there's anything of interest going on here for you.'

'I don't want you trying to get him married off,' his mother said.

'Another woman in this household would be one too many,' his grandmother said. 'She might think she runs the place, and as the matriarch of the family I'm perfectly capable.'

'Capable? At dealing cards, I'm sure. And how much have you lost at gambling overall, would you guess?'

'I always manage my cards well. Besides, you don't expect to win every game. The sport is in the playing. The camaraderie. The friendships earned.'

His mother snorted.

Then Pierce arrived, and both women seemed to try to outdo themselves in showing their devotion to him.

When Agatha and Marie appeared, the room quietened. Marie wore one of the old dresses, but Pierce almost tripped over his boots rushing to her. She appeared to want to stay in the background, but it wasn't possible. Her dress was plain, overly simple, but among his family she stood out in her lack of adornment.

His mother certainly noticed her, and her eyes turned to him, as if to ask *This one?*

He gave a quick nod of his head.

Pierce made himself available to the only women in the room he wasn't related to, flirting equally with Marie and her aunt. But that was Pierce. He'd once said that if a woman wasn't flirtatious then surely she must have friends who were, so there was no sense in ignoring the possibilities.

'Let us sit and enjoy our meal.' Gabriel extended an arm to the table.

'This is a wonderful evening,' Pierce said. 'Good food. Good company. And Gabriel.'

'And I'm equally pleased to have you here,' Gabriel said.

'I'm all for his staying unwed,' Pierce said, and gave Marie a smile. 'To keep you informed, that makes me next in line for the Viscountcy—after my two brothers, one of whom has been wed ten years and has no children, the other of whom has three lovely daughters.' He turned to Gabriel. 'I want you to know, Gabe, I would make a good viscount. I will be happy to taste all this food first, so you can be sure it is safe. In fact, I've heard that the wine could be tainted, so I'm going to make sure you will not get ill from it. I've been told a criminal will only poison the best wine. Are you sure this is it, Gabe? I wouldn't want you to get ill on a lesser drink.'

'That is not humorous,' Gabriel's mother said, and glared at her nephew.

'I'll test it for both of them,' his grandmother said. 'I could be on my last legs anyway.'

'Oh, please…let me pour for you,' his mother said.

Marie looked at his grandmother, and then his mother, and then at Gabriel.

He gave her the merest flicker of an eyelash, acknowledging the verbal duel.

'Well, cousin?' Pierce said. 'Have you been lost in any card games recently?'

'He was won,' Marie said. 'And it's obvious that Gabriel is an exemplary viscount and no one could fill his boots.'

'Because he's got feet the size of a barn,' Pierce noted to no one in particular, before taking a sip of wine.

His grandmother chuckled. 'I'm blessed to have such accomplished grandsons. They both take after me.'

''I thought I should spend more time here in case I missed anything,' said Pierce. 'And so I could visit my dear grandmother. It is wonderful to have a family gathering. We get together so rarely.'

Gabriel's mother glared, and his grandmother looked as if she'd just won the title of Grandmother of the Realm.

'I love these family dinners, too,' she said. 'We do not have them often enough.'

'They seem very entertaining,' Agatha said.

'Just ignore us,' Gabriel said. 'We test our wits instead of our rapiers.'

'You can ignore *him*,' Pierce said. 'But if Miss Marie would like to go with me on a carriage ride in the park tomorrow I'd be thrilled. Grandmother can be our chaperon.'

Marie tensed, then stammered, 'I—I would not impose upon your grandmother so.' Then she studied Pierce. 'And I think it would be best for me to avoid that.'

For a second her eyes locked with Gabriel's, and he reassured her with a glance.

His mother and grandmother saw it. His mother gave a soft gasp, and his grandmother grimaced.

'You have just reminded me,' his grandmother said to her daughter-in-law, 'I've never told Marie about your courtship with my son. I think it would be a wonderful thing to include in my memoirs.'

'Memoirs?'

His mother spluttered. Gabriel had never seen her do that before.

'Marie is writing the story of our family. I'm telling it to her.'

'What a thought! If you even get the facts right.' His mother tilted her head, and this time she gave a nod towards her mother-in-law and then frowned into her plate. 'And I suppose the odds are not in my favour on that.'

Marie took in a slow breath, and Gabriel didn't move.

'It's not completely decided to publish the memoirs.' Gabriel spoke softly but with emphasis.

'I can hardly wait to read Grandmother's recollections,' Pierce said.

'We'll see,' Gabriel said, easily enough.

'Gabriel. You must get this stopped. It's unthinkable!' his mother said, placing a palm flat on the table.

'I think you'll find it enlightening,' Gabriel's grandmother said, and then turned to Marie. 'We may need more paper.'

When they'd finished dinner his grandmother stood, tapping her lips with her napkin. 'I have so many stories to tell you, Marie.'

His mother rose, squared her shoulders, and addressed Gabriel. 'We need to discuss this.'

'We can talk in the sitting room,' Gabriel said.

'Did you encourage these…memoirs?' his mother asked, as soon as he and she were alone in the sitting room—or, as alone as they could be with his grandmother and cousin in attendance, both of whom had rushed in after them.

'No.'

'I should never have left this house… But my parents

need me.' His mother quirked a brow and stared at him, giving the napkin she still held a twist. 'One can only handle so much, and your grandmother is many times more than what is bearable.'

'You didn't have to marry into my family. I did warn you,' his grandmother answered.

'I like Marie,' Pierce said, his voice rolling like a cloud of cigar smoke. 'And I know I can speak for Gabriel. He likes her even more than I do.'

'She's fine for a tryst,' his grandmother said, 'as long as it's nothing serious. It is nothing serious, is it? You know I was jesting with that wager only because I really wanted those pearls.'

'Is that it?' his mother asked. 'Just a romance? Do be careful, Gabriel, you know how easily a woman can be hurt in a situation such as this.' She slid her index finger against her necklace, let it twist once, and then slid her finger back and forth several times. 'She's practically alone in the world, isn't she?'

'No. She has her aunt.'

'Sometimes it isn't so bad to be alone in the world,' his mother said.

'While I am friends with Agatha,' his grandmother added, 'Marie is better for Pierce. Because he needs someone like her. You need someone less adventurous, Gabriel. Like Rosalind. That's the perfect woman for you.'

'Marie should leave,' his mother said. 'I can tell this home is not the place for an unwed young woman.'

'She has nowhere else to go.'

'I'll invite her to my parents' house,' his mother said. 'That will be best for everyone. We can leave at once.'

'No,' his grandmother said. 'We've hardly started my

memoirs. And I haven't yet told her anything about *your* family history. You'll find a few surprises there.'

His mother choked.

'Dearest Flora,' his grandmother said, nonchalantly tapping her finger to her ear. 'I hope you will enjoy reading about your parents—from my perspective, of course. Both interesting people, from what I could unearth. They need very little embroidery—so to speak.'

'You would not dare—' His mother's voice broke and her fingers splayed.

'If you will all excuse me,' said Gabriel, standing and taking a stride to the door. 'I'm going to go discuss your departure with Marie.'

He had to. He could not let her live here among the wolves—particularly the family ones.

Entering the corridor, he made his way to her room, knocking on the door.

'Marie,' he called out. 'I need to speak with you.'

She opened the door. 'I have my things ready to leave. I expected this. We will have to return to my uncle's hunting lodge and hope the servants there don't realise he doesn't know we're there.'

She stepped out into the corridor, looking the length of it. His mother had just stepped into view, and his grandmother was almost elbowing her out of the way.

Gabriel took in a long slow breath, then took Marie by the arm and backed her into her room, shutting the door behind him.

Almost instantly someone rapped on the wood. 'Gabriel. This is most untoward. Don't damage Marie's reputation.'

His mother.

The door rattled and he grasped the latch, holding it closed.

'Would you mind me visiting you tonight?' he asked softly.

'Just don't bring anyone with you.'

Marie stepped away from the door and Gabriel opened it. His grandmother and his mother stood side by side, guardians of their viewpoints, and Pierce relaxed farther down the corridor, leaning against the wall, arms crossed, one foot propped behind him, humour in his eyes.

'*This* is why I don't visit often,' his mother added. 'But it's clear this time that I have stayed away too long. My life is being destroyed right before my eyes. And my parents' health and happiness are at stake.'

'Grandmother, as I pay all your expenses, and the costs of all this household, I am telling you that you cannot write the memoir,' Gabriel said. 'Not only do I need to maintain dignity for the family, in order to help with my financial ventures, it would also cause grief to Mother. And to my other grandparents.'

'I would like to see Marie do as she wishes,' Pierce said. 'And I would enjoy reading Grandmother's recollections. Grandmother, just send your billing to my man of affairs.'

'The Duke will not be able to continue our friendship,' his mother said, wringing her hands. 'Not with his daughter about to be introduced in society. He does not know all the details of our family life, and to have them thrown out into the world... I will have to disappear—as I did before, when I was married.'

His grandmother shrugged and sniffed dismissively. 'I will be continuing with my memoirs.' She peered around

Gabriel's shoulder at Marie. 'You might want to get a copy of the signed document I gave your aunt and include it.'

'I should leave this house,' Marie said. 'It seems I am causing an upset here.'

'You're just acting like one of the family,' Gabriel said.

'She's a better listener than anyone I know,' said his grandmother. 'She's like a grandchild, only better, because she doesn't argue.'

'I do like you,' Marie said to his grandmother. 'And your memories are so interesting to me. This family's life. Except today is not good. I must hope this is an aberration.'

His mother groaned. 'I wish that were true.'

'See?' His grandmother held her head high and gave a dismissive look to her daughter-in-law before returning her gaze to Marie. 'It is nice to have a female in this house who is agreeable. And who can be trusted to do the right thing.'

Marie didn't know if she could be trusted to do the right thing.

Gabriel's mother made a choking sound. She was adept at that. And she had a nervous habit of tugging on her ear.

Marie sighed inwardly. Leaving Gabriel would be difficult, but it would be better to do it soon. He'd noticed her for all the wrong reasons. He'd thought he could make her into something exactly as he wished. And she didn't want to be used that way. Seen as someone lesser, who had to be dressed a different way and have her hair changed. A poor woman to be rescued. One who would deal with his grandmother—as if anyone could—so he could do his duty and then retreat from his family while attending briefly the social interactions they provided for him.

And she had almost no family to add to the situation.

She would be earning her keep.

She looked at him, seeing the weary look on his face. She was an orphan who had always wanted a family, but she could see now why to him her lack of family members might not be such a bad thing.

Chapter Sixteen

'**I**'ve missed you,' Gabriel said, after she'd opened her door that night.

'Did you notice me only because I have so little family?' she asked, stepping aside.

She indicated the sofa and he relaxed on the lumpy object, still amazed at how its wear seemed to create a welcoming hold, and how the room full of misfit furniture was the most welcoming one in the house.

He wasn't holding her, but inside her room, on the sofa, it was as if she was clasping him. He'd never been in a room that embraced him like this, and it was all because of her.

Looking around, he saw her reticule, some papers, her shawl, a cup, a flattened bonnet... He relished the moment.

'I shall have to find another place to live,' she said, moving beside him.

He put an arm on the back of the sofa, and after the smallest consideration she snuggled into the haven he'd made for her.

'Your grandmother has spent the evening trying to tell me all the family mishaps she can think of. And your mother has pulled me from the room and insisted I give to her everything I've already written. She says her mother-in-law is a bad influence on everyone, including you. She has even said I can move in with her parents if I leave the memoirs behind.'

'Are you going to?' he asked. Their lips were so close he could feel the caress of her breath.

'No. I would feel even less secure than I feel here,' she whispered. 'I don't know her at all. But I do feel I know your grandmother. If a thought is in her head, she has no problem with speaking it. But I will have to find somewhere else to live.'

He didn't want to think of her alone in the world. True, she had her aunt, and she'd managed in the past. But he didn't want her to have to do that in the future.

'Are you sure you don't want to stay here?' He clasped her closer, surrendering to this moment of having her so near to him.

'I'm sure I *do* want to stay, but I don't want to be caught in the miasma of your family concerns.'

Her eyes begged him to understand, but he wanted her to understand as well.

'All families have hierarchies. Disagreements. Problems. Resolutions.'

'A family should give you a safety net. A place to return to when you tumble. And I don't know that your family gives that,' she said. 'They don't enjoy being together. And none of them seem to have ever learned how to talk to each other in a nice way, just in commands. Even you.'

'That's not as uncommon as you'd think.'

And it didn't seem to matter any more. He needed to hold her. To have her close.

'Because you have such a large estate, you can sequester

yourself away from them for the most part. And that's what you do, isn't it? Sequester yourself away from your family.'

'My family is used to having its own way. They've been surrounded by servants their whole lives.'

He didn't see that as a bad thing. Servants were much better at pleasing his family than anyone else was.

'Now I see why I get on so well here. In a sense, I've been a servant my whole life.'

Her face blasted him like the coldest winter air.

'No, it's not that.'

'It would be too much of a commitment to be expected to keep everyone happy here. No, if I'm to be a servant again, it will not be in a house where my heart is involved.'

'I do care for you,' he said.

It was true. The way her eyes lit up when she saw the gardens thrilled him, and he enjoyed seeing her excitement. Her pleasure in the plants moving from bud to bloom. How she stopped to enjoy and inhale the individual flowers' blooms. So appreciative of being able to see the leaves.

'I believe you,' she said. 'You like me. But in perhaps the same distant way you like the other women in your family. I would be perfect to live here, in your mind, because I could be someone you only saw on occasion.'

Now he wondered if she was correct—very correct—in her intention of leaving.

But then another concern edged into him. One of fear. Of loss. He didn't want Marie leaving. She was safe in his home. Protected from other men who might not have her best interests at heart. If she fell in love with someone like Pierce it would only be a matter of time before he moved on to someone else.

And he knew he risked losing her, but he had no choice

if he wanted to keep his family intact. To protect his mother and his grandparents.

He would speak with the publisher and find a way to have his grandmother's memoirs stopped. But it mattered to him that Marie didn't seem to understand his distaste for having his family's misadventures shared.

He couldn't understand her willingness to embarrass his family. She was seemingly unaware of how much pain it would cause to people he cared about to revisit the problems they'd moved on from. It seemed she took his remonstrations much as she had his instructions for waltz-ing—she let them go in one ear and out the other. She seemed caring, but he didn't know if it went deep enough. Perhaps it was a façade she'd developed because she'd had to show a caring manner to survive.

She straightened her shoulders. 'I have been mostly alone in the world except for Aunt Agatha, and if I am alone again it will not be the first time. I can take care of myself. I will survive. I don't like being cold, but I can be, and I can make do with very little. In fact, sometimes I think I am happier with less. I don't have to worry about losing as much.'

He met her gaze. 'It's not a bad thing to have something you don't want to lose.'

Pondering his words, she saw the truth in his expression.

'It's safest for me not to take that risk,' she said.

'Is it?'

He reached out.

She clutched him, hoping she would remember for ever what it felt like to be sitting close to him, in this cosy room, with comforting things around her.

For this moment in time she wasn't poor, but wealthy

beyond belief. Being in this small room in this instance, near to him, enveloped in his presence, was the closest she had ever been to heaven. But like all wonderful things it could not last for ever.

'By fortune of birth I was given a viscountcy, and by that same goodness I was given the means to train for it. I have been a good shepherd,' he said. 'And I will continue to be a good overseer. It is my heritage, and I must pass on the best example of it that I can. Instead of writing those memoirs, you could marry me.'

Somehow the kind words hit her as a spear into her heart. 'I'm not blackmailing you into marriage. Not now. Not ever. And I am deeply offended at the thought.'

These were not words she would accept from a future husband. A future husband had to believe she was such a part of his life that no other would do, and know that he would slay emotional dragons for her—even if the dragons were inside himself.

He could not wed her to purchase her silence. To end his duty of finding a bride.

'You could find a much better wife,' she said, moving away. 'Daughters of dukes and earls and viscounts and barons are all about.'

In a marriage to her it would hurt to see him wonder if, perhaps, he should have chosen someone else.

'You are not being kind to yourself.'

'I suppose not. But I've not found much of the world to be kind either. And I have lived in that part of the world more than I have resided in your world. Really, I can only touch the fringes of your life. I stand just close enough to see in, but not close enough to stay in it. Not close enough for you.'

'With a marriage to me, you would.'

'I would always have to watch my footing.'

Not just with society. But with him. She would never know if he was thinking of the mistake he'd made. Of the society women who would have wed him. The grandparents and connections his children would have had.

'I will not be reminded, even with my own words, that I am not the jewel you would have hoped for. A poor man who might offer to share his only crust of bread with me is better than a rich man who tosses me a crust of his fine bread.'

She knew she placed a high value on herself—to walk away from a marriage that would give her money, but no promises of the heart. But she had seen what had happened to her aunt, and the belittling situation she had found herself in. The tension.

'You would rather risk so much than stay with me?' he asked.

'It will be better for both of us in the long run.'

'I am sure Grandmother's stories are interesting to other people,' he said. 'But I've lived them. Tried to discount them. I do not want them published.'

'Most people have things in their family that they would rather not be discussed.'

'This isn't about "most people". It's about us,' Gabriel said. 'In this room, it is about us. But I will always remember that your choice wasn't to marry me, but to disregard me. You have chosen the wrong path.'

No, she hadn't. Because she had chosen herself.

Quicker than she had ever seen anyone move, he turned away from her.

'You want to betray me, and I will not let you. Not under my roof.'

'Fine. I will leave.'

'But I don't want you to go.' He faced her again.

'Your grandmother has shared her stories with me. She trusted me, and you should, too.'

'You're planning to profit from your closeness to my family.'

'Yes. I am. I already do. And if it were not me, it would be someone else.'

'Let it be someone else, then. Not you.'

She was torn. Torn between the look she saw in Gabriel's eyes and the chance she had to support herself. If his grandmother's memoirs were published and did well, then her aunt had another friend who was considering having her story written.

It would mean a lot to her—having that opportunity and possibly many more—and not only that, listening to his grandmother's reminiscences had been fascinating.

But one thing bothered her even more. Gabriel did not trust her to do the right thing. He thought her to be betraying his family. And perhaps he was right.

Was she selling her integrity? The way she had when she had agreed to undertake the changes in her appearance that he'd suggested? Making herself into the person he wanted her to be. Someone just like everyone else.

He'd seen that she was different. Been fascinated. And then he had tried to remove the parts of her that he'd noticed in the first place.

She should never have agreed to be anything other than herself.

True, she had liked the hairstyle, and she had felt beautiful in the new dress. But he had remade her, and she didn't think she could remain as that person. She was more comfortable in clothing that didn't matter. That didn't make her seem above others. And, goodness, she was not. She was just herself. An orphan who had been fortunate.

She had no choice but to continue her journey and take care of herself.

'You would be giving up a fortune, children who will have the best of things, and a status few receive.'

'I have never had status. Nor a fortune. And I don't want either if it means I would be indebted to you or anyone else for ever.'

His eyes looked pinched, and she suspected that now he truly saw her. Not the woman he'd thought she could be, if she used just the right cosmetics and the best fashions and became an accessory to him. But a woman with a mind of her own.

She could see it in his face. His wonderment at how she could say no to such a thing. But status was not important to her. She had no children, and might never have any, but she had made peace with that. And a fortune would be wonderful, but once she accepted it she knew she would be encased for ever in a world that would not let her leave. It would own her. A world in which she wasn't quite sure she could measure up to expectations.

She put her hands on her hips. 'I could not do that.'

'What do you mean?'

'If you were the richest man in London or the poorest it would not matter,' she said. 'I would not sell myself even for millions. It is not about funds. It is about strength. Mine. To find my way in the world.'

'Being wed to me would give you a stronger place in the world, and yet you don't want to step into it.'

He touched her jaw with one finger, drawing her face up so that she met his eyes.

'Almost the first thing you did was ask me to change my appearance.'

'You had no qualms about asking me to change my cravat and wear simpler clothing. It doesn't matter to me. It's just colours and loops on the piece of cloth I wear around my neck.'

'It isn't. Not for me. You wanted me to be more appealing.'

'I wanted you to be the best you could be. Just as I suppose you did with me. It was not about changing who you are. It was merely a style of clothing.' He laughed softly. 'You wanted me to reflect the colours of the past, and I wanted you to stop dressing from the past and appear current.'

'If we can't agree about something so insignificant—though really it isn't—how could we agree about things like child-rearing?'

He studied her. 'We should leave that to the experts. I hire the best in staff, so there would be no concern.'

'Children need to be raised by their parents.'

'If you hire an experienced governess she will know much more about raising a child than you. A child's life is too important to be treated lightly. You should take care and find someone who has knowledge of the best ways to rear one.'

She tapped all four fingers to her chest. 'I would want to raise my own children.'

'A good governess would not keep children from their mother. And I'd expect to see my children often.'

Elbows tight at her sides, she faced away from him and made two tiny fists. She pounded them into the air.

'I didn't have my parents close at hand. If I should have them, I want to experience my children. And I wish for them to know I am at their side.'

'That would be easier with a husband.' He pointed a finger at his chest. 'Such as myself. Children need a father. To be created.'

'Yes. I know,' she said. 'But perhaps a father should be in their lives, not just visiting them.'

'My father wasn't in my life. And he was especially irritating when he was. I did nothing right. I annoyed him. He said it was a cruel twist of fate that a man couldn't pick his children, and that he didn't think he would have chosen me, or his father would have chosen him, but that my grandfather and I would have chosen each other. We were alike in many ways.'

'I cannot believe you would be that kind of father. A parent should not desert a child.'

'What makes you think that fathers are supposed to be close to their children? It's not natural. Remember in the Old Testament? The father had a favourite out of the two brothers and you know how that turned out. Best for fathers not to get involved.'

'I'm guessing the mother was not in those boys' lives.' She tapped her cheek. 'They probably had a governess.'

'Perhaps I should withdraw my proposal.'

'You don't have to.'

She moved, and tried to ignore the crispness of his waistcoat, the gentle masculine scent that would give any woman pleasant dreams for the rest of her life.

'My first proposal ended with an errant arrow, and now this. I am becoming adept at rejection.'

'Goodness,' she said. 'A little rejection is only a hiccup in life, or an awareness that you're trying something new.'

'Why would you say that?' he asked.

'Because it has been so in my life, and I assume it is the same for others. I've been rejected by relatives, by a school for young ladies—as both a student and a teacher—and by a seamstress for an apprenticeship...' She paused. 'I think Aunt Agatha is the only person who hasn't rejected me.'

'I haven't.'

'Is that how you see it?' She tapped her chin and put on the most innocent expression she could muster. 'Remember the first time you saw me? You were consumed with opinions about my appearance.' She mocked a male voice. '"Change your hair. And your attire. You'll be perfect if you're someone else. Someone I can change on a whim."'

'That's not what happened. I only wanted you to be the best that you can.'

'I *am*. I am the perfect niece for my aunt. I agree. She agrees.'

'So do I.'

'After just a few changes... A few hundred changes.'

'Didn't you enjoy the attention at the picnic? Being the most admired lady there?'

'Ho-dee-holily-dee...' She strung out the nonsensical made-up word. 'Talk about stacking the deck. There were no other women their age for the men to congregate around. Strange how that happened.'

'You were the object of notice.'

'Just because it was enjoyable, it doesn't mean it was the right thing,' she said, trying to mind her tongue.

'You are an extremely rare and wonderful person. But I won't let you cause notice for my family in society.'

She studied him. Since biblical times or before people had been writing down others' stories. She was only following in their footsteps. And keeping a roof over her head was important.

'My aunt must have a home. And if you had heard her arguments with her husband, you would see why it was best that we left.'

Lord Andrews had not always been so treacherous, her aunt had said. True, he'd never been perfect, but he'd not always been so insufferable. In his own way, Aunt Agatha had said, he'd loved her.

Marriage was such a disaster that she was amazed the practice had remained in society. The words of that silly promise—'I do'—were only as genuine as the person uttering them.

She appraised Gabriel carefully.

Solidness looked out of the eyes staring back at her. He didn't lie. He wasn't going to let his grandmother's stories be told.

She swallowed.

He wished to marry her, he said, but she wondered if that was only because he had reached an age where he thought he should settle and have children and she was right there in front of him. He could wed and get the memoirs quashed in one fell swoop.

'You are not the woman I thought you were when we first talked.'

Gabriel felt splintered. A part of him ferociously wanted to wed her, and another part of him warned him that he should hesitate. He should not commit himself.

He didn't know if he would be able to give her the permanency of heart she deserved. Perhaps he was too much like his father. Perhaps he truly didn't know what love was, or how to feel it.

'I'm trying to be more like your grandmother,' she said. 'At least in my fearlessness.'

'I don't know how the two of you get along.'

'We're managing well. I like her. She's sardonic when she wishes to be and it's amusing to me. I sometimes burst out into laughter when we're talking, and she ends up laughing also. Should I never marry, nor have children, as I expect, then I will try to become more and more like her. And should I marry—when I am in my older years, I expect—it will be to a man who wears a simple cravat.'

'There are a lot of men who fit that description. There is one in front of you and you are not taking a chance on him. You are afraid.'

Perhaps she was wise to be. He'd seen so many marriages fail, and most times, if not always, the first blow to the union wasn't from the woman, but the man. At least with the kind of men he played cards with at the clubs…

'That could be true,' she said. 'But even if it is fear, it doesn't mean I'm not making the right decision. In a short time you will forget the passion we shared in our moments together, and only remember that I needed a home. Now, you know I can leave. But if I couldn't, would my words still have weight? Everyone who lives here permanently is either in your employ or financially dependent on you. That is so much power and you don't even realise it.'

'You say that I don't realise it? Perhaps I do. And perhaps I treat them all with dignity, and you cannot see the true value in that.'

His grandmother was the worst possible influence.

Marie had been corrupted by his grandmother and by her aunt's free thinking. She'd been completely ruined in a most unacceptable way, but he'd given her the opportunity to redeem herself with an appropriate union.

And she had thrown it back in his face.

Tomorrow, he hoped to see her at breakfast, and he would make certain to have an elaborate neckcloth. She would notice, and likely have her hair in the most depressing knot ever. Not that he truly minded. She would still be Marie, and he felt bad for angering her.

'Well. Goodnight… And an apology.'

The moment between them lingered.

'I'm not apologising.'

'I am. To you. I don't like it that we disagree. I still want us to be friends. It means a great deal to me. *You* mean a great deal to me.'

Her mouth opened, and she stared at him. 'I'm still working on the memoirs.'

He flicked a brow. 'I still care for you.'

Chapter Seventeen

⚜

He had awakened early—if one could call it awakening. He wasn't sure he'd been asleep, because all night he had been considering Marie's views.

Even her thoughts on child-rearing were different from his. He'd never pondered Marie's perspective before. A man such as he had so many important duties to attend to. He'd never thought of children as being any responsibility of the father except for the provision of shelter, food, education and perhaps, as they grew, training in affairs of the estate.

But Marie might have a point, he thought. Although he wasn't sure that a baby would even notice its father's presence, and the nursemaid and the governess would probably be offended if he was present. A situation like that would take some consideration. The children might grow up disliking their father if they had to be around him continuously.

'You are joining us?' His grandmother squinted at him when he strode into the breakfast room.

'I thought it would be a pleasant way to start the day,' he answered.

'That's not what you usually say,' his grandmother replied, and then looked across the table at Marie. 'I suppose you wanted to see me.'

She laughed, in a way that said she knew she was the only one to find it humorous.

Marie greeted him civilly and he nodded to her, amazed at the awareness that washed over him.

Her hair was curled in almost exactly the style the maid had perfected on her. It framed her face and her glasses, and the looser knot she retained crowned the view.

'Did I tell you the story about the cutpurse trying to steal from my friend?' his grandmother asked Marie, interrupting his perusal. 'I want you to be sure to include that. That thief didn't think he would ever be able to get away from me. It hurts more than you'd think, you know...to pummel someone. I thought I'd injured my arm. Definitely bruised my hand.'

'How would you have handled that?' Gabriel asked Marie, genuinely wanting to hear her answer.

He supposed she fascinated him because she'd been raised as an orphan, and that made her different from the other women he knew.

'Well, I have no complaint with how your grandmother reacted,' she said, smiling at the older lady. 'She certainly got his attention. I don't know how I would have responded. I rarely know what I will do in a situation until presented with it.' Marie studied him. 'Your neckcloth is exceptionally bright today.'

He laughed, touching it. 'I know. I chose it just for you.'

'How sweet,' his grandmother said, rising and putting a hand on the table. 'It's ugly. And now I must go to my room to recover from the sight of it. I'm going to jot down some notes for more events I want Marie to include in my story.'

After she'd left, Marie said, 'I can see that she might not have been the best person to raise a child.'

'She was a better mother than it appears. When Father was young she made sure to see him quarterly.'

'That's true,' his grandmother said as she put her head round the door and looked back into the room. 'I really can't blame myself for your father's problems because I didn't raise him. Now, come along, Marie.'

She stood. 'I will be there directly.'

His grandmother cleared her throat and then left.

Gabriel's eyes met Marie's and he smiled. 'I suppose you should leave.'

She stood and walked closer to his chair. 'This is for trying to get me to blackmail you so you could marry me.'

She tied two of the loops of his cravat together. Then she put a hand on his shoulder, not taking it away instantly, but letting it slide slowly down his back as she meandered from the room.

He wondered if he had searched her out on purpose. Not in the house. But in life. If he'd managed to find the one person who would say no to him.

Then he saw the truth of her words hidden in his thoughts.

The one person who could say no.

He'd never thought anyone could refuse him. He had a title and a fortune.

Gabriel suspected that his father had had a constant battle within himself to remain within the bounds of proper society. That he had had so many mistresses as a way of living more adventurously. More dangerously. He had chased things which fired his blood and gave him an appetite for more. Not taking care of himself so things felt more rigorous. More dangerous. More daring.

Until he had been emboldened enough to attempt a boat crossing that caught him in a storm.

Gabriel purposely didn't race to the edge of things like that. He had worked hard not to continue the family lineage that way. His mother had spoken with him every time she'd visited, and the one thing she had requested each time was that he repair the family honour.

She'd claimed that his paternal grandparents had let down so many people—servants included—and several times he had been walking in corridors when the servants didn't know he was about, and had heard discussions of his father's mistresses or his grandmother's antics. He'd never liked that.

He'd asked his father, and his father had told him it was not his concern, said he would have the servants sacked for speaking when they should be working.

From then on, he'd pretended he'd heard the tales from a friend. In part, it was true. One of his friends had mentioned something, but he'd called him a liar.

His father had told him to get better friends.

He'd watched his father leave the room, wondering how one would get a better father.

Now he pondered if his father hadn't got the best of sons, either.

He didn't blame Marie for refusing him. It might have been the wisest thing she'd ever done. But that didn't change the fact that he cared for her.

He found he had no appetite, and without Marie in the room there was no reason for him to remain, so he moved back to his bedroom. The bed had not been made yet. A huge bed. Likely made to his grandfather or his great-grandfather's specifications.

Only one pillow had been disturbed. Only one pillow had ever been disturbed in this room since he had taken it. It was presumptuous of the maids even to think he would need two. He walked to the bedside and ran his fingers over the fabric, imagining Marie's head on the second pillow.

The fear of never having her at his side again clutched him.

Gabriel could see his father's errors. His father had chosen not to give his heart to his wife. He'd chosen not to give his heart to his son, either—which really hadn't bothered Gabriel at all. He'd had the best of nursemaids, and then the best of tutors.

He needed to seek out Marie. He needed to learn more about her. Perhaps a man should see a woman more than a few times before he proposed, but with Marie it wasn't necessary.

In that instant he suspected the footsteps he'd been determined to avoid had been the very steps he'd followed. He'd been just like his father—only he'd not left a wife alone at home. Or a family. He'd merely avoided having them.

At teatime, the butler entered his rooms and gave him a message.

He strode to Marie's room and knocked.

She was at a little desk and, stopped her scribbling when he entered. There were papers on top of the sofa, and she was still dressed in her singular dresses, reminding him of a doll from the past. One who'd had some trials, as evidenced by the smudge of ink on her cheek.

She appeared comfortable in her surroundings. And she made his house appear more lived-in. Less an elaborate shelter and residence, more a place of solace. A better home than it had been before.

But he didn't know if he was imagining a world like that because of his age and his desires. Perhaps he saw a different person than she truly was.

He reached out, bending to lift her hand. Bringing her knuckles to his cheek by way of greeting.

'Once you try to publish this book there's no going back.'

He wanted so much to hear her say that she would not risk hurting his family.

'There's never been any going back for any of us,' she said, standing. 'Life moves at a gallop when it is good, at a crawl when it is bad.'

He kept her hand in his. 'You could disguise the incidents, so no one knows who you are writing about.'

'We've gone over this. Your grandmother wants her story told, and I believe it is an important one. Inspiring to others.'

'It's easy not to realise the true value of things,' he said. 'Like privacy.'

But that wasn't what he truly meant. Trust. That was more precious. Priceless, in fact.

'But your grandmother wants her adventures noted. She wants other people to know of the trials she's had.'

'There are two sides to every story—if not more. Particularly where my grandmother is concerned. She's been lighting fuses all her life. And when she doesn't light them, she gets someone else to do so.'

'I agree that it seems that way, and probably is, but that's the thing that has made her fascinating. Someone sitting at home and having what appears to be a dull life could live

vicariously through her, and see and appreciate the plain-
ness of their life in a new light. They will thank her for it.'

'Is that what you're doing?'

'No. I have always been happy for the brief moments
of peacefulness in my life, because I have seen so many
people who do not appreciate them. Some of them create upset for the excitement of it. They fashion their own
drama instead of traipsing to the theatre, but it is over a
stocking or a bite of pudding or a hair ribbon.'

'You understand that my heritage and my obligation to
my family name must come first?'

She clasped his hand. 'I appreciate that you're not rant-
ing and railing against me.'

'That's not something I've ever done. My mother and
father were quite businesslike as they discussed their dif-
ferences, no matter how much was at stake. Both of them
refused to be like Grandmother.'

'You are true to it,' she said.

'I asked you to marry me.'

'Because your family was annoying you.'

'Yes. But if a person knowingly lights the fuse, then
they should be aware of the fragments that might fly about
them. The destruction they could cause. Sometimes I can't
keep explosions from happening. I could not un-break the
window after Grandmother's first gunpowder explosion.
It was destroyed.'

She nibbled her bottom lip again. For the rest of his life,
if he saw a woman bite her bottom lip he would imagine
Marie.

He wanted to be certain she knew he wished her no ill
will, because he was going to make sure his grandmother's
story stayed private. He could understand Marie's wish not

to wed. To be able to take care of her aunt and herself. He hoped she could comprehend his duty to protect his family.

He would say goodbye, and she would see the sentiment in his gaze.

It seemed natural to kiss her, but as he was on his way to kiss her cheek she put a hand flat on his chest, stopping him. 'That will not cause me to change my mind.'

'I know.'

She stood and grasped the fabric of his waistcoat and pulled him close, but this time he stopped, just before their lips touched.

'I will not change my mind either, but you will always remain in my heart,' he said.

'I love you.' Her words were soft. 'But that doesn't mean I will be staying. It only means what I said. The book is almost finished, and my aunt is taking the pearls to be sold tomorrow.'

He knew the depth of his missing her would be great. Knew the emptiness that would follow him when she'd left.

He didn't know if he moved forward or she did, but their lips met, hungry, and their arms pulled each other close, and then closer. He ended the kiss, keeping his eyes shut, letting his lips linger at her cheek, and then enclosing her in a hug.

'Is this our goodbye?' she asked.

'No,' he answered. 'This is just our first step on a new beginning, away from each other.'

'I think a goodbye would be easier.'

A knock on the door interrupted them, and a maid entered.

'Miss Marie, did you know your uncle has arrived? He is talking with his wife.' She spoke quickly and left.

'I expected him to come. My aunt sent him a letter telling him we are not returning, and asking for the items she left behind to be sent to her. I doubt he has brought anything.'

Gabriel saw the sadness in her eyes, and knew he could not add to her struggles.

He would miss her. A lot. But it was for the best that he didn't care about her. That he distanced himself from her as soon as possible so it would be easier. Because he had recently visited the publisher. And it had been very cordial. Friendly.

The publisher had smiled and said, 'You scratch my back and I'll scratch yours.'

He would let the publisher tell her.

Chapter Eighteen

Marie was still in the little room, second-guessing herself, wondering if she'd let a lack of principles destroy her. She wondered if it was fair to Gabriel to tell his grandmother's story when he had done so much for her.

A crash of footsteps sounded outside her door and she raised her head, confused. Who would be running in the house?

Then the door burst open and her aunt rushed inside, arms splayed and chin quivering.

She stopped in front of Marie, tears forming. Pacing from side to side.

'What's wrong?' Marie asked, standing, feeling a knot in her stomach, knowing the news wouldn't be good.

'It's Reginald. He has left. And he has taken the pearls.' She clasped her hands, interlocking her fingers into a singular clasp and hugging herself. 'He asked me to prove I had not sold them. I was happy to do so. When I showed him that I still had them in my reticule, he ripped it from my hand. I told him I had promised them to you, but he wouldn't stop. He said I must go with him if I wanted them.'

She put a hand to her head.

'He wants everything to be unpleasant for me. He said they were only mine as long as I lived in his house, and he said I must return. I said I would never be forced. He stormed out, but I could not get him to leave the pearls.'

Marie gasped. The pearls were her aunt's security. Part of the marriage settlement Lord Andrews had given her before they wed, to prove he really cared.

Marie gave her aunt a hug. 'I will talk with Gabriel,' she said. 'He will help.'

Or at least he would help her aunt.

She touched the door, holding herself upright, letting her mind grasp the realisation that her thoughts had immediately turned to him and the belief that he would assist her. She comprehended that he was the only one she wanted to help her. The only one she truly thought could get the pearls returned.

She put a hand to her throat, considering whether or not it was fair to ask him for aid, but then she saw the tears rolling down her aunt's cheek.

She took her aunt by both arms. 'Don't worry. I will summon Gabriel.'

She rushed from the room.

Scurrying into the corridor, she ran to his rooms, hoping he was there, not knowing what she would do if he wasn't. At the door, she pounded on it, calling out his name.

Instantly, he opened the door, and the sight of him reminded her that he was not a dream. He'd been a real moment in her past. And now there he stood, tall, solid, not even wearing a plain cravat, but none at all. Waistcoat open. A ledger in his hand.

An imposing form. Rigid as a fixed blade.

He tossed the ledger aside when he saw her face.

'What's wrong?' he asked, grasping her arm. 'What has happened? Is someone hurt?'

'No. No. It's the pearls.'

He surrounded her with his arms, pulling her inside, hugging her close before he released her. 'They are just gems. Calm yourself.'

'They are not only gems. They are my aunt's security. Her marriage settlement. Our chance for a home. Please help us.'

She'd not seen him before like this. He was almost a stranger to her, and yet he was studying her with compassion, perhaps longing. Loss... And her heart tumbled a thousand times over, in less time than it took for her to say anything more.

She had to break the silence. Their eyes and bodies were speaking too much. Too simply. And she couldn't lose herself. She couldn't forget that she needed to be strong.

'Can you help us?' She rushed the words out. 'Uncle has taken the pearls. Aunt Agatha is in tears.'

He frowned, shaking his head. For an instant she thought he was disagreeing, and then she understood that he was reflecting on his actions.

'A wise man would only help you in return for a promise from you to give him the manuscript.'

'I can't. I've already promised it to your grandmother.'

He waited, arms crossed, stance wide. The blink of his eyes told her he was going to help her. He had already lost the battle within himself. He didn't relish it, but he would.

'And an even wiser man might do the right thing and help the people he cares about.'

He stepped away, reaching for the wrinkled cravat he'd removed and looked at it. He moved to the bell-pull and tugged on it three times.

'I can't let anyone else assist you.'

Almost instantly a servant arrived at a run. He told the maid to make certain the carriage was readied immediately.

'Do you need to take anything with you?' he asked, looping the fabric around his neck, giving it a simple tie, and doing up the buttons on his waistcoat.

'No,' she said. He was all she needed.

He fetched his coat and took her arm, and they waited at the front entrance until the carriage was pulled around.

She told him what had happened, and wondered what it would feel like to always have him at her side. Like a knight who would come to her rescue. A man who would thrust himself in front of anything that was charging at her. A protector.

The thought left her speechless. Only her aunt had ever seemed the least bit interested in protecting her. She'd never expected anyone else to come to her aid.

Now Gabriel was helping her. As if he was supposed to. As if she were his wife.

'Are you doing this for me?' she asked. 'Or for my aunt?'

'For you. But for her also. I have to. I won't turn away when you need help. I will always be here for you when you need me.'

'You don't have to. You promised me nothing. You owe me nothing.'

Then she saw something else in him. The reason his forebears were titled. The intractable promise.

He looked at her, and a smile wafted across his lips. 'Yes, I do.'

He looked across at Marie, sitting beside him in the carriage, prim little glasses perched on her nose. The outdated frock and the fringe of hair around her face gave her a rarity that soothed him. He'd never seen anyone who looked quite like her. Her mouth was pursed into a scowl, her eyes were tight, and her tiny brows rose above them.

He swallowed, shocked to realise the way his heart had wrapped itself around her. He couldn't help himself.

'Will you ever marry?' he asked.

Her lips thinned. 'I doubt it.' A soft smile flashed across her face. 'This would have been the time to take that direction. But…this book will be my marriage, I suppose.'

He squeezed her fingers, pleased she had not yet found out about his discussion with the publisher.

'I've been subservient all my life, in order to have food and a roof over my head. It has been my employment. But to have a husband… I would no longer need to be employed and yet I think that is what marriage would feel like. A job I cannot leave.'

'Many people leave it, even if their vows still bind them.'

'Like my aunt and her husband. And we are in the midst of that. It reminds me of how treacherous life can be after a simple vow.'

She studied the view as the carriage rolled on, and he reached and took her hand. He felt a light squeeze, and he pulled her knuckles to his mouth for a kiss before letting their clasped hands rest between them.

The carriage bounced and struggled in places, but continued on, and he supposed that was symbolic of their life. They were both going in the same direction, and would be feeling the ravages of life, but it would not be with any commitment between them, instead the knowledge of a deeper friendship in which disagreements would dissolve.

He hoped.

She wasn't going to take it well that his grandmother's memoirs would not be published. And now her aunt had lost the pearls.

When the carriage finally stopped, he took her hands after he'd alighted, helping her step out and tucking her hand inside his arm. 'How well do you know your uncle?' he asked.

She grimaced. 'He and my aunt had a terrific row just after I moved in, not long after their marriage, and not much has gone well since. He mostly kept to himself, and she and I kept to ourselves. Shouting wasn't good for him, my aunt claimed. And he did seem to disagree with everything she did.'

'Even people who don't appear to like each other may have a deep bond.'

'I've yet to see anyone whom marriage has made happy.' She wrinkled her nose and pushed at one of her sleeves, fluffing it. 'Not one person.'

He thought for a moment, more jesting with her than serious. 'It might be a clever ruse. People could just be pretending unhappiness so others are not jealous. A card game of sorts, with the winning hand kept hidden.'

She sniffed. 'Don't expect me to wager on that one.'

After stepping inside, he gave the butler his calling card.

The man read it, straightened his back, and took them into a room with drapes flowing into carefully arranged half-circles at their base, the fabric motionless even with the breeze bringing in the scent of meadowlands.

'I will fetch Lord Andrews immediately,' the butler said, leaving.

Lord Andrews' uneven gait announced his arrival, and his brows were knitted in a furrowed clump that looked difficult to contain on one forehead. He appeared like an ageing bull with a face damaged by years of running into hedges, other bulls, and possibly barn doors. He wore the narrowest cravat Gabriel had ever seen, and it was looped into a bouquet of knotted twists. Possibly about sixteen loops total.

He touched his cravat and gave Marie a quick glance. She responded with a smug nod and an overly polite greeting to Lord Andrews.

Lord Andrews stretched out a hand, indicating they both take a seat.

Gabriel relaxed against the sofa with Marie beside him. He spoke briefly with the man, complimenting him on the location of his house and the well-pruned hedges in front of it. Then he said, 'I wanted to talk to you about your plans for Lady Andrews.'

'Nothing to discuss if you're a friend of *that woman*. I have tried to be friendly,' he said, 'but I couldn't drink fast enough.'

Those eyebrows moved when he spoke of Agatha, and reminded Gabriel of a caterpillar struggling to remain in place while the ground moved around it.

'But you wed her,' Gabriel said.

'I was blinded by grief for my wife and *that woman* was already living here. I didn't grasp what I was doing.'

'You gave her the pearls, though.'

'It was a mistake. A huge one. I've taken them back. Even though they're fake.'

Marie gasped. 'You can't do that. You purchased them for your first wife, and you gave them to my aunt as a wedding settlement. They're rare—just as my aunt is.'

'They're fake. Just as fake as Agatha. And you.'

Marie crossed her arms. 'That is not true. They are real, and she is priceless. It's not her fault. She did what she thought best. And all because of a secret, everything changed. You're punishing my aunt but you're also punishing yourself.'

'Bah!' He waved a hand. 'Of course I'm punishing her. But they are fake. Probably why she likes them.'

Marie turned to Gabriel. 'We tested them. They're real.'

'How?' he asked.

'The tooth test,' she said. 'You rub them against a tooth. Real pearls are gritty. Fake pearls are smooth.'

'You heard the young lady.' Gabriel gave a shrug and rose, taking a step closer to the older man, knowing that few could ignore his words when he stood. 'She had tested them. They're real. Get them.'

'Paste,' the old man said, not retreating.

'I will come with you to retrieve them,' Gabriel said, 'or I'll wait here with you while Marie finds them. Tell her where they are.'

'Would you rather have the pearls?' the old man asked him, those caterpillar eyebrows stilling. 'Or would you prefer to have the letter in which your grandmother wagers you in marriage?'

'It was in the reticule,' Marie admitted, lips firm, lowering her head briefly before she lifted her eyes again.

Gabriel frowned. 'Get me the pearls. A piece of paper is only a piece of paper, and I don't care what it says.'

The older man went to a small cabinet and took out a folded piece of paper. He handed it to Gabriel. 'You can have it. It won't do me any good. Just a moment of amusing reading.'

Glancing at it, Gabriel put it in his coat pocket.

'Get me the pearls,' Gabriel repeated, commanding the man to move with his eyes.

'Fine,' the man said. He gave Marie another angry glance. 'She can get them. They're on my bedside table. But…'

His voice faded away as Marie ran from the room.

He glared at Gabriel. 'I should never have given them to Aggie.'

'Perhaps a wife is more important than jewellery.'

'You can see how well that is working out. Agatha brought my wife's daughter into my house without telling me who she was. A secret that would have been better kept for the rest of her life. She ruined the precious memories I had, and proved herself untrustworthy where I was concerned.'

'It's hard to keep secrets hidden.'

'Yes, but I would have been better not knowing. Just because something's true, it doesn't mean you want it splattered across your face.'

Gabriel agreed, but it would feel disloyal to say so.

Marie's returning footsteps sounded on the stairs, interrupting, and she entered the room with the pearl strands interwoven in her fingertips. Two strands, not overly large, with the outside rope having a larger pearl hanging from it. In her other hand she held an elaborate case.

'Agatha only wed me for a place to live.'

The old man studied Marie, challenging her to deny it.

'When I first found out about Marie I thought she was Agatha's daughter,' he said, taking a handkerchief and wiping his nose. 'I could understand that. After all, we all make mistakes in our youth. But the fact that they both kept the secret from me, and that Agatha brought her into my house as her niece… And then I discovered the truth.'

He pointed a finger at Marie.

'The courts would consider you my daughter. Don't you think a man has a right to know something like that?'

'Don't blame me,' Marie said. 'I should blame you for leaving your wife alone for two years.'

'I had to. I needed funds and I was helping a friend on a venture. I had no choice.'

'Maybe Agatha felt the same.'

'She should have told me about you before we wed.'

'Would it have made a difference?'

'I doubt it. I regretted it the moment I wed Agatha and turned to see the wrong woman at my side. It's true I gave the pearls to Agatha. I suppose I thought they would make her look more like my wife if she wore them. She was my wife's companion. Not mine.'

Now Gabriel understood Marie's viewpoint on marriage a little better. If she'd heard this man say that he'd turned and seen the wrong woman at his side...

Gabriel wondered if he would look differently at her after he'd read what she'd written about his family. If his feelings truly would change in an instant. They had when he'd fallen in love, and he wondered if people fell out of love just as quickly. He wondered if *he* would fall out of love that rapidly.

'Aunt Agatha is your wife now,' Marie said, moving to stand at Gabriel's side and holding the necklace so the light reflected from the huge pearl in the centre and the two huge bluish ones on each side of it. 'And I am not your daughter.'

Gabriel took the strands of pearls. He had no awareness of the stones, was only conscious of how close he was to Marie and the intensity of her eyes, thanking him. Again, his feelings for her intensified. Pounding strong within him. He wanted her to be happy, but he didn't know if his sincerity would fade as quickly as it had arisen. No feeling had ever intensified so quickly inside him. Not even hatred or compassion. He'd never had such strong emotions before. They were new to him, and they weakened him.

He'd raced here to retrieve the pearls for Marie and assist her. He'd helped others before. Many times. But it had never seemed that his life was at stake. That his happiness was in jeopardy. He was in her clasp as handily as the pearls were. But clasps could easily weaken. Could be destroyed.

Now Marie studied him, admiration in her gaze.

'We'll take them and leave,' Gabriel said to Lord Andrews. 'You're doing the right thing.'

Her uncle whirled around and one of his hands clenched, as if he could feel the necklace in his grasp, and his lips moved. At first he made no sound, then he spoke. 'I can't sleep without those pearls in my house. Last night I had my first night of good sleep since Agatha took them and left.'

'Perhaps there is a way you could have them back,' Gabriel said, an idea coming to him. 'You have a second house?'

'The hunting lodge. It's little more than a hut. I don't even like going there any more.'

'What if Lady Agatha would trade you the pearls for the lodge?' he asked. 'The law is that a man should provide for his wife,' Gabriel said. 'Whether you want her living here or not, that is a consideration.'

He levelled a stare at Gabriel. 'That would get two eyesores gone from my life.'

'The lodge desperately needs a new roof,' Marie said.

'I would have them both out of my hair?' he asked Gabriel, ignoring Marie.

'Yes, providing you pay the expenses for the lodge. A man should take care of his family,' Gabriel added.

'I'll do it for five years,' the older man groused.

'Ten.'

'Six, and I'll add enough to fix the roof and the floor. Trust me, it's needed. I will put aside the amount for that payment and the same for expenses on the property to be given to my wife in full. I want the paintings from the walls, but the furniture is of no consequence.'

Gabriel looked at Marie. Saw the quick upsweep of her chin.

'I'm sure she would be happy with that,' Marie added.

'Until everything has been agreed I will make certain to hold on to these.' Gabriel lifted the pearls. 'Plus, I will employ someone who will make sure the paperwork which allows the lodge to change hands is completed. The pearls will be returned when the papers are signed and the repair money is received. Until then, I will have them stored in my safe.'

Gabriel slipped them into his pocket beside the paper.

The property would still belong to Lord Andrews, so they would have to be careful in putting it in his wife's name. He didn't know how it would be sorted out, but his man of affairs would.

The older man thumped over to stand beside Gabriel.

'Let me touch them.'

His voice wasn't a command, but a request. Gabriel held them out, and Lord Andrews ran a gnarled finger over the pearls.

'If I release the funds immediately, will you have paperwork ready to be completed?' His voice softened. 'Without these, I have nothing. I never knew how much my wife meant to me. I never knew how alone I would feel when she was gone. That's why I wed Agatha. But after I wed her I was still alone. And then I discovered how I'd been betrayed.' His hand fell to his side and he shook his head. 'I thought marriage would bring back my world, yet I felt more abandoned than ever. What a jest.'

With that, he turned to leave.

'Why don't you try to talk with my aunt?' Marie asked, interrupting Lord Andrews' exit. 'She was a good companion to your wife. The two of you could talk about her. If you don't think of Aunt Agatha as a wife, but as a friend, perhaps you would get on well.'

'Do you think she would want to live here if she had anywhere else to go?' he asked. 'I don't.'

'I can't say. But she might want to live here if you were friendly to her.'

'I do need someone to advise the housekeeper,' he said. 'But I want the pearls back in my house first.'

'Then you will have no trouble with our men of affairs meeting and getting the particulars in order,' said Gabriel.

'The sooner the better. Tomorrow, even.'

'The hunting lodge will be set aside so it belongs to Lady Agatha and her niece,' Gabriel said.

'It will.'

Marie saw satisfaction in Gabriel's regard. They'd secured a house for her aunt, and funds for a time.

She only felt sadness. She didn't want to leave his house. But she didn't want to wed a man who might look at her after the wedding and see the wrong woman.

'We'll begin on the particulars today, after I have talked with Agatha to make sure she's happy with this, and I will get everything done quickly,' Gabriel said.

Her uncle gave a quick upsweep of his head. 'Send me a note if she is agreeable, and I will arrive at your house with my man of affairs to complete the transaction.'

'And will you talk with Aunt Agatha?' Marie asked.

'If I've time to spare, I might.' He glared into the distance. 'It seems, since she left, I don't know which direction is up and which is down. I was so angry with her. *So* angry. But living without her… She was…useful to have around.'

Gabriel gave him a nod, and they made their farewells.

'Useful to have around?' Gabriel said once they were alone. 'Faint praise.'

'More than she usually heard from him, I assure you.'

Once they were in the carriage, and it was rolling away, Gabriel said, 'We'll go via my man of affairs' office. His brother is very knowledgeable about property transactions. The sooner it is completed, the better off you'll be. We don't want to give your uncle a chance to change his mind.'

'He's not truly my uncle. Not even by marriage. Agatha worked as a companion to her distant cousin. My mother. When my mother discovered she was going to have a baby and knew it couldn't be her husband's, because he'd sailed from England months before, she decided to keep it a secret. Aunt Agatha helped her to conceal me, thinking eventually my mother would be able to take me in as a ward. But my mother didn't. And would become furious when reminded of me.'

When Marie's mother had passed away, Agatha had consoled Lord Andrews in his grief.

'After Lord Andrews asked Agatha to wed him, she said she wanted her niece to live with her, and he agreed. At first.'

'You don't hold a grudge against your mother?'

'No.' Marie gave a one-sided shrug. 'I would have hated to live with a mother who didn't want me. I would always have been thinking something was wrong with me.' She tapped under her chin.

'You must have had a miserable childhood.'

'No. A mostly happy one. I worked a lot. Laundry and cleaning and cooking and so on. I didn't really mind. The local shopkeepers were generally nice.

She moved closer, surrendering again to the joy of feeling that he cared for her.

'I couldn't change the fact that the woman who raised me often resented me but needed the funds.'

Then she paused.

Shaking her head, she said. 'A lady would visit me occasionally. A nice lady, who worked as a companion. She would always bring funds for my care. I suspected she was my mother, and I asked her one day, but she said she wasn't. The lady whom I lived with verified it. My mother had stayed in her house since before I was born, so the servants wouldn't know she was going to have a child.'

Marie had been disappointed, but the lady—Agatha—had done her best. Even if her visits had only been for a few quick moments when funds were delivered, or an occasional half-day.

Agatha had taken her on her first carriage ride. Such an adventure. A present for her thirteenth birthday. Marie had enjoyed having someone who cared about her, and when

Agatha had come to her after her marriage and invited Marie to live with her she'd been overjoyed.

Aunt Agatha had asked if she wanted to bring her clothing, and she'd said that she would like to leave it behind for more unfortunate people. But really she'd been wearing her best dress, and the only other had been too small for her and pinched painfully under the arms. They'd thanked the woman who'd cared for Marie, and Agatha had promised to visit.

When Marie had arrived at Lord Andrews' she'd been given a frumpy old dress that her aunt had apologised for, and bathwater. Bathwater in abundance. And soap. Soap that had smelled like a flower garden. That had been the only thing she'd asked for more of, and she'd kept the excess fragrant soap at her bedside, waking up to a room that smelled of bliss.

She'd felt like a flower arrangement when she'd stepped out of the bathwater and dressed in the old dress, which had hung off her, but it had been so pleasant to have a dress that was too large instead of too small, after a childhood of trying to squeeze into dresses she'd outgrown.

Getting to know the maids had been enjoyable, and soon they'd all insisted she must let them assist her and clean for her, or they'd be out of a job. She had pinched herself. And not awakened. She'd felt richer than any Midas.

She'd decided it was too good to be true, and that she would do her best to go along with whatever arose and be a wonderful niece…or, secretly in her heart, a daughter.

'Agatha gave me some mementos. She showed me a painting of my mother. Her husband had put away all her jewellery, but she gave me some handkerchiefs my mother had had. Showed me books she'd read. But really only the portrait meant anything, and I would try to see my resemblance in it. The rest of it—the handkerchiefs, the books, the rooms she'd lived in—didn't mean much to me. It made me angry more than anything. That she could have had so much and keep me a secret.

'I told Agatha I'd rather have mementos from her, and that, even better, I had memories of the happiness I always felt when she visited. Of the few times she was able to take me on a carriage ride or spend half a day with me.'

'You were fortunate to have her.'

'Your grandmother was the only person who would take in my aunt, and she encouraged her to leave a man who was unkind. She wants her story told. And I would like it to be told also. If being wayward is the only way to have a heart, then perhaps people should know it.'

'Are you including your own history in the memoirs?'

'No, this is your grandmother's book.'

'You could put a note inside,' he said, 'and tell your story…and Lord Andrews'.'

Her body tightened and she couldn't speak. His words had hit her with the force of a slap. Lord Andrews would never forgive appearing in a book like that. He would be furious at Agatha. The marriage would be destroyed with no chance of repair.

She unclasped her arms from around herself. 'Agatha is provided for, and I will not risk anything ruining that. It's the least I can do to help her procure a home of her own. I'll be able to take care of myself.'

She tried not to think of the words he'd said at the last. The duplicity of not wanting her own story in the memoirs.

Chapter Nineteen

The horses had seemed full of life when they'd begun the journey home, but they soon slowed, relaxing their pace. The excitement Marie had once felt at being in a carriage had faded, overridden by the need she felt for Gabriel.

'Can I see the pearls again?' she asked. 'They really don't mean much to me…except for their value in gaining Aunt Agatha her freedom. That is everything. She'll have a home now. A place of her own.'

He studied their bluish tint. To him, they looked as if they were worth little, but everyone else seemed impressed with them.

'They're just baubles,' he said.

She grasped them, letting her fingers dance over the orbs. Looking at the clasp. A piece of jewellery worth more than she'd ever owned in her life—probably more than Agatha had ever owned.

She returned them to him, anxious to get back to his home and tell Agatha the good news.

Then she looked at his face, and felt a river of emotions pass between them. She would be leaving his home, and she had to make plans.

She clasped his hand the rest of the way back to his

estate, and released it only as the carriage stopped at the entrance.

When they walked into the house, the light was already fading from the sky. She rushed inside to spread the good news and tell her aunt that the hunting lodge would soon be hers.

Her aunt clapped her hands in joy at the opportunity to live in the lodge, and agreed that she would prefer to exchange the pearls for a home.

'I'll put them away,' Gabriel said, and Marie followed him.

Once in his room, he locked away the necklace, and then, with just a look in his eyes, he seemed to be able to pull her into his arms. His hug was tender. His touch on the back of her neck consoling.

She wondered if he was caring for her, or just for a woman who had had so little affection in her life.

'You don't have to show me extra tenderness because of my past.'

A small line appeared between his brows. 'I wouldn't caress you at all if I didn't want affection between us.'

She felt cosseted. Consoled. Her heart expanded to the point of almost filling her eyes with tears.

She hugged him in return, wishing she could give him the same feelings he was giving her.

Staring up into his eyes, she felt her knees weaken, and yet she didn't fall away. He held her. His arms were cradling, soothing, lifting her.

She moistened her lips, wanting his kiss more than she wanted air.

He must have seen it in her gaze. Their lips met. A taste

reminding her of wine. Of comforting nights. Of dreams too good to wake from.

He pulled away, reaching to touch her hair, her cheek, running his fingertips over her face.

'This moment is my whole life,' he said, touching her bottom lip. 'You are the sunrise, the sunset, and all the hues in between.'

She reached for his cravat. 'A simple knot is so much easier to take off.'

'Prove it,' he whispered against her lips.

And then her fingers slipped, and she accidentally tightened the knot.

He reached up and put his hand over hers. In an instant the neckcloth was loosened, and fell to the floor.

'Nothing to hurry about,' he said. 'Nothing to worry about. We have all night, and I want this to last at least that long.'

He took her into his bedroom. Effortlessly.

Then he let her stand beside his bed, and he dropped a soft kiss onto her lips. The softest kiss she'd ever had. So much lightness from someone so much stronger than she was. She realised she'd been asleep her whole life.

He touched each hook on the back of her dress and she felt them undone, but he didn't remove the garment.

Instead, he stopped and slipped his waistcoat from his shoulders, dropping it. He pulled his shirt from his trousers, and then stopped moving.

'Since we have the whole night,' he asked, 'do you mind if we go slowly? If I hold you in my arms? If we just sit and feel the night?'

'I'm not sure,' she said, not certain she could wait, feeling her body crave him. 'But we can try.'

She sat on his lap, felt his arms around her, and he held her hands, moving his fingertips over them, watching them as if he'd never touched anyone's skin before and could hardly believe the tenderness of it.

She had never seen anyone's hands in the way she saw his.

Capable, strong, and yet so gentle.

He put his cheek against hers and somehow shut everything away from her. It was a gift he had—enclosing the world around them and making everything and everyone else disappear. Even if they were only together for this one night, he made it feel like a for ever moment. Stopping time to hold her close.

He ran his fingertips over her shoulders and pushed her dress aside, his lips capturing the soft skin underneath.

Helping him remove his coat, she pulled him closer, burrowing into his arms, and he wrapped her more warmly than any covering that had ever touched her.

Removing his clothing, and then hers, he pulled her onto the bed with him.

'Marie…' he whispered, and he made her name sound exotic, intriguing and intense.

Their kisses deepened and she tasted the moist miracle of Gabriel, marvelled that all was right with the world.

When his fingertips brushed over her breasts, holding her nipples before he gently grazed them with his teeth, she gasped.

Then she ran her hand over every plane of his body, memorising it, though she knew she would never be able to totally recapture the feel of him in such a way that it would remain with her for ever, as she wanted it to.

Kisses rained on her face, and then he rose above her,

asking her with just a slight change in his countenance if she were ready. She answered by reaching up and pulling him closer with all her strength.

A flurry of passion ignited within her and rose quickly to its peak. She clutched him, hanging on for life, and he responded, holding her against him.

'You don't have to rush away,' he said as she lifted her dress from the floor.

'I really should get back to my room.'

'Stay a little longer.'

She sat on the bed, her hand resting on the covers, and he moved closer, so he could interlace his fingers with hers.

'It pains me to think of you, a child alone in the world, with no parents for help. What if Agatha hadn't cared for you?'

He gave her hand the smallest squeeze, and she felt protected. Touched.

She stood. 'She did, though. And, really, almost everyone around me did watch over me.'

'A child shouldn't have to think about such things.'

'I didn't. I just survived. And I knew if I did all the right things, one day I would have a chance at something better. Aunt Agatha told me that over and over. I had all the answers. Truly, I did. I only needed one. I was simply to survive until I could get to a point to thrive. And now I have the luxury of choices. Not a tremendous amount, but more than I had before. I'm not finding the decision as easy as I would have hoped, though.'

'Do any of us truly have choices? Or must we just try to decide on the best option that might take us in the direction we should go?'

She understood how he felt.

'I don't want to be missed,' she said. 'I must get back to my room. It will be morning soon, and you are the only one in this house who isn't an early riser.'

'Let me help you dress,' he said. 'It will be an honour.'

'To be a lady's maid?' she asked.

'For you. Yes.'

She held herself away. 'You don't have to be so concerned. I was fortunate.'

He held her close and rested his cheek against hers. She knew her height was taller than usual for a woman, but she was still smaller than he was.

'What are your plans?' he asked.

'I will live with my aunt at the lodge and I will study botany. Or birds and flowers and weeds and nature. It will be grand to have such a world around me.' Then she whispered. 'And we will have a cook. And a gardener. What rapture.'

'I have a cook and a gardener and a vehicle.'

'You have so much,' she said.

'Yet you refuse to consider the impact those memoirs will have on me, even as you know what it would mean for your aunt to have her story included. Her husband would not take it well.'

He lifted her fingers and brushed them against the skin of his cheek, following the downward line of his skin.

'As I said, I will not be including Lord Andrews. It is too risky. He might rescind his offer to Aunt Agatha. And besides, their marriage has already been hurt by the past. That is enough pain for a lifetime. It is different for your grandmother, because your grandfather is no longer with you.'

'My mother is courting. Her new beloved has a young

daughter. A young daughter who may not be as strong as you. Who *can't* be as strong as you, given she has likely been sheltered by her father. She has already lost a mother, and her father will not want more grief in his family.'

'If your mother's sweetheart cannot deal with the truth of your mother's past, and she can't persuade him before they marry, then perhaps they shouldn't wed. It was horrid to see the upset when Lord Andrews discovered my parentage.'

She hesitated.

'The rows were horrible. Living in such an atmosphere was terrible. He might have been able to forgive Aunt Agatha if they had not wed. Marriage causes people to stop being sweethearts and become two rivals under the same roof—or, in your case, a person who is determined to retreat from everyone else.'

'I'm not retreating. I just have too many duties to be able to loll about all day, or spend large amounts of time going on about the weather, or playing cards, or chasing after a new sweetheart.'

'I have just realised that you have so many people who care for you that you do not even consider them. You take their affection for granted.'

'What do you mean?'

'Your mother, your grandmother, Pierce…' She shrugged. 'Even the butler cares for you. And your valet. The housekeeper. The cook. And it is not just because you pay their wage. They genuinely like you.'

'I try to be kind.'

'Did you know that some people have their servants face the wall if they happen to be in the corridor at the same time?'

'No. That's ridiculous.'

'Not to them, but to you it is. But now, in your own way, you are the one turning your back. You provide, but you retreat to your rooms. You let them walk by. You are kind and considerate, but do you really see them as people?'

'Yes. I do,' he said. 'I truly do. I am close to my valet and my butler, and the butler takes care of the rest of the staff. I don't spend much time with the female members of my household, but the butler sees that everyone is treated fairly.'

He moved to lift his cravat from beside the bed, wadded it, and arced it across the room.

'Perhaps you are the one who is inexperienced in this. Not showing feelings doesn't mean you don't have them.'

Gabriel studied her.

They had shared an intensity within an intimacy. He understood that she wanted to have a place she could retreat to, and he had given her that. She had options. A plan for her life.

She was looking at the backs of her hands and seemed to be rubbing something away from herself. Guilt, perhaps.

'I want to tell your grandmother's story, and that will give me the means to be on my own.'

'A noble goal. To control your fate,' he said. 'But at the expense of others? I'm not so certain.'

Just as she'd lit that fuse in the gardens, another was lit inside him, sizzling forward at a fast pace, leaving him speechless. The intensity of their lovemaking had deserted him, and in its place was a feeling of being used.

He'd done all he could to provide her with a way around publishing the memoirs, and yet she persisted in continuing on that path, claiming she needed to be on it to provide a roof over her head.

That, he could understand. A roof.

But she didn't need to destroy his roof to obtain it.

Damaging his family and his reputation was not something he could fathom.

She gathered her things, and he helped her dress, and then opened the door for her to leave.

Later, he missed Marie so much he wanted to search her out. But he didn't want her to know how much he missed her, so instead he went to his grandmother's sitting room. It was better that he did not see Marie again before she left.

His grandmother sat at her desk by the window, her pen in her hand and a small stack of paper and a perfume bottle in front of her.

'Just making some notes for Marie,' she said.

'Where is she?'

'I only know she's not in this room,' she said, sorting the papers and raising one so he could see it. 'A love letter your grandfather sent me.' She sniffed. 'He was always calling me his little frog. His favourite endearment. But he was the one who had to jump . I miss those days. I miss him.'

'Have you told Marie about those endearing names?'

'Of course.' Her face formed a mound of happy wrinkles. 'You should be proud of these memoirs. Yes, I embarrassed you, and I embarrassed my husband's family, but I had fun. Marie needs to learn about adventure.'

'No, she doesn't. It was providential that more people didn't get angry with you for the things you did. And your fortune was used to help smooth things over. You should stop this now. You're hurting too many people.'

She used the back of her knuckles to smooth the skin on her neck. 'My fortune was a smaller amount after your grandfather got a grasp on it, but you should thank me for that marriage. It gave you a title. And my father helped his grandson—your father—to rebuild the family finances, and taught him how to manage a ledger and tenants and everything but women. Probably easier to teach a cat to sing.'

'Don't judge all women by your actions.'

'It will be a mistake on your part if you don't take my actions into account. A mistake. If you wed some little flower petal like one of those women I invited to the soiree they will decorate your arm, and your house, and you will get on well. You don't need to wed a woman with my sensibilities. She would cause you no end of worry, and you'd be just as alone as you are now, but with a wife as an additional burden.'

'Do you consider the women in my family are burdens to me?'

'Aren't we? In your opinion?' She smiled to take any sting out of the words. 'Your mother keeps to herself…as you do. She stays away from London in order to hide from everyone. Now she watches over her parents, but she left Town originally while my son was still alive. She left you behind to keep an eye on your father. And you're still trying to make it up to her because you couldn't control him either. They both deserted you, and it still upsets me. And, no, I'm not putting that in the memoirs.'

She moved her foot and let her slipper dangle from her stockinged toes, then she gave a kick and the slipper hit the wall.

'You could quash the memoirs.'

'I could. But they will be published. Marie needs the

money. So does Agatha. And even if it I did stop it, Marie still has ink on her hands and wears those frightful frocks. Yes, you dressed her up well once. *Once*. But she went straight back to looking like a ragamuffin.'

His grandmother's eyes had never appeared so cold. 'It's for the best that nothing further developed between you, because you will always know that Marie was willing to sell your family to the highest bidder, so to speak.'

He didn't waver.

'Your choices are your own,' she said. 'Mine are mine. I gave this family funds through my father. I wanted the title of Viscountess. I charged my way into society and then I did as I pleased and let the men clean up after me. But I certainly looked the part. She doesn't.'

He clamped his teeth before speaking. 'She is beautiful.'

'I don't want you to wed her. Rosalind is perfect for you. The only way I can make certain you don't wed Marie is to show you how mercenary she is.' She waved a hand, dismissing his words. 'It has nothing to do with Marie's face, and everything to do with her presentation. She doesn't present herself well.'

One brow rose. She tapped the side of the perfume bottle.

'Marie is nearly a child of the streets. She truly is. She doesn't want it known—and that is to her credit—but Agatha talks too much—as do I—and she has told me the truth of Marie's birth, and how Lord Andrews found out and was incensed. She shouldn't have told me.'

'Grandmother, do you only allow friends into your home so you can gather information to hold against them?'

Anger tinged his voice, but her smile only grew.

'You and your grandfather and your father learned commerce one way—I another.' She still smiled. 'Besides, I do like Marie, but she isn't viscountess material. She doesn't give a fig about—' Then she stopped.

He controlled his temper, waiting to see what she'd say.

'Perhaps I am wrong. Perhaps Marie craves attention as much as I do. She is willing to write the memoirs, and she does get noticed with her spectacles and frightful frocks...' She hesitated. 'I don't think you will treat her right. If you wed Rosalind, I won't care. But if you wed Marie and chase after other women it will kill her. She doesn't trust marriage anyway. And I don't trust you to be faithful. Marie needs someone she can count on. And based on my experiences, and the people around me, I think she will be happier unmarried.'

'It is not your decision.'

'If you say so.' She shrugged, then changed the subject. 'Will you pass me my shoe?' she asked.

He didn't move.

'Fine. Ring for a maid to fetch it.'

He walked to the door, putting his hand on the cool wood.

She called out, interrupting his retreat. 'It's best she goes. Because you're noticing her too much. And you're too much like your father. You do have your father's smile after all.'

He flashed his teeth.

'Again, I do like Marie. But society will not forget the part she played in the inevitable scandal of my memoirs. Society is vengeful, and no one would ever be able to convince it of her being virtuous once she goes through with the publication. Society has to be respected in order to give its respect.'

'How could you do this to Marie?'

'I'm not doing it to her. She's doing it to herself. She's choosing commerce over love. Your grandfather had a title, and yet still, even to the end of his days, it was in everyone's mind that he wed for money. That's how I know that it never goes away. Never. It was always with him. I couldn't erase it. He couldn't erase it. It didn't matter how much we loved each other, it was always there. And even now, as his grandson, you are aware of it. Those secrets don't die.'

He walked out of the room. He couldn't dispute his grandmother's words. He agreed with them. The fact that Marie had shared his family secrets would always be between them if they married.

They would never be able to escape it.

Chapter Twenty

A fter his man of affairs finished the documents Gabriel stood with Marie and her aunt, and watched as Lady Agatha took the jewel case and gave it to her husband.

'I hope these make you happy,' she said.

With a flick of the latch, he opened the box, staring inside. He didn't raise his eyes from the pearls. 'If you've left anything at my home, you can ride in the carriage to get it, and it will deposit you both at the lodge afterwards.'

'Thank you,' Agatha said. 'I did leave behind some sketches. And a few mementos. But I must collect my things from here first.'

He raised his eyes, holding the pearls in his left hand. 'I've had a lot of time to think about it. I've watched everyone around me go on with their lives since my wife died, and I need to do the same. I want you to do so as well. I would like to see you and Marie settled into the lodge. And I might like to visit from time to time.' Then he took her hand and lifted the back of it near his lips, gave it a kiss. 'But only if there are no more secrets between us.'

'I hope you can forgive me for not telling you the truth about Marie. I had kept it private for so long I didn't even think about it any longer. And it didn't seem my truth to share. Plus, I didn't want to hurt the memory you had of your wife.'

'Can we take a carriage ride and talk about it?'

'That would be wonderful,' she said, taking her lavender-scented handkerchief from her reticule and giving it to him. 'Please let me speak with Marie a moment and then I will join you.'

Lord Andrews gave Gabriel and Marie a nod, and then left.

'That was the most compassion I have ever seen from him,' Agatha said. 'I hope it isn't a temporary state.' She interlaced her fingers. 'His wife truly did love him, and regretted that she had erred, but I could not regret it because it gave us you.'

She focused her entire attention on Marie.

'I am sorry for the grief it has caused you, and sorry that you didn't grow up in a grand house. But I saw your birth, and I held you, and I have loved you as my own daughter since that day. You were the best card I'd ever been dealt, and I wanted to hang on to you. Remaining as companion to your mother was the best I could do for both of us. I hope you understand.'

'Most certainly. Over and over. We cannot undo the past,' Marie said. 'And I am pleased about my birth. In my childhood the winters were cold, but I did have a grand time.' Marie smiled. 'I doubt I would have enjoyed growing up in Lord Andrews' house—plus, it was always like my birthday when you came. The other children around me never got such grand treats and adventures as you gave me. Sometimes I shared the treats with my friends, and on those days I was the most important person in all London.'

'You always will be to me.'

Agatha gave her a fierce hug, and scurried from the room, sniffling.

'I'm sorry for the grief that keeping me a secret caused her,' Marie said to Gabriel. 'But at least I knew who my birthing mother was. I had a good childhood. Not perfect, but good enough. And even if I think of complaining, then I wonder whom I would be trying to make sad.'

He noticed she ran her fingertips over the sides of her skirt when she said that. She'd spent her whole life wearing others' cast-offs and making herself happy with what life gave her.

The expression on her face changed. 'It almost made me feel special to be an orphan when I was growing up, even though I missed tales of my heritage. I could imagine my parents as I wished them. I have been fortunate. So very fortunate.' She smiled at him, but it didn't reach her eyes. 'And so have you.'

'It didn't always feel that way.'

He'd had so many duties that he'd had to study, hour after hour, and at family meals he'd had to listen to his parents bickering about his grandmother's antics. While neither had approved of them, they'd definitely not agreed on how she should be handled. But he'd known he was fortunate. Perhaps he'd looked from the window of his parents' coach and seen little Marie running errands and felt sorry for the sad child whose parents didn't have the wealth his did.

And now she was willing to turn her back on it.

'Do you like poverty?' he asked.

'No.' She laughed. 'I have seen it reflected at me from murky bathwater. It's not pleasant. But thanks to you that is no longer my fate. I want to thank you for helping me and my aunt—my very precious Aunt Agatha—and for making sure she has a home.'

'I am pleased to do so.'

The words burned his throat. He *was* pleased she had a home. Pleased Marie could be with her aunt. But he wasn't happy that he had given her the resources to walk out of his life. He had had no choice, truly. It had been the correct thing to do. The right thing. But he knew he would ponder over the choices he had made for a long, long time.

'I have enjoyed having you in the house,' he said. 'You've been a friend to my grandmother and she's been happy to have an audience.'

And he had been pleased to have her with him—even if he was disappointed that she had chosen to write his grandmother's story, and upset with the feeling of her betrayal.

'I am finished with my account of your grandmother's life.' She put a hand on his arm. 'I was shocked in places. She's not always been virtuous. I don't know that you should read it. She has said she has started making notes for volume two, and will contact me at the lodge.'

'I understand,' he said.

The publisher had reassured him that no one would read the memoirs. He would expect contact from the man soon—just as soon as the manuscript was submitted.

Chapter Twenty-One

The butler gave a light knock and walked inside the library. 'Lady Agatha only needed a small amount of help with her departure, and was happy to be on her husband's arm. Miss Marie seemed unsure about it all, but she left in the carriage with them.'

Hawkins held a parcel in his hand.

'And this arrived.'

Gabriel didn't move, his eyes on the bulky rectangular package.

'Would you like it on the table?' Hawkins continued.

'No.' Gabriel held out his hands. 'I will take it.'

Without excess movement, the package was placed in Gabriel's grasp and the servant left, making almost no sound. The door clicked shut, and the silence in the room oppressed Gabriel.

He held the story of his grandmother's life. The family's history and its escapades detailed for others to read for their amusement.

His jaw locked as the thing that had caused such a whirlwind in his life officially ended.

When his friends had asked about the rumours of his grandmother's behaviour he'd shrugged away the reports as exaggerated, and hoped they were. And after his grandfather had passed on he'd even hired people to keep watch over her, and to keep other people from hearing about her exploits. He knew they'd not be able to contain her completely, but they'd been able to keep others away from anything trying, and alerted him to her adventures. He'd even paid the scandal sheets to keep quiet.

Now the story sat in front of him. Knowing the details of his family life had been exposed in such a way angered him. But it was the fact that Marie was willing to profit by it that gave him a kick to his stomach.

He expected such a thing from his grandmother. She never found a pot she wasn't willing to stir. Dust she wasn't willing to kick up. An event she wasn't willing to make ribald. But he had expected more from Marie. He had thought her reserved, reticent, retiring.

Somewhere under that demure demeanour she had a cache of explosives.

Gabriel reached out and pulled at the string binding the wrapping paper and it came untied. The papers seemed to fall open to their title page: *The Memoirs*.

He ran his fingertips over Marie's name, written in small print under the title in tight, cramped handwriting. He could imagine her hand dipping the pen, then tapping it on the side of the bottle of ink, carefully putting her name to the title page.

His grandmother's reminiscences had been written clearly.

The chapters were sewn together in clusters, with one big stitch at the top left-hand side and threads hanging loose. Marie would have bent over the binding, her eyes studying it as she pushed a sewing needle and thread through the papers and then snipped it off and tied the strings.

He envisaged her working hard, putting her heart into his grandmother's story. Possibly sometimes amazed by the risks taken by the older woman. The events the older woman had attended. The men she had entranced.

He'd thought nothing inside should surprise him, but he read the first chapter and discovered he had not really known of his grandmother's past. These stories had been successfully hidden from him.

Then he wondered if the only person truly in the dark had always been himself. If he'd done all that work to protect his family's reputation so he didn't have to face it. If the rug he'd been brushing things under had been his own.

He could read no more.

He put the papers aside and looked into the empty fireplace. He would have to have it lit, just like that fuse had been.

And he fought the explosions inside himself.

Gabriel stood at the window, looking out over the perfectly tended grounds. Perfectly tended because his gardener had a love for nature. A wish to see things grow. But it was more than that.

He'd spoken to the gardener. Seen the man's face when he'd talked of getting a new plant he'd heard about and hoped might grow well.

He doubted the man even knew of the emotion that shone through his eyes.

And now he understood. Understood how the man would feel if he went to the garden and discovered all the greenery gone. Everything. Nothing left but ground. Barren earth. A place without growth.

He'd seen what loneliness did to a man. He'd seen it in Lord Andrews. A man who claimed he couldn't sleep without a specific piece of jewellery nearby because he hoped to feel closer to someone he'd cared about and lost.

Striding inside, he moved to his rooms and found the safe that was years older than he was. Using the combination that had been handed down, just as the house had, he opened the lock. He pulled out a box that had been in the safe for a long time.

Jewels not wanted by the women in his family. Left behind, more or less, by the women who'd owned them. Not worthy of them. Too insignificant in their eyes to matter. Too insignificant to be worn. Forgotten about.

But he'd never completely forgotten the ruby ring. It had meant more to him than any of the jewels he'd seen worn by the women in his family or anyone else.

He opened the box to look again at the ring that had once been his great-grandmother's wedding ring. And then at the other piece of jewellery she'd owned that neither his grandmother nor his mother had wanted—a gold necklace with one small misshapen pearl hanging from it.

The pearl was a baroque. Considered exquisite in former days. Different from the others.

He returned it to the safe and shut the door as he heard the lumbering crash on the stairs.

He knew what was to happen next and, as expected, Pierce walked in and found himself a spot on the sofa.

Gabriel informed him that if he wanted to keep his boots, he'd better take them off the furniture.

Pierce took a handkerchief from his pocket and daubed

at a spot on his coat. 'You have the clumsiest servants I've ever seen. They could spill air.'

'Why don't you stay a while?' Gabriel asked. 'You can drink here as easily as at your club.'

'I agree,' he said. 'Would you pour me a drink?'

'No.'

Pierce laughed, and rose to fill a glass, and then half filled a second one and gave it to Gabriel.

'Don't overdo it,' he said.

'I never do,' Gabriel answered.

The nights were interminable, and sitting with Pierce would be better than listening for Marie's footsteps.

After a half-hour or so of sharing tales they'd both heard before, Pierce said, 'So, why the air of melancholy? Have you finally realised you are in love with the errant archer?'

'That is not your concern.'

'Ah,' Pierce said. 'I saw the determination on your face when you pulled the bow string and aimed that arrow. You might not have known you were in love, but I did.' He checked the stain on his waistcoat again. 'Of course, that didn't change my plans to woo her away from you. No sense in making it easy for you.'

Gabriel let out a deep breath. 'She means more to me than anything else in the world.'

'So why is everyone tiptoeing around as if they're afraid they'll wake someone?'

'The household has divided into two camps. The females are congregating on one side, and the males on the other. The maids dart about and rush so they can do their jobs but are not seen as disloyal. The male servants are distressed with the maids, and extra-solicitous of me, if that is possible.'

'Servants divided in your household?' Pierce asked, his voice high, and then he lowered it. 'Well, Grandmother *does* live here. And I did speak to her just after I got here. Somehow her maid misunderstood my request that she water my horse…'

'I told the butler to gather the servants and tell them that they must all work together. He returned and told me the housekeeper agreed completely, and yet nothing has changed.'

'What is the disagreement?'

'I'd rather not discuss the particulars.'

'Oh, I'd rather you do. And don't be surprised if I already know. As I said, I did see my adorable and retiring grandmother before I came to you. She says what is on her mind.'

'I prefer diplomacy.'

You're too respectable. It amazes me that we get on at all.'

'We all need a roof over our heads, and coal and flour, and soap and meat, and puddings and breads…'

'I try to let my man of affairs take care of all of that. You should take a lesson.'

'From you?'

'Yes. And, since Marie isn't here now—I asked, so I know that it is her absence that is dividing your household—I suggest that I court her. Simple enough. We all get what we want.'

'Touch her and you will go out through a window head-first.'

'From what storey?' Pierce looked at his glass. 'Because she might be worth a few bruises. I can just imagine her at my bedside…coddling me. Holding my hand. Holding my—'

'You really want me to kill you, don't you?'

'It sounds to me as if you've already made some sort of commitment. Maybe you've decided you'd rather risk unhappiness with her than risk happiness with anyone else. I think Grandmother's phrase is *Better the pestilence you know than the one you don't.*'

Pierce stood, and claimed it was time for him to find more enjoyment, because being with Gabriel was about as much fun as watching a horse's tail swat flies.

Then the room became silent. Tomblike.

Gabriel stared at the walls surrounding him. The silence was too quiet. A night stretched ahead of him that would consist of hours broken into minutes…broken into seconds pounding inside him.

He was hungry, but not wanting anything to eat.

Tired, but unable to sleep.

Lonely, but with Marie all around him.

Chapter Twenty-Two

She crumpled the paper in her hand. She'd been betrayed. By the publisher.

Turning to her aunt, she said, 'I must return. Gabriel has the memoirs.'

Her aunt studied her face. 'I thought you'd sent them to the publisher.'

'Yes. He did have them. But now Gabriel has the only copy.'

'I tried to warn you. He is his grandmother's grandson. She is a good friend, but we agreed not to trust each other a long time ago.' She hesitated. 'I'll send someone on a horse to ask if you can borrow my husband's carriage.'

Marie agreed to wait, letting her temper simmer. She should have known this would happen. Gabriel had power and authority and he would not hesitate to use them.

After the carriage had arrived, Marie rushed out to it. It seemed to take for ever for the vehicle to travel to Gabriel's.

She ran to the entrance she'd always used—the one on his grandmother's side of the house. She rapped loudly, and a maid opened the door.

'What is the rush?' Gabriel's grandmother said, stepping into the hall, directly in front of Marie.

'He has the memoirs—Gabriel.'

Her mouth formed a huge O, and so did her eyes.

'Gabriel? He has done that? Oh, my... I never thought he would do such a thing.' She blinked. 'But while you were writing I did keep remembering things that needed to be included, and I did jot down a few notes of what I'd told you each day before I went to bed at night. You will have to stay here and rewrite it.'

'I can't stay with Gabriel here.'

'Why not? Just tell your feet to stay put. Don't open the door if he knocks. He's rather opinionated, anyway. He won't bother you. You won't have to see him. And I may invite Pierce to help you. He's so helpful...'

She could not live under the same roof as Gabriel any more. Their rooms would be too close. It would be too tempting.

'I don't have any clothing here,' she said.

His grandmother squeezed her eyes tightly shut. 'Goodness, I have an old dress or two you can wear. It's not as if you normally wear anything other than a frightful frock—except for the picnic dress. I'm sure you and the maids can sew a few flounces. You appear to be good with flounces.'

She sighed, more dramatic than any actress Marie had ever seen on stage.

'You think you are saving funds by dressing comfortably. But you're also doing something else. You're saying you are your own person, and you want to keep people at arm's length.'

Marie shook her head.

'You're good enough at sewing to make those dresses fit you better. You know how to rip out a seam, take out things and change them, and then sew the seam back. But do you do it to make your dresses more fashionable? No.'

'They're comfortable.'

'Naked is comfortable. Wrapped in a blanket is comfortable. Dressing in nice clothing can be comfortable also. Both of us get on well—and you know why? We're stubborn, and we don't really care what others think of us. But really, the one person we should both treat well…the one person we should both consider…is the only one who is being hurt by our actions. And that is something we should think about.'

She *did* think about Gabriel…about how the lines at his eyes had tightened and he'd appeared to be finding her wanting.

'People don't change much,' his grandmother said. 'They keep making the same mistakes over and over and over…for years. You think I haven't messed up that trick of hiding cards in my reticule many times before? Well, I have. But I keep on thinking that I'll get it right the next time, instead of realising I should get it right by playing within the rules.'

Perhaps it was true. What if the actions that had been the right ones for her in the past were no longer moving her in the direction she should take? What if she should change now and become an even stronger person.

'Your story means a great deal to me,' Marie said. 'I believe in what you said. The risks you took. I think you were being true to yourself.'

'I was being true to myself. But *only* myself. It took me years before I realised that I should be true to my family. And that is when Gabriel saw his grandfather and I together. That is when I learned that my husband was more important to me than anyone else.' She lowered her eyes. 'Sadly, we did not have a great many years left together at that time. But I treasured each day. Each moment with him.'

She studied her hands and patted the top of one.

'Perhaps I sometimes still make the same mistakes. With my family. With Gabriel's mother and with him. I need to tell the whole story—not just the part of it where I am uncaring and sometimes spiteful,' she said. 'I seem to have no trouble owning up to my mistakes, but perhaps I need to own up to the things I've done right also.' She lifted her chin. 'Perhaps you should examine your own motives, Marie. Don't wait until it's too late.'

'My only motive is to support my aunt.'

'True. True... And I'm sure you're not afraid of marriage. Your aunt says you've not been around many people who were actually married to each other in your life. She said that when you were growing up the woman who cared for you might have a different man entering the house every time she visited. She was thankful that the woman kept telling you about the dangers of losing your heart. That kept you on the right path.'

'I was on my own path. She told me that too. Time and time again. I have always been on my own journey.'

'True. And it is not a society one, like Rosalind's. She's perfect.' She enunciated the word with a little purr at the beginning. 'Have you seen the way she dresses? A veritable fashion plate. An asset to any family. She will let Gabriel do as he wishes. Over time, they'll both likely stray in their marriage, but on the outside it will appear perfect.'

She shut her eyes and her lips thinned.

'Rosalind won't take it personally, like his mother did.' She cleared her throat. 'I thought it was going to kill her until she swept her husband out of her life. And then it killed him. Because he just let himself go. To drink. To brothels. To chapel... But that was only the once. The last time...'

In that moment, as his grandmother watched her, she saw no laughter. No jesting. Just loss.

Marie took the woman's hand, but his grandmother tugged her hand away. 'Don't let me get all weepy. I want those memoirs published. They are the record of my life.'

'But you can keep a copy for your family to read.'

'Oh, now that you have a home in the country, my life has lessened in importance for you. Go and enjoy your weeds. You won't have any thought of what Gabriel is doing here in Town. He is a good man, and he knows his duty. His duty is Rosalind. She's spent her whole life learning to be the perfect wife.' She shivered. 'Not like you. Agatha said you were basically trained to clean. That's noble. Cleaning. But not for women like me or Rosalind or Gabriel's mother.'

Then she lifted the perfume bottle on the table beside her and stared at the ceiling. She sprayed the air, the rose scent cloying.

Marie stepped away.

'The manuscript must be with him. Make sure he hasn't burned it.' His grandmother lowered the perfume and kicked out a foot, causing her skirts to fly out at the sides. 'It will be such a trial to tell you all those stories again. But I will if I have to.'

'I will speak to him,' Marie said, and then she stopped and examined his grandmother. 'Rosalind may be perfect, but we both know that you don't really like her, and you yourself said that weeds are stronger than hothouse flowers.'

His grandmother crossed her arms, shook her head, and this time her purr sounded more like a growl, seeming to underscore her words.

'So? What's it to be? Are you a weed or a hothouse flower?'

Chapter Twenty-Three

Rapping briefly on the door, Marie heard him call out, 'Enter,' and she gripped the door handle and opened it.

Gabriel studied her. There was no warmth in him other than the demanding blood that ran in his veins. She'd misjudged him earlier. She'd thought he would eventually understand that it was important to his grandmother to have her memories shared. Important to Marie to be able to support herself. She had hoped other women would want their anecdotes shared as well. That women would learn of their heritage and want others to comprehend the trials they'd endured.

'You have my manuscript.'

He stood, tossing the pen he held to the blotter. 'Yes, I do.'

She moved until only the table was between them, feeling as though she were on some imaginary gigantic chessboard and she didn't understand the rules of the game or her opponent. She didn't even want to play.

'I want it back.'

'You were going to tarnish my family name,' he said.

'Your grandmother agreed,' she said. 'It was her choice.'

'Fair enough. Just as it is my choice to stop it.'

'I will just write it again.'

'And I will stop it again—and again and again, if I have to.' He moved around the desk. 'You can live in the lodge. You have your expenses paid for some time. You don't have to publish.'

'It is the truth as told to me by your grandmother.'

'I don't care if it wis carved in stone, embroidered on silk or written on a pearly gate. It is my family you were trying to destroy.'

'It's your grandmother's story. Her life. Her history. I would think you would want to know that it has been recorded.'

'And if you can profit from it, all the better?'

He moved back to the other side of the desk, opened a drawer and pulled out a few pages from the beginning of the book. He tossed them between them.

'Would you be so kind as to read it aloud?'

'I know what it says. Your grandmother and your grandfather had a fiery marriage. They lit each other's fuses.'

'Did you make this up? About Grandmother and Grandfather trying to throw each other out of a rolling carriage? Calling it "a little marriage disagreement"?'

'No. That's true.'

'This cannot be published. It cannot. And you claim she was betrothed to two men at the same time? This is a travesty for our family.'

'You see what I mean about marriage?' Marie said to him. 'Not one single person I have ever heard of has had a truly good marriage. Not one. Except perhaps your grandmother and grandfather. And even so they nearly killed each other.'

'You're right. I have just realised it. Marriage is a sham. This proves it.' He let the pages flutter to the rug. 'Marriage is best conducted with separate houses. Just as your aunt and her husband have discovered.'

'We do not disagree on that.' Marie gathered the jumble of papers, straightening them.

He stared at the desk, and at the crumpled brown wrapping paper. He held on to the string, twisting it around his fingers before wadding it into a ball and dropping it.

'I wish you weren't so upset,' she said, moving to stand near the desk.

He let out a puff of air through his nostrils. 'I don't know what I should do,' he said, looking at the papers on the desk in front of him. 'My other grandparents are frail, and I don't want them upset. However, I doubt they would even hear of these stories. But my mother is hoping to wed again, and her sweetheart often stays in London and is a stickler for propriety.'

He paused, and then sighed in defeat.

He opened the drawer again and took out the unbound papers. He ran his hand over the top and then gave them to her. 'Do as you wish with it. I will not interfere or speak with the publisher again.'

She put the previously tossed papers on top of the stack and lifted it without speaking.

'Grandmother has the right to live her life as she chooses, just as I do,' he said. 'Without her funds added to the family coffers and her father's tutelage we would likely have the title and little else.'

'Did you read any more of than the first few pages?'

'No.'

'Are you sure you are willing to let this go to the publisher?'

She had to ask. He could still change his mind.

Instead of answering, he shut the drawer.

'I knew my parents did not have the best match,' he said, 'but Grandmother, with all her flaws, always spoke lovingly of her union with Grandfather. And I remember her caring for him when he was ill. He might have been exasperated by her—many times—but they were always supportive of each other.' He met her eyes. 'Is that what you found? That they loved each other?'

'Yes. She has the fondest memories of him, and she says she misses him every day.'

'Does that not change your view on marriage?'

She cradled the pages in her arms and moved to the door. 'I hadn't really considered what I was writing...what it meant.'

'Perhaps you should. Perhaps I should. And...' His pause was a lengthy one. 'And perhaps everyone should. My parents had a distant marriage, and my mother never said anything about missing my father after he'd passed away. She didn't live with him most of the time.'

'I know.'

'Father shouldn't have strayed. Or perhaps Mother shouldn't have married him. Perhaps you're right about marriage.'

She clasped the papers closer.

'Let me write a note to the publisher,' he said, sitting at the desk, dipping his pen in the ink. 'I will tell him that he may go ahead.'

'You will?' She took a hesitant step towards him.

'Yes.'

She heard the scratch of his pen sliding across the paper and walked to his desk, watching him blot the ink. She put the manuscript on top of the wrapping paper and read Gabriel's note allowing publication.

He indicated she should place the letter of agreement on top of the stack, and after she did slipped the heavier cover over them and tied it.

She picked up the parcel and started to the door, pausing to look back at him.

Then she walked to the fireplace and tossed the papers inside the burning flames. Immediately the scent of scorched paper reached her nostrils.

In a flash, he'd jumped from the chair, hurled himself around the desk, grabbed a poker, and pulled out the smouldering, charred package.

He stamped on the burning spots. Then he stared at her.

'I can't do it,' she said.

'I understand.'

He lifted the papers from their burned packaging, avoiding the smouldering areas, kicking the string and the heavier covering back into the flames.

'But you're correct in that secrets can't be kept. And Grandmother has a right to tell her side of the story.'

She took the papers from him. 'You don't understand.'

Again, she held the pages towards the fire, but he slapped them away, sending them flying into the room.

'You don't understand,' she said again. 'I can't risk hurting the young women who might read this, and I can't risk hurting someone who might believe that living such a life without care can be safe or healthy. Your grandmother had a fortune at her disposal, and still she was scarred in the leg, almost fell out of a carriage, and missed out on much of her child's life because she was chasing adventure.'

She shook her head. This was not about his grandmother's story. It was about more than that. She didn't want any young woman finding herself in the predicament her mother had faced. And she definitely didn't want them to think that pretending lawlessness would lead to a romance.

'And I can't risk hurting you,' she said.

He put a hand to the back of her head and pulled her to him so he could kiss her forehead. 'Sweeting… This is not something that has to be decided now. Why don't you stay here again, try to keep Grandmother from lighting any more fuses, and give us a chance to get to know each other better?'

Gabriel woke from where he had dozed on the sofa as the dawn light began to show through his window.

He opened his eyes. His valet had arrived and left after opening the curtains.

Then he heard it again. A rap at his door. A light rap. A Marie rap.

He stood, straightened his cravat, and called out for her to enter.

She peered around the door, her spectacles firmly in place, in a fluff of curls and a sad dress that had seen better years. And still she was the loveliest woman he'd ever seen in his life.

This was the sight he wanted to wake up to every morning.

Then he saw the thin manuscript she held in her hands.

She held it out to him. 'This isn't the original. We've changed a few things,' she said. 'I left in the carriage incident—how could I not?—but we've added an explanation of how your grandmother regretted her actions and tried to learn from her mistakes and be a better person.

And how much she loves her family…and how much they mean to her.'

'Including my mother?'

'Yes. It took her a while to remember that, and she may have embellished a little. But she says she truly does like your mother.' She ducked her head. 'In short doses and from a great distance—which I didn't include. She says it has been her goal in life to give your mother long earlobes…but not with these memoirs.'

Gabriel took the papers and moved to his desk. He pulled out the wrapping paper that the publisher had used to cover the original manuscript. He took the string and wrapped it, and then he gave it to her.

'The butler will be able to have it delivered for you.'

She hugged it to her chest. 'You do not want to read it?'

'I think it is best that I don't.'

'I have talked with your grandmother, and she told me she does not want to damage your mother's romance.'

'I appreciate that.'

She ran her hand over the parcel. 'This is to be her chance to set the record straight. To offer an explanation of her errant ways. Not to embellish her adventurous ways, as it was at first, but to say how she has learned from them, and would now recommend only the straightest and narrowest path to everyone. And she has passed that on to you.'

'That's not exactly how she taught me to be upstanding,' he said. 'I learned to be so by dealing with her disasters.'

'Which she credits you for many times over. In writing.'

'You and your aunt became a family with no ties to bind you at all…except one. The heart. It is a familial love, and that is what I want to form with you at my side. The love of a family between us. Even if we never wed. Even if it is only friendship.'

He touched his neckcloth, and the simple knot at his fingertips reassured him. Made him feel closer to her.

'I liked it when you returned to the way you prefer to dress,' he continued. 'Still the beauty in you shone. I liked it when you told me the truth about your relationship with your aunt—how you appreciated the good things of your childhood and didn't weary yourself over the things you couldn't change, but celebrated the things you had, and worked to keep them. Not just for you but also for your aunt.'

Her eyes didn't give any evidence of what she was thinking, but it didn't matter. He had to speak what was in his heart.

'I like you tremendously. More than I've ever liked anyone before. *Anyone*. You are the family of my heart. The family I would choose if I had all the people in the world to choose from and the person whom I want by my side. This feels more like love than anything I've ever felt before. I adore you. And even if we're apart for the rest of our lives I always will. You are the one person I know I can love for ever.'

She hugged the parcel even closer, before putting it on the table close to the door. She walked forward and took his hands.

'I wanted to ask you something,' she said.

He waited.

'Will you marry me?' she asked, reminding him of a lost child.

But she wasn't lost. Because they had found each other.

'I thought you would never ask.'

'You are a risk worth taking,' she said. 'Though a very minor one. In fact, I would say I am the bigger risk.'

'You are no risk at all.'

He walked around the desk and hugged her close, shutting his eyes for a moment and enjoying the knowledge that they were standing together and she wanted to marry him.

'As I listened to your grandmother recount her tales again,' she said, 'this time telling me how you worked so hard to keep her safe and protect the family, doing all you could to make life the best it could be for her, I realised that you were the one person I want by my side always. Someone who truly cares about the people around him and lives a strong life, with all the actions everyone claims are important, but who also does all he can to make them happen.'

'You could have just said you like the way I tie my cravat.'

'There is that as well.'

He placed a soft kiss on her lips. 'We cannot wed soon enough for me.'

Chapter Twenty-Four

They'd waited three weeks before the banns were read. Gabriel claimed he was giving her time to change her mind, but that wasn't true, and he had reminded her every night how much he loved her.

And when she had told him her only regret was in being born out of wedlock he'd taken her by the shoulders and shaken his head.

'No decent person is a mistake, regardless of how their life started. Your parents had nothing to do with the way you turned out. You made the choice to be good on your own, and you make my life better. I need you.'

Then he'd paused, considering.

'In our years together I want you to accept that a person doesn't need to try to live life so cautiously that they may never have regrets, because then you will regret the adventures you didn't have. And I don't want you ever to regret our marriage.'

She'd hugged him with all her might.

He had put all his worry about the memoirs aside. Nothing mattered as much as having her for his wife.

And now here they sat on the sofa, side by side, and suddenly all his concern about what she'd written about his family dissolved. Nothing mattered except her, and she was curled beside him in a dressing gown, with her hair beautifully askew, loosened from her knot, and her eyes peering at him with love through her spectacles.

'What did you do with the remains of the original manuscript?' he asked.

'It's in a safe your grandmother has. She says she has mainly written it for future generations she might never know. She thinks if they read the published memoirs first, they will not be so shocked at what she calls her "true story". And she says she planned this all along, but who knows?'

She shook her head.

'She also says she hopes we have a little weed soon. And when I know I am going to have a baby she wants me to tell her before I tell your mother. I told her we would tell them both at the same time, and now she's pouting, but she'll be over it by morning.'

He wouldn't have believed it was possible for a person to love another as much as he loved her. He loved the way the spectacle frames encircled her eyes and the lenses seemed to magnify her gaze, and he loved her love for him.

She had seemed to bloom since their marriage, and she wore the ruby ring from the safe and the misshapen pearl, which she claimed to be the most amazingly beautiful one she'd ever seen.

His grandmother had made it her mission to get Marie to become the most fashionable woman in London, and in Gabriel's opinion she had succeeded roundly—though Marie had complained, laughing and saying, 'Once a weed, always a weed.'

Then his grandmother had said, 'Weeds survive.'

She and his grandmother had become even closer, and

he knew Marie kept his grandmother from needing any more fuses of any kind ignited.

In fact, his grandmother and his mother could now even manage to share an occasional cup of tea, if Marie cajoled them into being nice to each other.

'You will not believe what Aunt Agatha has told me,' she said, and didn't wait for him to answer. 'She doesn't want to stay at the hunting lodge. She believes her husband is falling in love with her. He has bought her a new strand of pearls. Her own, he said, because he wants her to create memories with them.'

Then she reached under the sofa and pulled out a book.

'The publisher has sent this. I want you to have it.'

'Let us read,' he said, and held out an arm.

She leaned into him.

He read the first few pages and then began the second chapter. He would never have recognised his grandmother. She'd been a hellion, always fighting to be the centre of attention, even in duels, and she was honest about her disguised efforts on the stage with a horrible rendition of an unfortunate song, but the repentant woman was dedicated to her family, had chosen the right man to wed at the last moment—and, through a series of misunderstandings and fortunate events, had managed to save the day many times over.

That was not how he remembered hearing the stories from his mother, but now he understood that his grandmother's memories would never be the same as his mother's.

'Is this Grandmother's true story?' he asked.

'I'm not sure. But it's the one she told me the second time, after thinking long and hard about it. And your mother helped us take some things out, and added a short prologue at the beginning, which says that some of these tales may not be exactly true, but parts of many are.'

Marie relaxed against him, settling in, and he continued reading. As he finished each chapter he saw his family through her eyes, and he felt closer to it and closer to her.

When he'd finished, he gave it back to her. 'It's flattering to my grandmother. It's flattering to my family.'

'I enjoy listening to her stories. She's different when she's with my aunt, and she's different when we are alone. She just reminisces and recalls the past.'

'You have succeeded in correcting the family history. I like it.' He lifted the book, but couldn't take his eyes from her. From the radiance he saw. He wouldn't have thought a simple compliment would mean much to her, but it seemed to mean the world.

'Gabriel… Gabriel?'

He heard his mother shouting in the corridor, and then she stepped into the room.

'You will not believe what that woman has done. She's wagering again. This time on *my* betrothal.'

His grandmother strolled in behind her. 'I don't know why she's complaining. The Duke himself wagered he'd wed her within six months.'

'Yes! She asked him when he was going to propose, which is entirely not her concern. And now she has talked him into letting her play the harp at the wedding breakfast.'

His grandmother nodded. 'I am very kind that way.' She clasped her hands. 'I like him. He's a little young, in my opinion, but that's not my concern. He'll make a good… um…son-in-law.'

'He's not going to be your son-in-law.'

'Well, I will be his mother-in-law by proxy, then. And

you can be my daughter-in-law again.' She tugged at her earlobe. 'I've missed having you as a daughter-in-law.'

Gabriel's mother groaned. 'Trust me. In my heart, your position has never changed.'

Then his mother saw the book in his hands. 'What are you reading, Gabriel?'

'Oh, dear,' his grandmother said, swooping closer. 'Is that…? Is that mine?'

Gabriel held it out to her and she clasped it in both hands. 'Finally.'

His mother coughed, but it sounded more like a squawk, and then both women left, arguing over who would read it first.

Gabriel interlaced his fingers with Marie's. 'That is the best I've seen them together in a long time.'

'We're so fortunate we have a big house.'

Gabriel stood. 'With a good lock on our door,' he said.

After latching it, he returned to open the bedroom door. Then he took her hand and lifted her to her feet, sweeping her into his arms and carrying her from the room.

'I'm so grateful to have you,' he said, giving the bedroom door a kick to close it after they'd gone through it. 'I look forward to spending many nights watching the stars with you and many mornings waking with you at my side. But now what I want most of all is to tell you how much I love you.'

'I love you too,' she said. 'You're the man who has made me believe in marriage and happy endings.'

* * * * *

*If you loved this story,
you're sure to love more of
Liz Tyner's Historical romances*

A Cinderella for the Viscount
Tempting a Reformed Rake
A Marquess Too Rakish to Wed
Marriage Deal with the Earl
Betrothed in Haste to the Earl